3800 16 0074644 4
HIGH LIFE HIGHLAND

D0119709

Ross Armstrong is a British stage and screen actor who has performed in the West End of London, on Broadway and in theatres throughout the UK. Among others, he has acted opposite Jude Law (*Hamlet*), Joseph Fiennes (*Cyrano de Bergerac*), Kim Cattrall (*Antony and Cleopatra*) and Maxine Peake (*The Deep Blue Sea*). His TV appearances include *Foyle's War, Jonathan Creek, Mr Selfridge, DCI Banks* and most recently, *Ripper Street*.

After gaining a BA in English Literature and Theatre at Warwick University, Ross joined the National Youth Theatre where his contemporaries included Matt Smith and Rafe Spall. A three year course at RADA followed and whilst there he won the RADA Poetry Writing Award. The idea for his debut novel *The Watcher* came to him when he moved into a new apartment block and discovered whilst looking at the moon through binoculars that he could see into his neighbours' homes. Thankfully for them, he put down his binoculars and picked up his pen.

He is an avid cricket fan and hosts a regular podcast for *All Out Cricket* magazine. He also has a monthly column in *You and Your Wedding* magazine as he prepares for his own wedding in 2017.

THE WATCHER

ROSS ARMSTRONG

HQ
An imprint of HarperCollinsPublishers
1 London Bridge Street
London SE1 9GF

This hardback edition 2016
1

First published in Great Britain by
HQ, an imprint of HarperCollinsPublishers Ltd 2016

A catalogue record for this book is available from the British Library.

ISBN: HB: 978-0-00-818118-5
C: 978-0-00-819275-4

Printed and bound in Great Britain by
CPI Group (UK) Ltd, Croydon, CR0 4YY.

For Catherine

7 days till it comes.

I look in her direction. About fifty metres away behind a sheet of glass stands a woman. Looking out at the reservoir. She's in the building opposite. I've spotted him in that building before, but not her. I've been watching him. She's about my height, my build. She could be my reflection. Except she couldn't because she's a little darker, has an air about her. European. Her hand rests on the frame of the door, softly. She is lost in thought. No, she is concerned. She scratches her bottom lip with her teeth. She wears lipstick. She has a tousled fringe. She has a light blue dress on, for the summer. I adjust the dial on my binoculars, to sharpen the focus. Her eyebrows, perfectly plucked, knit in displeasure. Her face is half lit by the early evening sun streaming through her window. North facing. Or perhaps it's not her window. I certainly haven't spotted her before. In there. With him. Which is strange.

She takes a careful step backwards. Steady, feline. The sun recedes now, kissing her features goodbye. The dark of the room smooths over her face, like a sheet, enveloping her. She's harder to read. But I can still see her. She's so still. Careful. Intense. Pensive. Every muscle in her face firm and poised. Rich with intent.

She's still lit by the gentle glow of the room. But only just. Softly, so softly. A single lamp perhaps. A femme fatale. Shadowed. Like from a 1954 movie. How quickly they all turn into models. Through my eyes. All the people behind the windows in the building across from where I am now. Like they're posing for me. For a photo shoot. How well they perform. How beautiful. It's almost like they know.

Without thinking, my fist at my side turns into a gun. I lift it. Slowly. Until it points right at her. If I pulled the trigger now perhaps the glass of my window would shatter, then hers would too and the bullet would strike her between the eyes, one inch above the bridge of her nose. Her skull would break. And she would fall.

Bang. Bang.

Oh, God. She's looking. She looks in my direction. And she sees me. She's got me. In her sights. Her face tightens. But it's her body. Her body doesn't move a muscle. And neither does mine. I'm still. But not frozen. I'm ready. Poised. My elbow rested on the sill. My left hand gripping my apparatus. The right fixed in its gun-like pose. I hold firm for some reason. I'm not embarrassed.

She breathes in through her nose. Her chest lifts just a touch. Through my sights I see her eyes refocus. Her pupils shrink a fraction of a millimetre. And she stares me down.

Meaningfully, she raises her hands to her dress and, keeping her eyes on mine, she delicately lifts it and shows me her right thigh. A purple bruise. And above it, further still, a burn. She's looking right at me. Oh, God. Showing herself to me. She holds it there. Then glances behind her. Sees something. Lets her dress fall. Maybe she's not alone. It's so still here.

Then, from behind me, the rumble of building work begins. Metal crushes concrete. Maybe it was always there but I'd drowned it out. With my focus. They're still working on the last few buildings between this one and the park. As I stare at her, the noise of machines and the crunch of the wrecking ball goes on. Behind my back. They crescendo and then dip inexorably. A heavy drone. A wall of sound, dipping and rising. I look at her. And she at me. She could be trying to tell me something. Is she play-acting? Is she pleading for her life? Trying to communicate something? Woman to woman. The corners of her mouth rise into a kind of smile.

Rumble. Rumble. Rumble. Rumble.

I'm going to call her… Grace.

From nowhere, a hand fixes around her throat and pulls her into the darkness. Her arms and dress flail forward as she's dragged out of sight. She disappears. My breath, which only now I realise I was holding, leaves me suddenly.

My home phone rings. I jump, clutching my sweater. Resisting the urge to cry out. It gets louder and louder. As if it's getting closer. Homing in on me.

It's strange. My phone ringing. Because it never has before. Not since I moved in. I'd forgotten it was even plugged in.

Ring, ring. Ring, ring.

My hands grip my jeans, needing something to hold on to. As I brace myself. And turn to look at it.

Ring, ring. Ring, ring.

It's strange, you see. Because no one even has the number. No one.

Not even you.

Something crashes against my window. I fall and put my back to the solid white wall. Out of plain sight. I'm breathing so hard now. Shaking. The hairs on my arm stand on end. My heart is beating out of my chest.

The glass is cracked. I daren't turn my head. But in my periphery I can see something. Pressed against my now cracked window. Don't Turn Your Head, I tell myself.

But I can see something. Out of the corner of my eye.

Don't Turn.

I can see something. Sliding down it. Slowly. Dreadfully.

So I breathe in through my nose. Bite down hard on my tongue.

I turn my head. And look.

Part One:
The Look

42 days till it comes.

HS – *Passer domesticus* – Wetland – Good vis, wind light, 12 deg – Singular – 2 leucistic patches, buffish, pale supercilium, rich dark streaks on mantle, female – 16 cm approx. – Social, dominant.

I thought I'd send my findings over to you in particular. As I hoped you of all people might understand. We haven't seen a lot of each other recently of course, but I've had a think about it and there are a few things I want to say. Even if I'm not that keen to say them to your face exactly. Or on the phone. Or Skype, or the other platforms.

I'm not up for it. I don't want a scene. I'm not keen to 'have it out'. Woman to man.

I had thought I'd made everything pretty clear. Had said my piece. Is it piece or peace? I never know. But either way, I thought I'd said it. And I thought that was it. For ever. Between me and you.

But now I think about it, there are a few more things I want to touch on. Want to prod at maybe. Without having to look at you and feel guilty or inhibited while I'm saying them. Without you butting in or anything.

It's probably all my fault. I know. I know you think it is. I know that's why you think we're not talking. But hear me out, OK? I want to say a few things and be heard. That's all. A friendly ear, without the glare of your eyes. Without any judgements.

I hope this doesn't sound too severe! It's not meant to be. You know, it might be fun. To help you remember a few things. Maybe hear some new things too. Things you don't know. I had this sudden urge to tell you. So much has happened since I made my decision.

I know the notation isn't always right but cut me some slack, OK? This is how I've always done it and you know I like to do things my way. Also, don't get all 'the way you do' if I'm telling you things you already know, you're never too old for a refresher. I don't mean to chastise, you are always so patient with me. You always have been. I just need someone to talk to. Someone at a distance to share my findings and the way I'm feeling, so maybe we can make sense of it all. Together. Someone level-headed. I know you're not a trained therapist! But we used to talk, when we were out there. Look. I think I might be getting myself into some trouble.

I don't know. Aiden thinks I'm stuck in a rut. Mentally that is. That's what he says. Mentally and emotionally. And financially. And creatively and career-wise. Which is always nice to hear. I didn't ask, he just volunteered this information. Apropos of nothing. He wasn't just being a dick. But he wasn't joking either. He's almost definitely right.

Aiden told me all these things this afternoon. God, he's

a clever arsehole, isn't he? It's like he can see the inside of my head. He's staring at me now, grinning slightly as he leans against the window. He looks handsome as the light streams in around him. We're both tapping away opposite each other on our celluloid keys. A proper modern, alienated couple.

He's on his laptop and I'm on Mum's old typewriter. Maybe you remember the typeface. The font. I found it in the move and thought it'd be nice to get the old thing out. Aren't I retro? I feel like the woman from *Murder, She Wrote*. Only problem is I can't make any mistakes on this thing or I'll need Tippex and I hate Tippex. It stinks. So I type carefully. And if I say things I regret. Well, they just have to stay.

He shoots me a look and a smile that says 'make me a latte would you?' and I will, because that's always my job now for some reason. We've got this new machine, it's like we live in a coffee shop. I've bought some hazelnut syrup, to add some definition to our flat whites. And some sprinkles to lightly dust over our cappuccinos and cortados. It's all very middle class. We're Cameron's children, you'd wince.

I don't move a muscle. If he wants a coffee he can ask, like a normal person would. He looks away again. But even though his eyes are down he knows I'm looking. I can tell. His face lit by his screen. Smiling so smugly it's practically demonic. Cross-legged like I am, as if each other's reflection. He's silently trying to get a rise out of me.

'Coffee, please, ducky,' his look says.

He can tickle me by barely moving a muscle. Make me giggle with the way he sits or the rise of a single eyebrow.

He can clear his throat and it feels like a jab in the ribs. A soft hum can be a gentle hug. That's how close we are. We send each other our thoughts by the smallest vibrations.

He's found a new way to make me laugh. He uses this stupid voice he's been practising. I can tell when he's going to do it. I see the thought drop in. Then I see him smile when he's about to do it. I see right through him. He looks up now to give me the full force of it. Here it comes.

'You tapping avay your leetle thoughts, huh? Using zee leetle grey cells?'

I smirk, despite myself. Cheeky bastard.

'I am zinking about the brown mark, above your elbow, on the back of your arm.'

He's decided it's time to stop for a moment, for one of our micro chats. A tiny ellipsis before we dive back into our worries and fears. A wry smile envelops my face.

'My birthmark?'

'Yez. Your mole.'

'My… freckle.'

'Your tea stain. Yes.'

He's dropped the voice now. He's got serious. Or as close as he gets anyway.

In the silence, his eyes wander over me.

'I was just thinking about how it's like a small button. I've always thought of it like that. Then I remembered I had a dream where I could press it and it would make you lose your memory. What do you think about that?'

I pause, breathe in through my nose and consider this. 'I think you're a very strange individual.'

'Interesting you should say that. Very interesting,' he says. Nodding, narrowing his eyes and archly taking me in as if he's some sort of Buddha-Yoda, enlightening me with his abstract bullshit. He strokes my ankle, then makes to go back to his work.

'Did you then?' I say.

'Did I what?' he says.

'Did you press it?'

'It was just a funny dream. I thought I'd tell you.'

'You pressed it! And now you're being evasive,' I say, throwing my shoe at him. It's meant to be playful but I hit him in the head quite hard.

'*Ow!* Oh God. Oh, my God. My eye. I think it's going to have to come out,' he says, overreacting wildly in search of a laugh. Which somehow he gets out of me.

'Oh, my God. Tell me what happened next in your lame old dream?'

'It's not a lame old dream. It's a nice dream,' he says.

I hum to myself. Then breathe audibly. Rolling a bowling ball of disdain between us.

'It's not a nice dream. Is it? It's not lovely, is it? It's actually quite horrible.'

'I think "horrible" is a tad extreme, honeybear,' he says. This is one in a line of creative love names he's taken to calling me. He uses them because we're not the kind of people who would use them.

'Well, I only say that because it's a controlling, manipulative, latently sexist dream, in which I am essentially a doll-like creature to be played with at your whim. But, now I say it out loud, maybe you're right, maybe that's fine.'

His face contorts in thought. Then pauses. Then gives me a look like he's about to cut through this whole conversation with something utterly brilliant. A real showstopper.

'Don't let anyone else's dreams control you, Lily. For you are the master of your dreams,' he mumbles with a degree of earnestness.

The room cringes.

'Wow, that's great, Aid. You should put that in front of some clipart of a sunset and whack it on the Internet. People love that sort of shit.'

'Well, laugh it up, Lil. But your reaction to all this is very telling. You care too much about weird signifiers of what you are to others. You are the master of your fate and your–'

'Yep, got it. Don't worry, I'm fine as I am. But, thanks for the pop psychology, Pops.'

I'm irked but it soon turns to flirtation. It always does in the end.

'That's OK, honey… badger,' he says.

He absorbs my mocking. It's one of the many things I like about him. His discretion. His lightness of touch. He's self-effacing and utterly pretentious at the same time. And somehow I'm still intrigued as to how exactly he does it. It's a puzzle. The sort of thing that keeps a relationship going. He glances back at his screen again. Six, eight, ten taps.

'Oh, one more thing. What happened when you pushed the button?'

'Ah. Hmm,' he mutters. 'Dunno. As soon as I pressed it, I woke up.'

Without formal ending, Aiden's eyes fall onto his computer. I am to consider this conversational cul-de-sac over, as we segue seamlessly back to our own worlds. Then he peers up over his device and smiles at me for a second. Full beam. All of him there, without any side.

Then he disappears behind it again. And the tap-tapping goes on.

As I look at him, I see the binoculars sitting at his side and I get up and grab them in an instant and see what I can catch. I'm limiting myself to two sightings a day; I don't want to get obsessive. You know how I get. That's why I'm writing to you above anybody else. Because you know me, what I'm like. I fancy seeing one more bird while there's still a little light. A wood pigeon or a goldfinch. Just a little one. You know. Just for a bit of fun.

35 days till it comes.

BT – *Cyanistes caeruleus* – Grassland – Magic-hour sunlight, still, 18 degrees – 10 flock – Bright yellow breast, black chest line, male – 12 cm, perhaps – Excitable, jerky hops and aphid swoops.

I've never been creative. I'm more a facts and figures type. My oeuvre is no great loss to the artistic world. I'm the only person I know that literally cannot paint. Not on a canvas, or wall, nothing. You may say this isn't a thing, but it is. Even when I started painting the flat Aiden would say 'long, smooth strokes' and I'd try to do it but somehow I couldn't and he ended up doing the whole room himself, telling me to 'just watch and make funny comments to keep me going'.

Hey, you know what? This is creative. Ha, Aiden, ha! This will be my project that will lift me from the partial doldrums. Maybe engage my heart a little as well as my graph paper head.

But I think what he really wants to know is, when I'm

going to get back to my book. I know this because he said it today. He said:

'When are you going to get back to your book?'

To which I sighed. Then thought. Then replied.

'Aid, enough sweaty academics have written Hitchcock essays, I don't think I need to throw in my tuppence. It's rehashing. It's a remake of a remake. It's just regeneration.'

He raised his eyebrows to this. I knew it without even looking up. I felt it.

'Sure, agreed. Damn right. You give up on those dreams. Anyway, I mean, it's not like nobody told you Film Studies doesn't make anyone any money, honey.'

'Oh, don't do the dad jokes, Aid. My dad did them all at the time.'

'You don't need a degree to work in Saturday Night Video!' He roared.

'There we go. Thank you!' I shouted. I read his mind. I always do. We're that close.

'Well, it looks like it's Medical Market Research for you for ever then. Sounds like a strong plan. Is that the plan?'

'Trust me, this was definitely not the plan.'

No, not even the most left field career adviser would have put me here. Except one. The left field career adviser that is London: with its ever-shrinking career opportunities and economic demands. Bugger off, London. I'd move back to Chesterfield, if I didn't think it'd make me end it all. I'm serious. I would. But it would. The way I'm feeling now, at least. Everyone always said I was just like my mum. I hope I'm not too like her.

I go out on the balcony and my gaze runs past the trees to a flock of starlings, dancing around above the reservoir, swooping up into the bluing evening sky. I try to get a better look when they rise higher, hoping the moonlight will give me a better view of the plumage. Then I focus on the moon instead. We used to do that sometimes, didn't we? It's so clear tonight. If you look hard enough it actually looks like a place, not just a star or whatever. It's mad to think people have had their feet all over that big rock in the sky, isn't it? I know it sounds stupid, but it is weird, isn't it? Then, absent-mindedly, I let the binoculars run to the block of flats on the right side, Waterway it's called. All the blocks have got these serene 'natural world' names, to convince everyone they don't live in a pigeonhole in North London and work in new media. We even have a concierge. Don't ask me what they do. But he wears a uniform. I don't think he can handle dinner reservations, like in a New York hotel in the movies. I think he mostly signs for post and solves 'parking disputes'. Of which there are many. It's that sort of building.

There's a light on in the penthouse. And I've always wondered how big it is in there and I stand and stare. I stare at his Habitat curtains, which I saw in the shop the other week actually. They don't look super posh or anything. Then I stare at the swing chair he's got on his balcony, that does look expensive. And then I see him. Look at him. There he is. The million pound penthouse guy. Doesn't look that impressive. In fact he looks downright odd at the moment. What's he doing in there? I look closer. I analyse.

His back rises. Up and down he goes. A slight sheen on his back. He's in his pants. This fair-haired (sweaty) man of average height, who has actual abdominal muscles, which I catch briefly in a reflection, is doing squats with dumb bells in his hands. With his back to me. No idea I'm here. Seeing it all. And he's in his pants.

He looks ridiculous, a real cliché. He mechanically turns ninety degrees to his right, so I can see his moist, blush aspect in profile. He's gurning, how bizarre, how odd. It's like a music video now as Aiden's '90s Trip Hop spills out from our bedroom. He dips and straightens mechanically, as if to the music. It's hilarious – does he have no shame? What curious manoeuvres. What an odd gait. How little shame he has in his natural habitat. Can't he see that people can see him? If they look close enough.

And then he stands, turns and looks right at me. Without thinking, I duck, and I'm giggling like a schoolgirl. I disappear from his view. Gone in an instant. I peek up again and he can't see me. I think he's resolved his mind was playing tricks. He thought he saw something, me and my apparatus, but then resolved it was his imagination or… no, he's venturing out, arse partially exposed. He's on his balcony. He's looking for me, but I'm behind a wooden garden chair, hiding like a child. He can't see me. I'm safe. I'm in the hide.

'What the hell are you doing?' Aiden shouts from inside.

33 days till it comes.

Chaff – *Fringilla coelebs* – Wetlands – Red-rust breast, female – 8 flock – Chirruping but sad-seeming – 16 degrees, light rain – 15 cm.

Oh, shit. I'm in trouble. Aiden called me into the bedroom after the peeping incident and took on a grave tone.

'We've bought our first flat here, Lily, we are pretending manfully… and womanfully… to be adults and you are out there… er, perving on Jeremy…'

'Can we call him Gregory?'

'On… OK, Gregory… on Gregory the account manager as he bellows at you in his skintight underwear while the woman below dashes out to see you crawling back inside on your hands and knees…'

I can see him smiling though, all the while. Just that tiny smile in the corner of his mouth that lets me know he still loves me. That it's all OK really. That little smirk I fell in love with. Followed by the smallest snort and snicker. He's still there. That man I fell in love with.

I know it seems awful, but it was funny. It's amazing what people do when you're not looking. Not the pant squats as such, I understand that, but it was the look. That expression on his face that he must only use when he's on his own.

It's like the birds. But they know they're being watched, they're ready for it somehow, they're 'natural show-offs'. We used to say that. But humans are incredible. They're these amazing, living breathing things, that get up to things and have these looks on their faces. I'm not going to prescribe spying on people as a remedy for your aches and pains, but I do have to say there is something about it. Just something. Something thrilling.

I think we got in just in time here you know. The whole thing's being regenerated, it's a twenty-five year project. And yes, that is another word for gentrification and no I don't think that's awful, it's nice round here, it's beautiful. And we scraped together the money so we deserve to live here.

I do feel sorry for the people in Canada House, though. Some of them have lived there for thirty years and they're being turfed out. Half the place is boarded up already. The others are just waiting until they get the shove too. 'Rehoused,' they say, but who knows. You hear stories about people being forced to pay rent in new builds they can't afford. You hear stories of people becoming homeless. Or, worse still, getting moved to Birmingham. That's a joke, I know you were born in Birmingham. I went to one of the exhibition centres for a conference and it was fine. I mean, nice, it was nice. Yes, I know there's more champagne drunk per square mile than anywhere else in Britain, so they must be celebrating something. Yes, I know. And they have more canals than Venice. Although I've always thought it was the quality of the surroundings people enjoyed in Venice, not just the raw statistical length of the canals, but there we are. But it's really nice here, you'd like it. It's so sad to think that people who grew up here can't stay.

There was a quote in the paper that read:

'... the people in the newbuilds across the road tend to avoid the people in the old council estate...'

And, if that's true, it's awful. But I'm sure it can't be. I mean, as soon as I got off the Tube today, I crossed to the newbuild side of the road, but that's because they spray water cannons on the building site, to disperse the dust or something. I didn't want to get soaked by the mud and brick dust from the houses. It gets in your face and hair. I don't want to be covered in what's left of those poor people's homes. I mean those poor people. Not 'poor' people. Poor as in their plight. Not economically. I do. I do feel bad.

But I only mention this because just as I crossed the road... This is awful. Just as I crossed the road I looked up and that's when I saw her. I looked her straight in the eye. Jean. She'd been used as an example in the *Guardian*. She's the one who'd given the quote. There was a photo and a big piece about her feeling like she was

waiting in line for the guillotine, seeing homes demolished all around me. Seeing the building works get closer and closer. As I wait my turn to be slung out. It's like a death sentence.

It's awful. It really is. But what did she want me to do as I left the Tube, stay on her side of the road with the mud and brick from those houses spraying me just so I could give her a hug or something? Because, that's pretty much what I plan to do now actually.

I can't tell Aiden because he'd be worried about the rumours of what goes on and the sort of people that we're told lurk around those flats at night. But I'm sure it's scare-mongering. It's not like I'll be wandering about looking for her. I saw her. I saw her go into her home. I saw her and I thought, *Now I know*. So as soon as I'm ready, I'm going to go and see her. And apologise. For crossing the road. For everything. I'll see how she is. What she's like. It'll be interesting. Maybe take her some soup. Would that be condescending? People like soup, right? Perhaps we'll be friends.

I saw a Missing poster today, stuck crudely to a lamp post as I cut through the estate. A girl from over there has disappeared. It seems. Into thin air. I won't tell Aiden. People go missing all the time. But he worries about that kind of thing. He really worries.

One last thing. You really can't tell anyone about what I tell you when you read all this. Not Aiden, not anyone. In fact, especially not Aiden. If I ever do change my mind about seeing you. And we come over to you or we decide to have you here. If that does happen. You can't say a word about this.

It will always be between us. Just us. You and me. For ever. Just like our bird stuff. OK? I'm serious. So, no matter what happens. No matter how old and senile you get.

Remember that.

My phone goes. *Bleep bleep*. And we both know who's texting. And we both know what about. But no. No thanks.

I'm not ready to talk yet.

30 days till it comes.

WFC – Tippi and Janet – Waterway – Blonde and red – 2 flock – Relaxed, feminine, serene – 19 degrees, under cover of night, a light breeze – Both around 5′ 6″.

I turn off the light. Binoculars in hand. Aiden has a beer on the go and he's giggling at the ridiculousness of it all. I was looking at the moon through them. Sipping some wine. He finally noticed what I was up to and mistook it for something more sinister. I don't know what. Having another perv at Gregory perhaps. But now he knows he can be involved and it's all quite silly and fun, he loves it. He's really up for it now, in fact. It's become a game. It's so funny.

We roll down the blind and leave ourselves the smallest gap at the bottom to look through. We make sure all the lights are off and I walk him through it all. You would love this. It's like being back in the hide, but better. I get my elbows in place on a magazine and look up, playing with the focus dial and looking for a light on in the Waterway building. I flash past a couple of darkened ones, probably owned by overseas investors, so many flats are empty here. Then I see it. Lit up like a Christmas tree. A couple. At it. Not sex. Just at it. Living. You can see their whole room.

'OK, get the notebook out. The one I got you from the Japanese shop. Come on. What do you see?'

'The Waterway building?' he says, flatly.

'Good, that's habitat, make eight columns and put "Waterway" in the third slot. What else?'

'They're fashionable looking, they're pristine, like they're in costume. Maybe they work in—'

'*Woah*, there, cowboy, let's stick to the facts for the columns. How many of them are there?'

'OK, Lil… there are two of them. One blonde, one redhead.'

'Good! Two flock! Put that in column five and the colour of their plumage, blonde and red, in column four. We don't know their names so we'll pick some later for column two. We'll do a brief weather description for column seven. Something about behaviour in six and an estimated height for the last column. I'm good at this so let me suggest five foot six for both. It's a skill. You can get better with practice. It's my party trick, have I never told you that? I'm usually right to the centimetre.'

'Inch.' He smiles. He loves corrections. He loves a bit of control. 'Is zis your farzer's method? Tell me about your farzer?' he says.

I look at him, maybe a beat too long.

'It's my method. So. For column one I'm going to say… WFC. What do you think that–'

'White… female… couple.'

'Very good! Very. Good. Now…'

A lesbian couple. They're a lesbian couple! How exciting! Not that it's unusual or anything. It's just that I don't have any lesbian friends and I'd really like to. I would've voted for the marriage thing, if they'd asked me. Definitely. I'd have knocked on doors. If I'd lived in Ireland or something. I heard a podcast about people knocking on doors over there, changing people's minds. It sounded really cool. It's a no-brainer.

Look at them. We could be friends. We could have lesbian brunches. Or a lesbian book group. I'd love to have a lesbian book group. And now I have some lesbians.

'They've got a globe that lights up. They've got a record player. They've got a retractable punchbag. On a stick. They've got… an oak bookcase. They have blue fairy lights. They have a Dualit toaster, like we do! Ooh, they've left the Country Life butter out. Perhaps one of them thinks they might fancy some more toast in the not too distant future. They've got… cushions from Heal's, not cheap those ones, I've seen them online. They've got a tall fern in the corner where the exterior windows meet. They've got a pink orchid. They've got a twelve-bottle wine rack. They've got empty bottles ready to go down to recycling. They've got a bike in the corner, even though there are racks beneath the building. Oh. It's a Brompton! It folds. They've got a Chinese-framed print of the original poster of *Nights Of Cabiria*, the Fellini movie, and I think… yes… it's limited edition!'

'How do you think they do it?' he says.

'What? Keep the place so tidy? They both do their fair share, I'd imagine.'

'No, the sex. The two-woman sex… thing.'

'It's pretty much the same. Just with two of one thing, rather than the other.'

'Yeah, but…'

'God, you've led a sheltered life. Use your imagination. In fact, don't. Don't, do that. You're ruining this.' Sometimes he needs a scold.

'I mean, do you think they're a "get into their pyjamas" kind of couple? Or d'ya think at some random moment the blonde might just grab the redhead, throw her on that wooden table and just… give her one?'

'I wouldn't have thought so, they're varnishing it. They're only half finished.'

'How can you tell?'

'The difference in the colour of the wood. There's newspaper on the end there, look. And by the sink, brushes in a glass jug.'

'Bloody hell, you're good at this.'

'And, now I come to think of it, I've seen these two before.'

'Where?'

He holds my gaze.

I look away from him.

Shit.

'Wow. You. Are. Mental,' he says

'Don't say that. It's not nice,' I say, breezy, but firm.

Whoosh! A plane shoots overhead. They come very close here. It's like they're getting closer every time. The women look up. You can see their pale, white necks. Janet strokes Tippi's red hair. She dyes it. Must do with that shade.

Footsteps plod along the hallway. We pause. And give each other that grinning look of recognition.

'Uh oh. I zink our znext-door neighbour ist home,' Aid says, his eyes twinkling.

Soon, I'll tell you about the man who lives next door.

Part Two:
The night. And the day that followed.

20 days till it comes. Night. 10 p.m.

SWM – Cary – Parkway – Brunette – Singular – Pensive – 21 degrees, under cover of night, windy – 5′ 10″.

Cary has his favourite Breton top on. He's recently got one of those new haircuts. It's slick on top and shaved at the sides. It's the haircut that would occur if De Niro from *Taxi Driver* became the third member of Wham! He probably works in Shoreditch. It's probably a normal haircut there. He's finishing the look with a red scarf/neckerchief. Which is bold. I get the feeling he's been plucking up the courage to do this for a while and surprisingly it looks OK. He's dancing around a bit, probably to electronic sounds. I wish I could hear what band or DJ. I really wish I could. To get a better idea of it all.

His mates arrive and they do ironic fist pumps. They're probably going out somewhere actually. 'Mate 1' has a Hot Chip T-Shirt on. One of them disappears and then comes back and pinches his nose. Then the other ones disappear and do the same. They start playing on the Wii and it's competitive. One of them licks his teeth as he flings his controller forward, lets go of it and it smacks into the window. It's kicking off!

They're all laughing but Cary doesn't find it so funny, he probably only part owns this flat as part of that scheme. It's not as posh as the Waterway flats but it's nice, same floor plan as ours. He knows the window isn't broken or cracked but he's telling them:

'Dude, careful, these windows cost a fortune.'

Yes, I think that's what he said. And he's right, I bet they do. They wouldn't be cheap to replace. He thinks there's a mark. There is a mark. He's got a cloth. Oh, he's pretty much got it. Oh, I see. It wasn't a proper mark.

'How's Tippi's table coming along?' Aiden says, without looking up.

'Er, not bad, I think. Looked like it was nearly done and drying about an hour ago.'

'Do you think they sanded it first? I might do something like that.'

He never does anything like that. Not any more. He barely even leaves the house.

'I'd imagine so, Aid. I imagine they've done it with a few tables before, mate.' Doing my mock-urban-upper-middle-class voice.

'Oh, I'd imagine so, babe. I imagine they sell them online actually. That's what I imagine. Babe.' He loves it when we do this.

'Oh yup, that's what I imagine too. It's probably reclaimed. From some suburban yard, somewhere you wouldn't have heard of, mate.'

'Oh yeah, mate. I imagine it's difficult to tear Tippi and

Janet away from the reclamation yard. There's so much there you can… er… er…'

'Reclaim, babe?'

'Well, exactly, mate.'

I'm not sure who we're making fun of really. Everyone, I suppose. And ourselves.

Oh dear! Oh no. Cary. You poor thing. You poor little hip, upwardly mobile thing, you're bleeding. Ouch.

No sooner had 'the lads' put 'cloth-gate' behind them, when catastrophe struck again. I caught it in my sights perfectly. I could see it before they did. Those boys in their high spirits were larking about on their Wii. And Cary was standing way too close to the action. I thought, someone's going to get hurt here. And bang! He caught a controller right in the face.

He's bleeding quite a lot. From his top lip. The one with the mohawk is looking for something, maybe ice. While 'Mate 1', still clutching the blood-flecked controller, apologises profusely while pacing from foot to foot.

I'd call an ambulance but I don't think it's my place to. It might prompt a few questions. Like: 'Who the hell called this ambulance?' 'Dude, is one of us sending messages out into the airwaves without knowing it? By mental telepathy? Or, like, some other discreet human transmission process we're as yet unaware of?' And 'Hey, bloody hell, man, who's that woman staring at us through her binoculars over there?'

I think an ambulance might be a bit extreme anyway. I'm sure it'll stop bleeding in a moment. I still wish I could help. I'd go and give it the once-over myself if I was a doctor. But I'm not. No. I'm not a doctor.

'You're obsessed,' Aiden mumbles.

'No, I'm not. People always say that sort of thing about women. She's mad, she's mental, she's obsessed. You should know better. You write good women.'

'I think I just write people. Hopefully. But you're right. Sorry. I won't say that. It's stupid.'

'I'm just interested.'

'Yes, and you're good at it. It's probably from your past as an "avid birdz votcher". You big old geek.'

'I was never a birdwatcher.'

'What? Of course you were. Told me on our first date you were.'

'I certainly never said that. Let me educate you a bit. *Birdwatchers*: go to their local park, with standard gauge binoculars and mark down all the little birds they see in the local area. *Birders*: may go to other countries, recreationally or professionally–'

'*Professionally?* Who pays them to do that?'

'—or wherever, in search of more birds they haven't seen to add to their Life List. There are around ten thousand varieties of bird, even the most ardent birder is unlikely to see as many as seven thousand in their lifetime. Now, those that *go birding*: may visit specific hides and spots to see birds for an afternoon and may also keep a book or list of what they see, like the *birders* do. And lastly, *twitchers*—'

'Ah, twitchers!' He snorts.

'*Twitchers*: set their sights on a particular rare bird and travel specifically to find it.'

'Oh right, and which one are you?' he says.

'Well, you couldn't say I was a twitcher. Which, incidentally, my friend, is so named because one of the most famous rare bird searchers, Howard Medhurst, had a rather nervous disposition, if you must know.'

'Like you. You have a twitch. Yes, so that's what you are.'

'No I don't. No, I'm not...'

'See, there it goes. It's a long blink and your cheek goes a little too!' he says, grinning again, the cheeky sod. Thinks he's ruffled me.

'Really? I... I've never even noticed I do that.'

'Vell, you doo. So zere,' says my Austrian psychoanalyst. His eyes narrow as he takes on a darker tone. He smiles, half concerned, half like a predator, sizing me up. Then speaks exactingly: 'So... I suppose ze real qvestion iz... vot are you... searching vor?'

A knock at the door. I'm saved from my interrogation. I answer it. Aiden sits there not even thinking about getting up to answer it. He simply stays there on his arse, like plankton, like he always does.

'Dr Gullick?'

Aiden suddenly shoots up, excited, shifting himself into a position where he can see me but the woman at the door cannot see him. He is wide eyed and open mouthed. He eyeballs me.

'Yes, that's me,' I say.

'Could you please help me. It's an emergency,' she says.

'Yes. Yes, of course,' I say, swallowing hard and reaching for my black leather washbag. Here we go.

I told you. I am not a doctor. As you well know. But this does tend to happen from time to time.

19 days till it comes. 11 a.m. Work.

WM – Phil – Desk by the door – Brown hair – Very singular – Open, friendly, maybe too friendly – Air con broken, sweaty, temperature unknown – 5′ 11″.

There's a tall fern in a plain white porcelain pot in every corner of the room, you know the kind. Blackening bananas litter an enamelware fruit bowl. And people have started to sit on awkward seats that force you into a position somewhere between 'riding a penny-farthing' and 'kneeling while being held at gunpoint'. It's good for the back they say, but what you gain in posture you must lose in dignity. There's no place like home. And this really is no place like home. They say that in twenty years' time everyone will work from home. We'll communicate with colleagues and clients purely through the net and companies will save millions on the office space. I'm counting the days.

I turn off my phone because it's been ringing again today. I don't want it interrupting me now. There was even a voicemail. And we both know who's calling. Don't we? But, no. I'm not ready to talk, yet. Take the hint. I spend most of my time at work talking on the phone. To people in far off countries. People I don't know. And have no desire to. This is how it goes:

'Could I ask how you found the seating arrangement during the conference?'

'Was there enough seating in the relaxation areas?'

'Interesting, what sort of seating would you like to see for the conference next year?'

'OK. OK. Uh huh. Right. Did you… Ha ha. Oh, of course. Well, I… of course.'

Did you ever hear that rumour about office temperature? That an ancient office law comes into play during summer if your air con is broken? Which is probably more likely to be enacted if your windows don't open. Apparently they worry in this place that if they did open everyone would spontaneously jump out. Opting for the sweet release of death rather than filling out another spreadsheet.

That rumour. About that law. That states that if someone is officious enough to take an official reading with an approved thermometer. And the mercury inside hits that magic number. You all get to go home on full pay? Yes? You've heard that one? Well, apparently, that rumour is complete bollocks. I'm so tired from everything that happened last night. I just want to sleep.

I know that rumour is bollocks. Because Phil, who has the desk by the door, has just attempted to invoke this medieval law. He used a thermometer he oddly happens to have in his drawer. He's that kind of guy. Then he went to confront our line manager with his findings. He did all this because I asked him to. He's the only one I speak to. The only guy in the office that seems even vaguely interesting. The only one who shows any sign of a possible personality, now Lena and Rob have moved on to better things.

In a moment of desperation I Skyped him a cry for help. It was a nice moment. It went like this:

Gull1978: Get me out of here.

KentishPhil: Why?

Gull1978: I'm sweating. Even my sweat is sweating. It's like I'm bathing while I sit here.

KentishPhil: Graphic. You look tired.

Gull1978: Thanks. Couldn't sleep last night. Again.

KentishPhil: I understand.

Gull1978: Get me out of here. I'm serious!!!!!

KentishPhil: OK. Have a plan.

Then he tried it. He reached for his thermometer. Took a reading. Then very skilfully and with the utmost charm took the findings to Deborah, in a valiant attempt to bust us all out of here. Deborah laughed, said: 'That isn't really a thing. I've literally never heard of that rule. Sorry to disappoint you all.'

We all laughed it off and secretly seethed. She patted him on the shoulder. And asked him if she can get the Friday report by Thursday.

'If you were to design a perfect conference for cardiologists, what would it look like?'

'Well, just, say anything you like.'

'Really?'

'Lots more toilets. OK.'

'Hotel provision closer to conference centre, good.'

'Free hot dogs? Ok. Ha ha. Very funny. No, you never know.'

'How about a water slide? No, just joking there.'

'No, I know that wouldn't be appropriate.'

'Yes, I know heart disease is Britain's biggest killer.'

'Yes, I do know that.'

'Sorry.'

From out of the window I see a plane go by that could be headed anywhere. The sky is so blue. The plane cuts through it at tremendous speed. Everyone in it has a comfortable seat and someone is bringing them coffee and a decent enough meal. They are heading to Barbados, or Tenerife, or Ibiza, or Honduras, or Tuscany, or Agadir, or Cephalonia.

I think about that Missing poster again. It flashes into my mind occasionally.

I look down at my trainers. I've still got blood on them from last night.

Back to Last Night

20 days till it comes (Dr Lily Gullick). 11 p.m.

WF – Me, Lily – In an apartment at night – Light brown hair – Married, but utterly singular – In the mirror – Could be a doctor, in another life – 5′ 7″.

To cut a long story short sometimes our Internet goes down. We had to call out a local guy in the end because our provider takes so long to actually send someone to fix it themselves. Our guy says there aren't quite enough sockets in the building for everyone. So every so often someone's Internet guy changes around the sockets, pulling one out at random so there is a free socket for whoever is paying them that day.

It's like there were three in the bed and the little one said roll over, so they all rolled over and one fell out. Maybe that's not a good analogy. There are twenty-two flats and twenty-one phone ports, so it's like musical chairs, let's put it like that. At any one time, someone in the building doesn't have a phone or Internet connection.

And you can't even get a mobile signal round here because we're too close to the water, apparently. They can't get a transmitter close enough or something. So you have to boost your phone signal using an app and your Internet connection. So if you don't have the net you haven't really got anything. You're stranded.

So our guy, nice guy, Dexter, big guy. He has the idea of putting a sticker on our port that reads 'doctor on call'. He's done it before he says. It works.

The first time we got a knock on the door was four months ago, 4 a.m.

'Please, the concierge told me there was a doctor in the building and he gave me the flat number. I'm so sorry to disturb. It's my husband.'

Aiden was flat out, so I was the fall girl. Dr Gullick. It sounds good, doesn't it? Trustworthy somehow. You can imagine a Doctor Gullick. I don't know any of the Dutch side of the family. Maybe there aren't any anymore. I know it's a Dutch name but I feel as British as they come. But I'm sure the original Gullicks, the Dutch Gullicks, were good people. Maybe they were doctors. Who knows, maybe something will kick in. It's not the prettiest name of course. It means 'small bald man with no beard'. Did you know that? Hardly flattering for a gal. But there we are.

I looked at her as my brain adjusted to being awake. I finally figured out what on earth the woman was talking about. The thoughts connected in a couple of seconds. A concierge must have stuck his head in behind the phone port panel at some point and clocked the sticker. Made a mental note to tell people not to pull that one out at all costs. Which was our plan. This, however, was not.

I considered explaining, imagined her face as I told

her about the ruse. Maybe I could tell her it was Dexter's idea. Lay it all on him. He's a big guy. He could take it. Maybe she'd see the funny side. But I didn't do that. I couldn't take the shame of it. Not that I loved the alternative either. Both were pretty shitty options. It was a less heart-rending but more socially awkward version of *Sophie's Choice*. Anyway, somehow I instinctively reached for my leather washbag, which could be generic enough to have my 'doctor's equipment' within it. Nodded. And we left.

I gave her husband the once-over. Sharp abdominal pains had kept him up all night. I put my hands on his bare stomach. What a strange interloper I am. It's funny where one little lie can take you. His skin felt clammy and warm. I'm not sure what I was feeling for. A rumble. Or a kick. I applied gentle pressure and then dug my fingers in. He groaned. Skin is the kindest of fabrics. It felt like more intimacy than I'd had for a while. He breathed heavier and my breathing changed too. His stomach tensed. He groaned again. It wasn't arousing or anything. But it was something.

They waited for the verdict. I opened my mouth but nothing came out. Just a hiss of air. They leant in. The moment seemed to linger on forever. Words failed me. Stage fright. The three of us exchanging glances. In this abstract ménage à trois. Me, dressing up. Them, waiting. They have no idea. There's an intruder in their home.

My silence was starting to seem like the harbinger of bad news. The doctor with the test results wields such power. For a moment, I enjoyed the thrill of this. But I had to speak. I finally found the standard NHS Direct response falling from my lips:

'It's difficult to make any assumptions without getting an X-ray. It's your call, if you think this is a 999 emergency then I would pick up the phone now. If you think it can wait till tomorrow, go straight to your GP and wait in line to be seen that day. They'll usually fit you in at some point in the morning.' Like a bad actor, I fumbled through it.

Then I went back up to the fourth floor, crawled into bed and went back to sleep.

But now, here was another patient altogether, standing in my doorway with a subtle tremble moving through her lower half. A classic neurotic. Her problem? She couldn't sleep. Imagine for a second being a real doctor and being woken up for this when you have a double heart surgery the next morning. Or whatever doctors do.

She took me to her room, told me stories of stress. I think there was a rash involved. I don't know if she was hoping I had a secret pill stash or whether she seriously is ill. Physically or mentally. I wouldn't know. I'm not an expert. I'm not a doctor.

Either way, she can't have been so upfront with the concierge. Surely he wouldn't have revealed my 'identity' for that. Or maybe this was a classic palm off.

I made her sit down. Put my hand to her head. Then took her pulse and nodded sagely and improvised.

'I'm afraid even if I did have something to help you sleep it wouldn't do any good. I know this isn't what you want to hear but you need lovely, natural sleep. Just breathe in through your nose for fifteen and out through your mouth for ten. It's the best medication I can provide. Try it now, in for fifteen. Good. And out for ten.'

As I knelt at her bedside I was reminded of Mum.

'Thank you, Doctor.' I got a warm feeling when she said this.

'As for the rash, I can give you something for that.' I searched in my washbag for a cream I sometimes use for athlete's foot. I wonder what that'll do for her. Cure her maybe. Or maybe there's something in it that's bad for her. I hope not. But I don't know. Not a doctor.

I keep my bag low so as not to reveal that rather than a stethoscope and thermometer my 'doctor's bag' contains only tampons and hair clips.

'You can keep the cream. Now, please, get some rest.'

I head back to bed again, stowing the bag under my arm and trying to seem inconspicuous.

My phone goes and I hit reject straight away. Then there's a voicemail. Another one. I have a brief listen on the way back to upstairs.

'If you don't answer, I'm going to come round there. I will. No matter how far it is. I'm coming. You know what? That's it. I'm coming—' I hit Delete.

Then I see a figure in the hallway.

The guy next door: Lowell.

19 days till it comes. 2.30 p.m.

Knock, knock.

Phil knocks on my desk and asks if I want to go for a cigarette. I wake from another daze. I don't really want to go. But it's awkward not to. 'Awkward' is the predominant word I associate with him. I look at him and imagine it emblazoned across his forehead.

I don't smoke but he says if I hold one I get a free ten-minute break, so I do that. Outside the sun shines and he talks. Which is nice because it saves me doing the heavy lifting.

'. . . Until you're feeling like, hmm, I don't think I can actually take it any more, because my ribs are hurting. Then the movie gets kind of thoughtful. Then a little weird. Then kind of sad. Which is... you know. Then it gets really funny again and then it ends.'

'Sorry, what were we talking about?'

'Adam Sandler's *Click*.'

'Is it good?'

'Yes, of course it's good. He can pause and play time. He

finds a magic remote control. It's probably my favourite Sandler film. You like films?'

'Yes, I do. Never seen one of his films though, to be honest.'

'You like films, but you've never seen an Adam Sandler film? Oh, my God! What…? What's your favourite film, would you say?'

'*Psycho*.'

'Wow. That's… I don't think I've seen that one. Is that a black-and-white one?'

'Yes.'

'I don't tend to watch those ones.'

There's an awkward pause.

'Listen, just so you know. We all know.'

A pause.

'We heard. We know. So, I just wanted to say that,' he says.

'You… know?'

'Yeah. We… we know. And it will get better. I promise.'

We head upstairs again. What do they know? I suppose I haven't been hiding it well. I want to leave. I have to leave. That must be it. Everyone in this office has been looking at me and they know. I hate my job. And no, Phil, it won't get any better.

I can't concentrate on anything. For a moment I think back to Cary and his poor face. I hope he's all right. He always calls his mother, every night at seven, like clockwork. I'm not a great lip-reader but I'm pretty sure he always signs off with 'I love you'.

Phil is nice. He's a good guy. A simple guy. Certainly. But there's nothing wrong with that. Just looking at him calms me down. He's like a lava lamp. He's a bit like Lowell in that way. Ah, Lowell.

I like Lowell. Lowell lives next door. Which brings us back to last night.

20 days till it comes. Night. 11.45 p.m.

WM – Lowell – Riverview – Fair, curly – Unusually, in a 2 flock – Dependable – Interior – 6′ 2″

He is American, I think. Actually it might be one of those international school accents, which means he could be from anywhere. Switzerland or Swaziland. Hong Kong or Hawaii. Singapore or Kuwait City. He is balding but has a good head for it. He is subtly well built, muscular. Would seem formidable, imposing, if it wasn't for his kind face. Which puts everything else into context. It's worn like a travelling salesman, but soft like a foster parent. He seems bookish but with a superhero jawline. He's the kind of man that could never be an accountant. But in actual fact I think he is an accountant. But some sort of posh one. For a big charity, I think. He does some work for a local organic bakery too. I don't know what, but I don't think he bakes the bread. Management, advice and sums. You'd want him on your *University Challenge* team. He's a winner. You'd trust him to hold your baby.

He glides past me in the hallway. It's nearly midnight. He has casual khakis and a white shirt on. He looks like he should be sanding a boat on a beach somewhere. Barefoot, with a little dog running around his feet. He looks like a '90s Gap advert, designed specifically to show you that he is a man. A healthy man. He's with a woman. They're sensibly dressed. Equally dependable looking. In a gentle, middle of the road way. He is holding her up and she has had more to drink than him. He's an extreme moderate. Always a couple of G and Ts but not so many that he's ever out of control. I imagine – we've never been out for a drink. He's never been in our flat and I've never been in his. We're not close. But we'd like to be. Aiden has a man crush on him, I think. He jokes that he once saw him cycling and he swooned. We have friend ambitions on him. He's always good for a 'stop and chat'. I've never seen him with a girl before. Good for him.

'Lily. How are you this evening?'

'Hey, I'm good. You? Up to no good I assume?'

'Oh yeah, you know how it is. This is Sarah…'

'Hello,' she says, perfunctory but warm.

She smiles. Weather girl teeth. I hope she sticks around. Maybe he's unlucky in love. Or just has exacting standards. Who knows? He's dependable more than exciting. Maybe that's it.

'Well, we'll love you and leave you. As they say,' he quips.

'Do they say that?'

'Yeah. Yes, I think they do. They do to me anyway.'

'I don't believe that for a second. 'Night.'

The funny thing is I do believe that. He has the extraordinary skill of looking just a touch downtrodden even with a perfectly nice woman next to him. Maybe he never makes it to the second date. Maybe once they see the inside of the flat they run a mile. Maybe there's terrifying taxidermy everywhere. I wonder what it's like in there. Inside his flat. And inside his head. For that matter.

I was thinking of all these things as I slid into bed. Trying not to let on I'm thinking about another man. I wonder what exactly he's doing to her next door. I wonder if Aiden would be jealous If he knew that's what I was thinking about. He's dead to the world anyway. As I lie there considering Lowell's possibly poor sexual technique.

These walls are well insulated. But not that well. But still, you never hear anyone cry out in passion. No banging from his side of the wall. Poor Lowell. And poor Suzanne? Sandra? Simone? Cecily? Sally? Samantha? Sophie? Sarah!

That's the one.

I don't want to boast, but I'm sure we've made our bedposts bang against the partition wall a few times. I'm sure he's heard us. But you never hear a peep out of him. Not to be crude. But I assume you know how it all works. You know we were trying for a baby after all. Up until recently.

Night. 12.30 a.m.

Midnight is long gone.

One a.m. comes along and goes. I think of Janet and Tippi's orchid. I think of Cary's bloody lips. I think of Phil's lava lamp face. I breathe in for fifteen. And out for ten. Like I used to tell Mum to. But it doesn't work.

Two o'clock arrives. And I am still in the land of the living.

I think of how many others in this building are staring at their ceilings as I do now. How many are dead asleep? I wonder how many of these rooms are even occupied. It's tough to keep track of your neighbours in a place like this. No matter how hard you try. It's hard to make connections. That's not what everyone wants. Hardly anyone wants that these days. They mostly just want an Internet connection and a funny video of some cats or a horse.

People come and go here. No sooner are they set up than they're looking to get out. The prices are going up all the time, which somehow translates into impermanence. People are renting for now, but looking to buy. People are buying, but looking to get something better soon. I overhear people talking about Flipping the Place On and Making a Tidy Profit in a Year or Two. I hear them say I Might Buy Another One Off Plan and By the Time That's Built I'll Have Flipped That One On Too. People are here for the week but jump in the car to get away for the weekends. People looking for a chance to leave the city for good. Everyone seems to be trying to escape this place, in one way or another. But me. I'm here to stay.

Then there's the people in far away countries who buy places for their kids to move into some day. Or just have them as an investment. Never bothering with the hassle of renting the place out. So they sit there like empty shells. As if haunted. Sometimes I wonder if they are haunted.

It's difficult to see back into a building you're already in. To see what's going on above. Or below or to the sides. Binoculars don't work like that. You'd hear the sounds if the rooms weren't pretty well soundproofed. Sometimes I think I hear crying through the walls. From above or below. Then I think it's just my imagination. But even crying would at least be something.

So I never know who lives here. I never hear them or feel them. Suddenly around a corner will appear a guy in flip-flops with a trendy full beard and an Antipodean accent. I'll have never seen him in my life before. I may never do again. Does he really live here? Is he an intruder? Is he a ghost?

Maybe ghosts haunt spaces, rather than rooms. I often think this. What I mean is, even though the four walls around me have only existed for a little over two years, and we're led to believe your home must be at least twenty years old, preferably fifty, to qualify for a haunting, someone did once live here. In this space. In the old block. The one they tore down so they could build this one instead.

The other one was built in the early fifties. Plenty of time for anything to occur here. What were their lives like? What did they do in here? In this space where I'm lying. Were there births? Deaths? Sex and arguments? In this space. Are these things the ghosts?

This morning, on the way to work, I stopped and watched the wrecking ball bash open a building, like paper. Brutal, efficient. You could see the insides of two or three homes in a row next to each other. One was painted dark blue, its walls now facing the open, its chest to the wind. Their flat became one big balcony.

The people inside never considered it would turn out this way. No ceiling or exterior wall. Only a tiny ledge of floor left at the back.

The next one was wallpapered. Probably in the seventies by the looks of it. Browns and beiges. The light switches were still there. I noticed. But I knew by the next hit they wouldn't be. They fell forty-five feet to the ground and were swept efficiently into a skip.

The third flat was a garish pink. Like the inside of a body. Light colours, to make the most of the meagre space.

The three homes sat there. Blown open. For me to see the remnants and adornments of the lives that used to live inside. Like a cross-section or a doll's house. It's a ten-minute glance, just for any lucky bystander that happens to be there at the time. By the eleventh minute, the three will be completely destroyed in two firm swings of the forged steel ball.

On the wall of the pink flat was a crucifix. It glinted in

the light. Visible to the naked eye. I watched the metal sphere hit it. I watched it drop, along with the concrete, dust and wires. And, without stopping for a second to consider what they had destroyed, the machines swept past and gathered everything up. Next, it went into the skip. Then into a lorry. Then the landfill.

Yes. Without a thought. The little cross. The residents prayed to. Would be buried beneath tons of nameless rubble and debris.

As I lie here, thinking these night-time thoughts, I wonder how many people are thinking the same things, at this very same time. Awake. Somewhere in another part of London. What if we could find each other and connect. Just as I'm thinking these things I notice something in the top right corner of my window. A single light still on. In a flat in Canada House. Unless I'm mistaken, it's number forty-one. Jean's flat.

I pull on an old jumper and some trainers. Carefully, so I don't rouse him from wherever he is. From his slumber and dreams. I can't tell him where I'm going. He'd say I was 'mental' again and it'd just make me angry. Really angry. Then I really won't be able to sleep. I grab my keys. My phone, just in case. And leave.

I've never been through the estate before. Just before I close the door I grab a handmade flick knife. Aiden bought it for me on our honeymoon, in Buenos Aires. I shove it in my black washbag. Just in case.

I'm walking through the estate at night. It's warm out here tonight. One of those warm restless nights. But I'm surprised to see no other lights on in any of the apartments. Or the estate. No other night owls in Canada House. Just number forty-one.

I skulk around, staring at the building. Many of the other flats are boarded up. Metal slats applied firmly to windows to keep things out. The weather, squatters, animals. The left side of the building is almost completely empty. Its guts hanging out for everyone to see. Glassless windows, dusty exposed brick, graffiti. There was a rumour that these houses once doubled for Warsaw in *Schindler's List* and, looking at them, I can believe it.

A yellow ADVANCED WARNING NOTICE tells us that the demolition of Alaska House, the largest of the blocks and the next one to go, will begin on 29 September. One of the roads behind it will be closed off for a while. This is their biggest job yet. Their masterpiece. Until then we have a few weeks' silence and grace. Before the rumble starts again. I pass the Missing poster too. It flaps away gently in the wind.

Jean lives on the right side of the building. The occupied side. Still waiting to be rehoused. There's definitely an eerie feeling round here. The place is too empty. Or maybe not empty enough somehow. I can't decide which yet. But as I'm thinking this I hear something and stop to listen. My thoughts drift away, I stand there listening. I could be imagining it. But I think it's the sound of someone breathing.

I turn and brace myself. Nothing. I keep my senses open. Searching for whatever is telling me everything's not quite right. Then I hear the sound of shoes scraping across gravel. Shit. I turn again to face it. Nothing. Perhaps the echo of my own feet. Rebounding off the concrete buildings that surround me.

The steps to her place are only twenty metres away, but I decide to break into a jog. My heart is beating hard, it's gothic out here. The street lights are out. Either turned off by the council or smashed out by someone more sinister. This is stupid. I've never done anything like this before. What is it I'm looking for? No time to think. Come on. Move your feet.

I get to the stairwell, breathing hard now. Cars intermittently light me up as they fly past thirty or so metres away. By their passing beams, I put one hand against the wall and tread carefully up the flight of concrete stairs that leads to her floor. I can't see the hand in front of my face when the car headlights drift away. I tread carefully. No light for five seconds, fifteen seconds. Nearly there.

I hear a distant engine that should soon light my way. Then something wet underfoot. I squelch in it. I try not to look down. The car approaches, I don't want to look back now. This is Jean's route home. Every night. Jesus. The flash of light comes. Blood on the ground. I look back.

Dead. Covered in hair. I put my hand to my throat and then mouth and only just manage to avoid screaming, knowing that would echo loud and long into the distance. I rumble and shake on the inside. It's a huge rat. Ripped open. Over thirty centimetres long. Dead. I gag a little. Disgusted but sighing in partial relief – it could be worse. I get to the top of the stairs.

I turn forward again. Then hear the sound of something fly past my head. Bats. There are a lot of them round here as we're near the water. They're cute in a way. Then a metal pipe swings past my ear and I dive to the side. I hear the sound of the air as it narrowly misses me. I reach inside my bag instinctively and grip the knife. A blood-curdling scream. A car passes, lighting the pipe again, clearly held in a gloved hand. It's like a nightmare. But I am definitely awake.

'I'm going to fucking kill you!'

I breathe deep, gasping from somewhere deep within my lungs as I ready myself to attack. The one advantage of the dark is that my attacker can't see me either. I stay quiet, jumping back out to face them head on. My fist tightens as I flick open the knife, keeping it concealed within the bag until the last moment. I breathe in once more.

'You fucking—'

As the car comes past I stare at her face to face. Both our hearts pumping fast. The cold, damp night air filling our nostrils. Jean holds a pipe above her head. She's a biggish woman. I would say it would crack my skull right open. If she uses her full force. I hope she doesn't, but then maybe that's what intruders get.

'You stupid cow. What are you doing?' she says, letting the pipe fall to her side.

I can barely get the words out. I hold up my hands. 'I'm sorry. I'm so sorry. Please don't... er... hurt me.'

She looks at me and recognition flickers across her face. A frown.

'Get inside. We should get inside. Now.'

Night. 3 a.m.

WF – Jean – Canada House – Grey perm – Alone – Wary. Tough. Gives as good as she gets – A warm evening, with European breeze, Pitch-black night – 5′ 6″.

'People like you shouldn't be hanging around here in the dark. You stupid girl,' she says, suddenly becoming a Mother Superior.

'People like me?'

'Beehives. That's what they call you. Bloody beehives. After that posh pub – the Beehive – they opened that all you yuppies go to. I knew when that arrived it was the beginning of the end for us.'

'I'm not. I'm not a... yuppy. That's not who I am.'

'Well, whoever you are, *they* can spot you a mile off. You're a different species. And you'll be an endangered one if you hang around here at night. You lot need to stick to your side. They don't much like me. So they certainly won't like you. And if they don't like you, you know about it.'

'Who are you talking about?'

'The kids. The ones they couldn't find places for. They're still here. They broke back into their own homes, some of them. Mostly in the Alaska House. Sleeping on newspapers. Making their way any way they can.'

'But I thought everyone had new places to live?' I say quietly. Guiltily.

'Yes. And if you believe that you'll believe anything. They got us out all right, with promises of bigger flats "just that little further out". The ones that stayed, our places are falling down and no one is coming out to fix anything no matter how much I ring up the council and threaten them. The others ended up in places like Ipswich. I mean, where's Ipswich? It's not my home. But some came back and stayed anyway, hiding in the building. 'Cos their lives are still here. Their jobs are still here. Whatever they consist of. I'm not saying they're criminals. Least, they weren't before. But once things start to slip. Once you break the first couple of rules, the rest don't seem so hard to break either. Every morning I wake up and someone has pissed opposite my door. Every morning I clear it up. I see everything round here. And I've seen some things. Drugs and drink is just the start of it. I've seen blood on the pavement. And I've seen it shed in front of my eyes too. But no one cares about the things that people like me see. Don't hang around here, you silly cow. Get back to your end. And lock the door when you're there.'

You couldn't call her kindly. She probably once was, but her manner had been hardened by the last couple of years. She looks ten years older than the photo in the paper. Her hair wasn't so grey then. But inside, the place is still a home. Pictures of children and grandchildren smile out at you from behind floral frames.

'They're in Portugal now. They only call once a month, at most. I should've joined them. Bloody freezing this country.'

She's right, it is cold in here. I'm not sure how, outside is quite warm, summertime spreading smoothly through every other corner of London. Jean's place has its own Arctic microclimate. Like the cold has soaked into the walls. She explains the price of fuel has gone up and her state pension doesn't allow her to be reckless, even with heating. Everything has to be thought out. Everything perfectly stacked. Enough tinned food for a nuclear holocaust. And, along with the metal pipe that sits next to the door, a cricket bat and an old fire poker are there for self-preservation.

For a moment, my eyes linger on a statue that sits on her kitchen sideboard. A cream-coloured monkey, sitting on a rock. Serenely smiling out at me. His ears are a curious shade of lime green. His belly is brown. And, on his head, the monkey balances a bowl. Which Jean uses for spare change.

Below the bowl, the monkey's hands cover his eyes.

A noise from the other room. I stand and grip my bag again, placing myself in front of Jean, ready to do who knows what.

'Ha ha, that's just Terrence,' she says. Now highly amused. Her King Charles spaniel puppy bounds into the room. She reaches for a treat and strokes his head. He comes to greet me too. I was never good with dogs, but luckily Terrence is good with me. Jean seems brighter suddenly with Terrence around. Younger. She is a different person all of a sudden. You can see what she would've been like with a family around her.

'I was up late. I saw your light on. I know it's strange, but I just wanted to say… I read the article, and I would never cross the road to avoid you. I'm sorry all this has happened to your home. I like it round here. But I'm sorry me being here means that… means that you're being forced to leave. I think that's awful. Terrible. And, in some way, I feel responsible. I'm sorry. For that.'

'Oh, don't worry about us, love. We're already sunk. We're just waiting till we hit the bottom. And there's nothing anyone can ever do about that.'

I am embarrassed to say it, but I want to come again. To help with things. If there is anything she needs help with. She doesn't look happy about it but she doesn't say I can't either. I punch my number into her phone and promise her again that I won't walk through the estate after dark. It's a promise I plan to keep.

I decline her offer to borrow one of her makeshift weapons, saying I'd run back and be safe. Not revealing I have a knife with me. Or that I had been a few seconds away from plunging it into her side when we first met. I chance a hug. She doesn't move for a second. But I hold on. Her body, at first rigid, softens. There we stand, two people who can't sleep, holding each other up. Gradually, her arms come up and curl around me. I haven't hugged anyone like this since Mum. As this thought passes through my mind, I squeeze harder and she does too. Her daughter was a long time gone. Something distinct passes between us. A noiseless whisper. Or a secret. Then I feel and hear her breathe, as some held emotion drifts up from her chest and then out and away. We all need a hug. She touches my shoulder and then ends the clinch abruptly, almost with a push. But, when I look up, I see a grudging acknowledgement in her watery blue eyes. I nod, both of us avoiding full eye contact as my feet scuff her floor and I turn and put my hand on the door handle.

I turn back for a second because I think I hear her say something. But I don't think she did. This, however, gives me a chance to smile at her properly and she gives one back like she's out of practice. I stroke Terrence, open the door and hear it close and lock behind me as I hustle off quickly down the concrete stairs. The stench of piss fills the air.

I run, while trying desperately not to look like I'm doing so. I can see my flat and imagine being safe in bed with Aiden any second. I look around me, even more self-conscious on the return journey than I had been on my trip over here. I am ready for someone up to no good. Ready to give as good as I get if anyone tries anything. I try to stay inconspicuous but my own breath seems deafening in my ears, echoing hard around the estate, making me a target. It's hard not to feel paranoid when someone has just told you to watch out. Then, from the corner of my eye, on the fourth floor of Alaska House, I see a metal slat pull open. A car speeds past, beeping its horn wildly in the distance, and its headlights illuminate the outline of a face. Startled by the starkness of the noise and silhouette in front of me, my breath falls away. I feel like I'm winded. As I stagger back to catch it and breathe deep, I look closer. A pair of eyes glisten in the window. I look straight into them. As they look back, accusingly. Then I turn and run.

19 days till it comes. 5.32 p.m.

I head out of work and hurry to the Tube. Marching towards home and to my bed. Every day at work is exactly the same. I don't know if I can take much more. I just have to zone out and let it happen to me, I suppose. Sorry. I'm falling asleep even now. I need to sleep.

'Is that blood on your shoes?' A shout comes from behind me.

It's Phil. A bit indiscreet. What if I was a serial killer? He would've just blown my cover. I give him a look. How does he know I'm not one? He could be getting himself into a lot of trouble.

'Sorry. I sort of blurted that out, didn't I?' he bumbles.

'Yeah, you did,' I say coldly. I'm tired.

'Whose blood is it?'

'Not mine.'

'OK.'

'All right?'

'You make me pretty nervous.'

I'm walking hard and he's struggling to keep up. I'm not slowing down though. If he wants to talk so much he'll keep up. I've got to get back and have a chat with Aiden. I'm worried about him. He's deep into his book. He barely leaves the house. I said I'd support him while he wrote it, so I'm the one paying the rent. I'm the one paying for the food deliveries too. He's done the same for me in the past, but this is different. He's a shut-in. He doesn't go out on his motorbike or anything any more. He never talks about our possible baby. He just sits by the window tapping away at his laptop. Morning, noon and night. He's really letting himself go.

'I know this isn't perfect timing but I wondered whether you fancied a drink some time?'

'What? What kind of drink?' I say, as if the word 'drink' seems somehow alien to me.

'You don't have to decide that now. You can have anything up to the value of six pounds. Which will get you most things these days. Well… in Yates. Not other places. But we could go other places.'

'You know I'm married right?' I stop for the first time and look him in the eye.

He looks back at me. I'm not sure I like how he looks at me. He's very keen.

'Er… yes, of course,' he says, falteringly. He stops altogether for a second.

Then tries again. 'I mean as friends. Just for a chat. Just to pass the time.'

'Oh, a friendship drink. Maybe. I'll let you know.'

'I'm sure you're very busy.'

'I am.'

I'm through the barrier and he knows he gets a different line to me so he's talking very fast.

'But if you need to let off steam any time. After work. Someone to talk to…'

'I'll think about it. Thanks.' I'm civil as I head off in the other direction. He's nice. I'm tired.

'Not that you need anyone to… Wait!'

That does stop me in my tracks. That was loud. A few people make faces as they pass by me and head down to the elevator. He's making a scene. I make a face that says, *Go on then. What?*

'I've seen you. I watch you. When we're at work.'

Oh, God. He's either searching for a romcom moment or he's about to throttle me. People flow past me and onto the escalator and down to the Underground. And I have to stay there. In his awkward tractor beam. Until he's finished.

'OK, Phil. See you tomorrow.'

He stares at me. Meaningfully. But I'm not entirely sure what the meaning is.

'I just like you, that's all,' he murmurs. It would be cute if it wasn't so awful.

Romance is a curse. The amount of unwanted gestures that get foisted on women in this city is incredible. All those sensitive London blokes that think they're in a kooky movie. Someone should tell them, *Real life isn't like that, love*. Supposed 'romance' has become an excuse for men to do what they want. To shout across crowded rooms. To talk in stupid voices. And, worst of all, learn to play the ukulele. Today's version of 'romance' is just another thing women have to withstand.

I point at him, make a gun sign with my fingers and fire. Pow, pow. Then I step onto the escalator.

'See you tomorrow then, Li...'

I'm halfway to the Victoria Line as his voice fades away in the crowd.

I wonder what he wants with me. Maybe he doesn't even know, at this stage.

At home, I collapse into bed. Kick off my trainers and turn my head to Aiden. He barely even looks up. Just taps away, his back leaning against the window. Not even a 'hello' or 'how are you?' I'm not sure who he's become. I barely recognise him. I breathe out heavily. My head falls back onto my pillow. Last night has given me such strange thoughts.

I don't know what it is about last night. But it's bringing things back to me. Some unresolved things. Again, I know you're not a therapist.

But if I do let you see me again. If I let you. If you do pay us a visit. If you really must cross the Channel and come and see us. If you can manage that trip over on the ferry. And everything else.

You've got to promise not to say those words. You will promise me that. You have to. Or you're not coming anywhere near me. No matter how much you say you can help.

I know you think I'm overreacting. But please. Don't say them.

Those words I'll never forget.

Don't say: This is how it started with her too.

Part Three: The Woman in Canada House

18 days till it comes. 10 a.m.

I slept for fourteen hours straight. I look at my phone and, luckily, it's Saturday. I had no idea. The days seem to merge into one. Aiden must be in the bathroom. He's not making much noise in there. Maybe he's in the bath. Stagnant. Like a soup. Still tapping away at his laptop all the while.

'You OK in there?'

No response. I slept too long. My head hurts and my brain is heavy. My limbs feel like they're carrying weights. I pull on some jeans and a shirt. I hate the feeling of putting on clothes when I haven't showered. I hoist up the blinds and let the light flow in. It's so bright. My eyes struggle to focus and then a crowd come into view. In the top right hand of my window. In front of Canada House.

'Just going out for a second, you need anything?'

No response. I still need to talk to him about his behaviour recently. Who am I to talk? I know. But, still.

I squeeze my trainers on and head into the hallway and then the lift. Using it for a few flights of stairs always seems pointless but I want to check I don't look too mad in the mirror. I tie my hair back, spray under my arms and throw my black bag into my rucksack. I guess I'm using it more in the way that Superman uses his telephone box. I tap my fingers against the metal rail as I wait for the door to slide open. When it does, I hurry to the glass doors, push the green release button to let me out of the building and the fresh air hits me, making me feel a bit sick.

I squint in the bright daylight. The crowd gets thicker as more bodies join it. I could call Jean and ask her what it's all about rather than join the rubberneckers but I only think of that when I'm virtually there. On second thoughts, I don't even have her number, I only gave her mine. There are faces I know from the newbuilds milling around, people from the council side too. It's a real community get together. But, God knows what it's all in aid of.

Then I feel it. There it is. That chilly feeling is here. The one that goes through the flesh and into the bones. The sort that makes animals stampede. The 'we need to talk' text. The Unavailable number that calls and asks for you by name and beckons you to 'sit down' because 'we have some news that might be difficult to hear'. Cary is eating a Cornish pasty at the edge of the group. Perhaps someone has erected a snack stand. He gets up on tiptoes to try to get a better look but doesn't want to venture in any further. I'd say hello but that would be odd. He's never met me.

I walk past the Missing poster and glance at the blurred picture of a young woman's face on it. It says she was a local student. The number of the local police sits underneath her photograph. I wonder where she went. I wonder *when* she went. I feel like this poster has always been there. Much like a flyer for a gym or cheap long-distance calls, I always imagine these things are not meant for me.

I push through the bodies. They seem to be crowded around an open door. It's a weird sight. They stand in neat rows like a perfect audience for a Covent Garden street magician. But they're being held back by an invisible force that allows them only so close. Some police tape that exists only in their imagination. Because the police are nowhere to be seen. Maybe no one has thought to call them yet. Maybe no one wants to, far better to keep that level of danger in the air, like a theory dangling, unanswered. It's more thrilling that way. Or maybe it's just not that serious. I'll join the throng and find out. I like to sit and watch as much as the next man.

My breath gets shorter though as I get closer and see they're standing, looking up at the open first floor door to number forty-one. Further up the stairs, directly outside her door, more people stand, gawping and ruining the view for those on the ground. Too many bodies in the way. They're stock still, staring at what I can't see. They part suddenly and a young boy shouts as something flies past everyone at knee level. It's Terrence. I feel like he's an old friend even though we only met a few hours ago. The night before last. When I was here.

Terrence barks wildly. Spooked or just seeing an opportunity to play. He finds me and comes to say hello. I stroke his head and peer past the faces and into the flat. Then I see her. There, face down in the middle of her kitchen, surrounded by her family pictures and an overturned dog bowl, Jean. It's strange how stupid people are in crowds. How insensitive to the moment. The import of the situation ripples through their bodies but their brains struggle with 'what's appropriate' and the result is an open-mouthed gawp. Some hold phones, unsure whether to use them. A bloke in shades scratches his arse. They are all overcome by this unusual Saturday morning drama and have no way of coping with it.

A man is venturing into Jean's flat, watched by the crowd. He heroically shrugs, looking down every so often, afraid to touch her in case he gets whatever she's got, then wanders out again. Women mumble. Men rub the back of their necks and scrunch their faces. There are boys in hooded tops here too. A bearded man in his pyjamas, with a French bulldog, who definitely lives on our side. Even the nervous woman is here, who I taught to count to fifteen. She sees me and reacts, eyeing me, excitedly. Instinctively, I turn to leave.

'Doctor! Let this woman through. She's a doctor!' she bellows.

Oh, God. They perk up now. Their indecision has a leader. I turn, hold up a hand, as if to say, *Yes, it is I, your saviour*. Someone even starts to clap, but it doesn't catch on. I am jostled up the concrete stairs and inside number forty-one. Despite ardent promises to myself that I would come clean, that I wouldn't let this happen again, it's happening again. I suppose this isn't the ideal moment to mention to everyone that I'm not actually a doctor. That it all came from a misunderstanding with my phone and Internet cable. Public declarations are for Richard Curtis films. And I'm not good in front of crowds. I'm the kind of girl that would rather skulk around in the wings.

They all have their eyes trained on me. I want to get out of this as quickly as possible, but it's difficult not to take a look around while I'm here. It's very much as I left it. The cupboard, half open, shows her array of tin cans still tightly packed. I crouch down, sensing I've spent a moment too long surveying the place, rather than tending to the matter in hand. I must get back to playing Dr Gullick. Dr Gullick, who has certainly never been in this flat before and isn't wondering what exactly happened here in between the time she left and now. Dr Gullick, who heals the sick. I crouch down to tend to her, without any idea what Dr Gullick will do next, but I have to do something, to please the assembled masses. After all, she may still be alive. But then, people who are alive aren't usually blue.

I take her pulse with two fingers, pushing my hand between her chin and the floor to get to her throat. She's cold. I've never felt anyone so cold. But then I've never felt a dead body before. I put the back of my hand in front of her nostrils, doing my best work from what I've gathered from old episodes of *ER*. No breath. I imagine her sitting up, gasping as the crowd reels, someone screaming at the back. She tells me to 'get off, ya silly cow', picks up a wooden spoon and throws some beans into a pan, muttering to herself all the while. But she doesn't do that.

I take a leap of faith and open her eyelids. I don't know why. Getting into it? Curiosity? It's so intimate. My middle finger and thumb pulling apart the tissue paper eyelids of this formidable woman. I try desperately to hold back my gasp as I stare into her, the pupil dominating her eye. Doctors tend not to squeal. It doesn't engender much trust.

Her eyes were so alive, so fidgety last time I saw them. I look into the pupil now and I'm struck by the emptiness of it all. How quickly we can all become 'the body'. Where has the rest of Her gone? I'm struggling to come to terms with something. I've never seen anything like it before. Never been confronted so directly by what used to be an idea, death and nothing. No literature, television drama or gossip can prepare you for its glare. It's so mundane. It's a familiar tune. Hummed many times before, which will be hummed many more. And it chills me how quickly I can shrug it off, take the torch from my keys out of my pocket, shine a light in this whale's eye and play out the final part of the artificial inspection. At the last, somewhere between the role and myself, I touch her hand and hold it for a second.

I turn to the crowd who proclaimed me their leader and shake my head. Some sympathetic groans. A couple shuffle away at the back shaking their heads. It's as if they've just found out the bloke who comes to clean the windows isn't coming this week. Even death itself seems an anticlimax I suppose, especially if it's not happening to you. Or if you weren't staring into the face of it.

'Can someone call an ambulance, please?' I shout to them all.

'Isn't she dead?' a voice comes back.

'Yes. I believe she is, but either way an ambulance will have to come and take her away.'

'Why? If she's dead, she's dead,' the voice comes back.

'Because we can't just throw her in a skip and be done with it.'

It comes out before I can stop it. I'm angrier than I thought I was.

'She has to be pronounced officially dead. They'll take away her body to be examined.'

'Oh. You don't think there's... er... foul play, do you?'

replies another voice. With a tone that suggests the speaker thinks he's in an episode of *Diagnosis Murder*. Rather than reality.

How detached we all are. Safe in our tiny dwellings. Hidden from the natural world, our windows and TV screens soft lenses that beautify. I feel like I'm the only one that really feels sometimes. If that's not too narcissistic a sentiment.

'No. I don't think it's… "foul play". Personally. But that's not up to me to decide.' Just a dash sardonic. Classic Dr Gullick.

In reality, I can't say whether there has been 'foul play' or not. It looks to me like a woman dropped stone dead and gave herself an almighty whack when she hit the ground. But maybe that's the way it's supposed to look. Because, maybe, someone gave her an almighty whack first, and then lay her on the ground to make it look like the injury was caused by the fall. She's certainly gone down hard.

I could be more sure about my assumption. If I turned her over. But I don't want to do that. I'd be scared to move her. I don't want to 'contaminate the scene'. Plus, I probably shouldn't leave any more of my fingerprints in this place than there already are.

So I can't be sure exactly what caused that blow. But then, you see, I'm not a doctor.

As someone volunteers to dial 999, I take one last look at her. A young woman dials as she holds her boyfriend's hand. I think they live further down on the estate. I'm sure I've seen them before. I scan the other faces in the crowd too, just to check.

Before I go I have a last look around the place. I poke

my head around the corner to see the living room more fully than I did the night before last. Then, coming back to the kitchen, I see a strange thing. The black metal poker she kept by the door. Is gone.

Her other weapons. The cricket bat and pipe sit by in their usual place for safe keeping. But not the poker.

Perhaps she needed it for something. I wonder where it is now. It wasn't the sort of thing she'd ever be without. It was for her own protection. Jean was all too aware of the sorts of people that hang around here at night and what they're capable of. I wonder if anything else is missing.

I play a quick game of spot the difference. The room the night before last. Versus the room today. I spy something else. With my little eye.

The porcelain figurine. The monkey. No longer smiles at me from the sideboard. She could've moved it, or broken it, after I left, I suppose. But by the look of the dust around it, I'd say it'd sat right there since about 1982. I don't know why she'd choose last night to finally throw the thing away.

Someone's been moving things around. And I'm the only one that would know it.

'Well, there goes another one,' a passer-by drops, a touch macabre. And anyway, who was 'the one' before this one? The student from the poster? I make a mental note to look into that. I wonder what her story is. I guess I'm developing a far keener sense of civic duty than I've ever had before. I've grown a conscience. I've grown curious.

There's not so much care on display on the estate this morning. As if her death held a lower price for everyone else than it did for me. An old lady dies. So what? After the interest of it, everyone just goes home and sticks the TV on.

'I've seen blood shed in front of me,' she said the night before last.

'But no one cares about the things I see,' she said. And that's how it feels this morning. Like this is just going to be it. Her relatives in Portugal will be informed, appropriate tears will be shed for Grandma, as her bones hit the trough a thousand miles away, her insurance barely covering an empty ceremony, as in a distant room the relevant form is signed, and only I will care that someone may well have bumped her off. My only question is, why anyone would want to do that?

I walk away, slotting my black bag into my rucksack as I go. Relieved no one has got the chance to see inside it and catch me for the fraud I am. I'm going to have to stop doing that. Or invest in a stethoscope. I take out my phone to see if Aiden is worried about me. But there's nothing from him. I see one missed call from a number I don't recognise. I don't usually answer calls from numbers I don't recognise. But then I don't usually call them back either. Which is what I'm doing now. I'm doing a lot of things that don't make me feel myself lately. I turn as I call because it's ringing. I don't hear it through my phone, it seems to be coming from the direction of the crowd.

Christ. It's coming from inside number forty-one and now the assembled mass hear it too. Late drama shoots through them and a man in shorts is heading back into her flat. He picks up the phone from her sideboard, shrugs and puts it back where he found it, as I make my way out of there. I put up my hood and head quickly back to my place, undetected.

I look at my missed calls and find she had tried to call me at five-thirty this morning. And, all of a sudden, I'm thinking a lot more seriously about that missing poker and figurine.

16 days till it comes.
The Ivory-billed Woodpecker.

Unknown – Unknown – The Neighbourhood – Unknown – Unknown – Killer – 15 degrees, clement – Unknown.

'Caroo! Caroo!' I call, as I stand on the balcony with my binoculars.

'What the hell are you doing?' Aid shouts from the other room.

He's perked up a bit recently. I had a good chat with him last night. Finally. But not about him. About me. And my things. My supposed issues. Don't you find that sometimes happens? You mean to talk about the problem with them and it somehow ends up coming around to some problem with you. It was like that.

It was mainly about what happened the night I went to Jean's flat. Yep. I came clean. About Jean, about the face that watched me, and everything after, including the phone call. He was pretty good about it really. Once

I'd looked him in the eye, stroked his face and promised never to do anything that dangerous again. I told him of my best intentions and played the episode down.

I told him everything I saw over there. Then we discussed what we should do next – which, we concluded mutually, was pretty much nothing. Because behind his stories of adventure, which people seem to lap up, Aid is really a pretty straight guy. I cringed at his fears. His lack of adventure. He's such a theorist. The most daring he got was to discuss calling the police, telling them all I know and leaving it at that.

I didn't tell him I've already done that. I didn't tell him I went to the police station straight away, to call it in, to tell them what I knew. I didn't tell him they stared at me, like he does sometimes. I didn't tell him they exchanged glances that clearly said, *This one's a bit odd*.

I thought I heard a snigger after I mentioned the porcelain monkey. I had to repeat it. 'Porcelain monkey,' I said. And the main one in the brown suit smiled gently and asked how I knew all this. I said I'd been there and seen it. A while ago. And the poker.

I didn't tell them it was the night before the night she died. I didn't tell them about playing doctor. Of course I didn't. But I said I'd been there. I put myself at risk by doing that. But I thought it should be said. I thought they'd want to know. But the one in the brown suit just stared at me and asked me about 'when I was here before'. I said I'd never been here before. In fact, I don't think I've ever been to a police station before. Never, in my life. I said he must be thinking of someone else.

I'm sure I saw one of them mouth, *She's fucking mental*.

Can you believe that? I'm sure I saw him do that. Hardly professional, is it? So I stared at him. I stared him down.

I know my porcelain monkey isn't exactly a pile of bloody clothes or a smoking gun. But it is something, to me. They don't know their arse from their elbow over there. It was a disgrace.

But I didn't tell Aiden any of this. None of it. I didn't tell him they virtually told me to sod off.

So having sat there, listening to Aid's sensible words and telling him I'd put all this behind me and think nothing more of it, we hugged each other close and I felt properly loved for the first time in a long time. Then I got down to business and started planning what I was actually going to do.

'I'm pishing!' I shout back. Which you already know, of course.

'You're pishing off the neighbours, that's for sure.'

'Aiden, have you any idea how often that joke is made in birding circles?' I don't, we never moved in birding circles, but the answer's 'a lot' I'd imagine.

'It's *quite* annoying,' he said. Delicately so as not to crack the porcelain of our glued-together relationship.

'I'm trying for something I haven't seen before. Something rare.'

It's true, that's partly why I'm doing it. I'm still enjoying looking at those birds. They relax me. But it's not the main reason.

'What? A rare one, round here? Which one?' he says.

You see, the main reason I'm pishing is so the neighbours see me, hear me. I'm looking to scale up my binocular use and I don't want people to think I'm peculiar. Actually,

I don't mind them thinking that at all. I just don't want them to think I'm looking at them. This way, if they see me with the binoculars, they'll think:

Look there's that nutty bird girl again.

Rather than:

Oh, shit, that bitch is trying to work out if one of us killed Jean.

Yes, Jean was killed. I know that now for certain.

'I'm looking for an ivory-billed woodpecker,' I say.

Now, you may now be at the stage where you're reading this and you're thinking: *Come on, Lil, there is no way you'll see an ivory-billed woodpecker in North London.* I know. It sounds hilarious. But let me explain. It's more of a metaphor. I'm looking for something that is hard to find. A person hiding in plain sight. In a crowd. That doesn't want to be seen. So it's really more of a metaphor. Aiden doesn't know birds so I can tell him anything and he'd believe me.

Do you remember telling me about Phoebe Snetsinger, the woman with the malignant melanoma who spent her family inheritance travelling around the world? She was killed in a road accident in Madagascar, I think.

There was David Hunt, who was killed by a tiger in Corbett National Park, India, in 1985, while twitching. Very exotic.

Then there was the glorious Ted Parker, who travelled around North America and saw an incredible 626 species in one single year, from all over the continent. I think he survived.

Why I mention all this, is very simple. Birders are natural adventurers. This is the world you introduced me to. We're risk takers. You. Me. And the others. Yes, some of them came to a sticky end. But there are many that extended their life lists way beyond what they thought was possible. Because they weren't afraid. It's time for me to take a few risks.

I'm sure you'll understand. Someone murdered Jean and if I don't do something they'll get away with it. She'll just disappear as if she was nothing. I'm not going to let that happen. There are still signs up for that missing girl too so I doubt anyone has come forward about her either. I can't find anything about her being found, on the web anyway. I did find out that she was a lawyer in her final year of her pupillage, a bright future ahead of her. Then one day she was gone. This place is a black hole.

Yesterday, twenty-two hours ago to be exact, a sign went up outside Canada House, appealing for witnesses to a possible break-in at Jean's place. A break-in! Meaning it's highly probable they believe it was 'foul play' but no witnesses have come forward to support this theory. My sights were trained on that sign and its passers-by for almost the entire day yesterday. I got two hours' broken sleep. But that's about it. Not one person stopped and took the number. One thing I've picked up from every police-procedural drama to *Crimewatch* is that 'the first twenty-four hours are crucial'. So we're running out of time.

If we're relying on the estate being filled with benevolent witnesses who love volunteering information to the police then we really are sunk. To some it's a time drain, others just don't want to keep that kind of company. Many might be scared of the repercussions, either from the killer or the police themselves. After all, half the people round here aren't supposed to be here anyway. Either way, no one is offering the police anything by the looks of it.

'There it is! I think I see one!' I shout.

'Really? Is that good? Is it rare?' he says, getting up, but not quite brave enough to step onto the balcony. He's a shut-in. I told you. He's putting on weight. I worry about him.

'I'd say so, come out here, come and have a look,' I say, teasing him a bit, as I know he won't. He hides away nowadays.

'No, I don't see anything from here. There doesn't seem to be any birds out… that I can see anyway.'

'Just because you dipped out doesn't mean I didn't see anything.'

'What the bloody hell does that mean?'

'Dipped out? Means you didn't see anything. And now your gripped off. That's when you're annoyed that you dipped out.'

'OK. Whatever,' he says, heading back to the bedroom.

What we know, is that I'm engaging in Suppression. That's when you have information that you don't want to share with the other birders. Remember? I know that's not playing by the rules. But that's the way it is.

All day I've been thinking about how they did her in. I'm starting with the question of cause of death. Sadly for our killer, I'm guessing the angle of the blow or something about the wound itself told them it was carried out by an attacker, I'm guessing with a blunt instrument, hence the sign asking for witnesses. They wouldn't be pursuing a break-in otherwise.

Another thing I do keep thinking about is that statistic about most people knowing their killers. Is it a true stat? Or is it contaminated by some bias? That's what you have to find out in market research. Where the flaws are in the statistics and what the real story is.

Does it seem like most victims know their killers because it's easier to catch the ones that do know the victim? There's a trail, coherent clues that lead to suspects emotionally related to the subject of the case. Whereas, when the killer doesn't know his victim as such, their crimes tend to go unsolved. Skewing the statistics somewhat. Creating a bias for solved crimes being committed by killers who know their victims and not stopping to consider that a large percentage of the unsolved crimes could be carried out by virtual strangers, who by their nature are going to be harder to track down. Better to kill someone you don't know is my conclusion. If I was going to kill anyone, I mean. You're so much harder to find. Just a tip for you there.

Jean saw people, but she didn't really know anyone. Same as me, I guess. And the same as most people in these buildings. Progress has driven us all inside. We're a world of introverts. Cohabiting strangers, flung together by fate. All with motives, all with mystery, all suspects. That's why I've got to go back over there. To the estate. The nastiest side possible. I'm looking for something, I don't know what, a clue, information, someone must know something over there. Someone must have been keeping their eyes open. Even if it's someone you ordinarily wouldn't want to meet on a dark night. If what Jean said was true, I won't need to find them. If I hang around long enough, they'll find me. I'm going to go over there. Soon. I'm going to make some noise and see who appears when I do. Then I'm going to cause some trouble.

My phone rings.

I was deep in thought and it startles me. But I manage to keep my cool. Aiden can't know what I'm up to. He can't see I'm on edge or it'll ruin everything. But staying cool is going to be harder now. Because the number that just called me is Jean's number.

It cuts out before I can get to it. Just two rings. Damn it! I stare at it wondering how the hell it's possible. My head is spinning. I feel sick and there's only one way to cure it. I'm going to have to move my plan forward. Speed things up a little. If someone's toying with me I need to strike first or I'll be a sitting duck. I didn't start this as a victim and I'm certainly not going to end it as one. Better to stay moving, go at them head-on.

I was going to save my plan for tomorrow night. But we're losing valuable time. It has to be tonight. I try a return call but it goes straight to her answer machine. She'd recorded a message herself – people don't tend to do that much I've found, not any more. As if offering the world their voice would reveal far too much of themselves.

'If you wanna leave a message, then do that,' she says, bluntly.

Hearing her voice again is uncanny. That word academics use to describe something spooky, unusual, almost unreal. A whisper from beyond the grave. So who called? Has she risen from the dead? Or was it the police trying to find out who she last tried to contact? I still don't much fancy talking to them. They'll take what I know and give me nothing in return. My hands quiver, so I clench them, steel myself and decide to get moving.

As I pack my bag, my hand stops over the flick knife. Of course I won't use it. But better safe than sorry. I put it in my washbag. I feel like I need something. This is stupid. I've never done anything like this. You know me. But please know I have to try to find out what happened to her. This is the only way I can think to do that. But don't tell me that it's dangerous. I know that.

Don't tell me this is the sort of thing my mum would do.

Don't you dare.

When the clock hits 2 a.m., I'm going over there.

Part Four: The Twitch

15 days till it comes. 2.02 a.m.

I don't have a plan. I said I had a plan but when I think about, as I creep from my bed and into my clothes, it's not really a plan. I think about stuffing some trousers and a shirt full of newspaper and putting them next to him. Like I'm sneaking out of my dorm in a teen movie. But Aiden's not waking up. I know. I can sense it.

No, it's not a plan. It could be the outline of something. But it's not coloured in yet. It's a sketch at best. I'm taking it over there to see if someone can fill it in for me.

I grab my bag and casually walk downstairs, pulling my baseball cap down, throwing my face into shadow. I don't need to be quiet for any particular reason I don't think, but I sneak down the stairs anyway. I don't know who hangs around in the hallways in my building at night, but if they're there then they're probably up to no good. I'm going to tread carefully. Keep my eyes open. I'm being paranoid of course, but if it gets late enough every place gets reduced to the status of a haunted house. Even if it's lit by automated fluorescent lights. Anywhere can spook you when it's quiet enough. That's what this place is doing to me as I descend the stairs, silently. Ghost-like.

As I press the green button and make my way into the clammy summer air I see the moon bounce off the edge of the reservoir. Sometimes this place has a clear enough sky to look like anywhere else than London. There's a constructed romance about it that shouldn't be able to exist around a place built in 2012. It could be Hawaii or Monaco. The sculpted gardens, watered every morning by sprinklers that rise silently from the ground, keep the place in a state of abstract perfection. The moon hits the dew on the grass and it shines idyllically. The flowers smell fresh and new.

They're always changing things. Pulling up plants that have been there for a matter of weeks in favour of something fresher. To keep the residents happy, to keep that sense of wonder, that 'out-of-the-box sheen'.

I think I see another pair of eyes looking at me. Oh, God. I gasp and reach for my backpack. Then I realise it's my reflection in the spotless glass of Resident's Tower. The last newbuild before the small road that currently separates the new estate from the old one. Before the project moves over the road and turns everything into the new. Consuming everything that came before. Rendering it dead and obsolete. The middle-class land grab.

The iron gleam disappears behind me and I head into the bare bones of buildings that stand like scarecrows, bearing down on me with toothless grins.

I'm trying to stay under the radar, silent, because I don't want to get set upon before I make it into the bowels of the place. As I walk, I busy myself by thinking of the possible motives anyone would have for murdering Jean:

1. A mistaken belief that she might have anything worth taking: the missing items could suggest someone was clearing up after a struggle. But you probably wouldn't have to kill her to take what she had anyway. And she wouldn't talk if you did rob her. She was savvy. But it has to remain a possibility.

2. Some sort of revenge attack: maybe one of them took a verbal or physical beating from Jean at some point. She was an imposing woman. She wasn't the sort to hold her tongue either. Maybe she gave as good as she got and someone got rid of her because of it. Maybe something hot-blooded in the night. Teach the old woman a lesson.

3. She said she saw everything that went on around here: she said it pointedly like she did little else other than keep her eyes open. Neighbourhood Watch. She could've seen something she wasn't supposed to see and got bumped off because of that.

4. Motiveless drug addicts: I find this to be the least compelling but let's file it at the top of a pile under a subheading that reads OTHER. There are probably motiveless crimes that happen around the city every day and I generally picture them as performed by desperate addicts, the criminally insane or both.

Who knows whether this holds any truth or is merely a photofit scenario my mind has created, built from news reports and fear mongering. A child's drawing of villains formed from the myth of an evil and deranged underclass that are coming to get us.

Motiveless. It's at least a possibility. And everyone is findable. Everyone should be punished for the bad things they do. Everyone lives somewhere. On this occasion it falls on me to figure out where. And we're starting right here.

5. 5... 5.

I get to my fifth possible motive but get distracted. I'm distracted by the size of Alaska House. It's the biggest of all of them and it dwarfs me as I look up to it and gasp. I take in the full eighteen floors, feeling unsteady on my feet for a moment, then allow my eyes run down to the fourth, where the hooded eyes spied me before I retreated into the black, two nights ago.

The charcoal sky and imposing purple clouds paint a gothic picture. If it were on a canvas it would look like an asylum. These morbid images aren't helpful but they're the only ones I have. I hate to generalise, but it looks terrifying in there.

If the rumours are right, these buildings that surround me are partly inhabited by people that shouldn't be there. I turn, a polythene bag shoots past on the wind. The smell of piss floats by too and makes me gag a bit. These homes were once reserved for families of good people, they've been stripped to their skeletons and what remains is pretty unsavoury.

A crash of glass and metal against the ground. I turn, readying myself to confront whoever has come to meet me. It's a fox, tearing apart a bin bag he has brought with him from God knows where. I gather myself and look past where he is dragging the bag and see that a doorway has been created by someone wrenching a metal slat from the concrete it was bolted into. There's a few like that in each building. That would take a lot of strength or some decent equipment.

I look up to the building above. Some of the slats have

similarly been torn off higher up, revealing blackness behind them. I'm getting closer to the makeshift doorway. I'd rather not venture in. I'd rather something came out and met me here, in the air. It doesn't feel safe in the open, far from it, but at least it's easy enough to run in one direction and see how far I can get if things go that way.

I poke my key torch into the crack and it sprays light into a concrete hallway. Inside, graffiti leads up the stairs. Spray-painted pictures crudely adorn walls. Some are the figures of men.

One shows a child with a gun to his head. Another shows a man stabbing another man in the eyes with one pair of scissors and cutting at his throat with another. The last shows a man strangling a woman. At least I think that's what it is. Maybe they're like a Rorschach test. Do you know what a Rorschach test is? They show you scrambled images and you tell them what you see. Sometimes you see what you want to see. Do you understand me? Sometimes you see what you want to see. It stinks in here. It's damp. It smells of shit. There's something growing in there.

I'm not going in there. So I take a shot at drawing someone out. Someone I can talk to. I suddenly yelp, a huge pishing call that echoes off the buildings.

'Caroo! Caroo!'

It's a huge, violent sound, drawn from within me. It stings the back of my throat to make it. I hear it echo back maybe for a second and a half. It sounds like the noise of a mad man. I'm scaring myself. But I do it again.

'Caroo! Caroo!'

Nothing. I do it again. I wait fifteen seconds. Another

ten. I breathe in through my nose. I breathe out through my mouth. Nothing.

I wait, desperate for a sight of something. Quite quickly, without me realising it, things have slipped to a strange, uncanny place. I stand here, begging someone to arrive with a knife or implement to bludgeon me with. A street kid with a lust for blood that we read so much about. A huge Eastern European who wants to smash me to pieces for no reason at all. They may not be here. They may not exist.

Come out. Come out. Wherever you are. I want to talk. I want to know the things you know. The things you've seen.

The things normal people sit and worry may come and break down their door I fantasise about here. I beg them to come and find me. But it looks like I'm going to have to make them come out.

'Hello! I'm here!' I shout, at full volume.

But the dark says nothing. The estate shrugs. I look at the crack in the doorway, choose to leave my flick knife in my bag. I don't want to accelerate anything that may happen in there. Then I lift myself inside. This is not how it was supposed to go.

The air feels damp in here. The torch lights my way past the graffiti, which looks like arrows, beckoning me to climb higher. I feel like shouting. But I want to wait a bit longer. Before I let them know I'm here. I don't try to muffle my footsteps or tread carefully though, that kind of thinking is long gone. I tread firmly and honestly. I am what I am. Come out and see me.

I feel like a sacrificial lamb. Walking into the arms of its killers. I grip my bag hard and unzip it. I root around for my flick knife while struggling to keep the torch straight. I stumble, using my hands to break my fall. I need to sleep. I've kept such strange hours these last few weeks. I hope they won't be the death of me. I run my hands along the wall. The sound feels like it's being amplified. Maybe it will rustle up something nasty. If Jean's place had it's own Arctic microclimate, this is the opposite. Heat has clung to the walls. Like we're in Morocco all of a sudden. I breathe in the heat. I'm sweating, it really is hot in here, how is it so hot?

I continue my ascent, getting closer, closer. But to what? The pressure gets to me and I shout again. I want it over now. Whatever it is. My terrible squawk leaves my body, as I do it I take out the flick knife and I drop the torch. Footsteps. I hear them loud and clear. I grab for my knife again but I can't find it. I'm losing my cool. In fact, I think I lost it some time ago. Someone appears to squawk back. Fuck. Fucking hell.

I search for the torch. My hands grapple through moss. Through glass. Through piss. I can't find it. All I have is blackness. As the footsteps get closer. I think I'm bleeding. If I was back home in my hallway and the lights were out I'd be close to hot tears with frustration but there's no time for that. My hands scramble artlessly along the stairs behind me as the noise is almost upon me. The footsteps get closer.

There it is. I find my knife and flick it open. Here I am. Come and get me. I lie low, still no light, my hand not calling off the search just yet, it rustles around. But if they want to attack in the dark then so be it, I have my weapon, it's a fair fight. I'm not scared.

But that feeling has just kicked in, the instinct to

bolt, but I cannot retreat even if I want to. It's too late anyway. The footsteps get closer. I hold firm, grit my teeth and make a promise to myself that I'll get out of here alive.

15 days till it comes. 2.32 a.m.

Boom. Rattle. Rattle.

I lie low, one hand still scrambling, the other ready to attack as the noise of feet comes closer. I plan to attack at shin level, dig the knife firmly into the flesh and through to the bone. If possible I'll rip around the back too, straight through the Achilles' tendon. I have no idea if this will work and couldn't care less at this point if it's necessary. How quickly we all become Rambo when the stakes are high enough.

Boom. Rattle. Rattle.

My right hand still searches, my left tightens its grip on the knife.

Boom. Rattle. Squeak.

What the hell is this thing heading towards me?

Rattle. Scrape. Rattle.

It is so dark, I shake glass off of my hand and feel blood and piss drip from it.

Bang. Squeak. Boom.

It's on me. I quickly change hands, remembering I'm better off using my right if I'm actually going to attack. My left hand brushes the floor and I feel the jagged teeth of my keys, I grab them, turn on the light and stab tentatively into the dark all at the same time. A squeal.

The tiny light flashes clean up the stairs and I see I have narrowly missed. A living, breathing thing. A huge rat. As large as the one I saw near Jean's flat. They scuttle past me, echoing so loud against the walls that they could've been an army. My hand shakes as I put my knife away again. All I made contact with was the floor. But I still scared myself.

I've never liked rats. I've always been afraid of them. But my mind is in a different place now. I could've killed an actual, living thing. Its heart could've stopped beating and it would've been my fault. The floor would have splashed with red, its tender puny heart would've stopped. Its life would've ended and mine would have gone on just as normal.

Don't judge me. The dark plays tricks and I'm so scared. I stare at the blade for a moment. It's no toy. The knife is as sharp as the salesman promised. It's a self-defence blade, handmade to guard against car jackings, the salesman boasted. 'You could take a full-grown man's leg off with it.' But he also conceded people mostly bought them for the craft.

I merely thought the handle looked nice. I'm putting it to better use than I could've imagined. But I hope I don't have to actually use it. It stinks so bad in here. I'm nauseous. I blow out and wave my hand in front of my face. I want to repel the moisture and smells away from me. But I carry on still. Up the stairs. Here I come. Sticking to my task. Sticking to my promise. Graffiti arrows pointing the way all the while.

At the top of the fourth floor I see something. Slats had been pulled away from doorways up until now but this one has been completely wrenched from its hinges. I wonder who did that. It sits bent and flung aside on the ground, a neat-looking red rug lies at the entrance to the hallway. My torch only goes so far, as it stalks down the hallway. They'll be ready for me by now. I've caused enough of a racket on my way up to let them know I'm coming.

The hallway is lit by a series of small lamps. They have an eighties feel, some of the shades look fire damaged, the sort you might find in a charity shop or a skip outside the newbuild side. The sort of thing we wouldn't even bother selling on eBay.

Their interior design. Our cast-offs. Our dirt.

It occurs to me that they could still be asleep. It might not be too late to retreat without a face off. I could turn round, make my way back with myself mostly intact, get a shower and forget all about it. But I'm not going to do that. I've got some issues to resolve.

I wipe down the knife with my jumper, almost gagging at the smell of who knows what from when I dug it into the concrete and matter next to the fleeing rat. I think they are asleep. I think I'm going to have to wake them up.

I count six doors in a row, all just ajar. They look repainted. It's cleaner up here somehow, the smell not so acute, it's almost civilised. I creep down the hallway. The lamplights flickering as I go, a dog barks somewhere in the distance and I try not to jump. I try to settle myself with my breathing method again. I try not to freak out. I settle on the first door, it seems the cleanest way to go.

I don't want to go too far in and get trapped from either side, particularly if there's a lot of them.

I brace myself, hold my breath for a second and then kick it open and run in. It's dark in there and there is no sign of anyone. I turn my key light on and scan the room. I'm almost disappointed.

A sink, toothpaste. A toothbrush sits by it in a red plastic cup. A mirror leans against a wall on a roughly hewn desk. To the other side, two sleeping bags on a mattress of magazines and cardboard boxes. The room is covered in piles and piles of newspapers, I turn and trip over them. I rise and stack the ones I have knocked over back up. I was always an excellent guest.

I leave the room and move to the next door. I look at it. Imagining what the hell might lie behind it. The half man, half human behind the bins at night. The 'desperate addicts' that exist only in my imagination. Imaginary needles sticking out of their imaginary arms as they salivate. I see a picture show of terrible images. Wild animals.

I breathe, and kick the door open and, when I see what's before me, I scream. An eagle. A crudely stuffed taxidermy eagle stares at me from the other side of the room. A golden one, God knows where it came from, I struggle to imagine it was ever alive, ever real.

I scan the rest of the room with my tiny light. This room feels less like a home but no less well put together. On the right side there is a record player and some old LPs. The basin similarly has a toothbrush as well as shaving cream and a razor. The slat has been removed here in favour of some ragged curtains.

Crates lie around the floor, perhaps doubling as seats. I smell something like gas and turn my torch leftwards to see an old electric heater oozing liquid, sweating onto the concrete. It's off, luckily. I have a feeling if you turned it on it would kill someone with what it emitted. They'd have no use for it in this heat anyway. Summer is still here, with a vengeance.

Then, my cloud of light lifts and hits something stranger. A well-preserved kitchen. A toaster, an electric frying pan, a plug-in grill, cereal, various other foodstuffs piled into a corner. This is not a nightmare. This is a home, or something like it.

I flash past it again and catch a face. A human child's face. Staring at me. He looks scared, he is about six or seven, he murmurs, too scared to move or cry, his face scrunched, his hands dirty. I pause, unable to speak, I put my hand to my chest and mutter 'God', then I walk towards him.

Then my phone rings again. I put my hand to it in a flash, but before I can get to it, something hits me in the head hard and immediately I know I'm bleeding.

I stagger back, my body in shock, as I turn to face what's behind me.

15 days till it comes. Time: Unknown.

WM – Unknown – Alaska House – Shaved head – 2 flock – Aggressive – Sweat drips from the walls – 6′ 1″.

I see him. Around six foot tall, tracksuited and holding a big piece of brick. My vision blurs as I look at the outline of his jaw, shrouded in his hood. The brick has specks of my blood on it. Mine I assume. Somewhere behind me, the child is screaming

He doesn't scream in fear. He shouts a kind of war cry which is intended to knock me further off my guard. It works too. I'm thinking about my mum suddenly. I'm so sorry. She was right, I so often was a 'silly girl' and now I've grown up to be a 'stupid cow'. What was I thinking, hanging around at night, poking my nose into other people's homes? What was I trying to achieve? The big one in front of me raises the brick high above his head. Higher and higher.

It will soon to come crashing into my face. The foundations of which will not survive the blow. All I can do is wait for it. I stagger. Here it comes.

'Go on then. Finish it off. Just do it!' A disembodied voice screams.

He pauses.

He takes a breath, but it doesn't take him long to recover. His stature says he's not afraid. He can do it if he really wants to.

'What are you waiting for, just finish it off, do it, *come on*!'

From behind him the child lets out another raw scream and the big one grips the brick harder.

'Put that down, for fuck's sake. What are you doing? Put it down *now*!'

The voice changes tack. It is hard and guttural, the stuff of eighties horror. Sharp, shrill, but full of intent. My mind falls back to *Hellraiser*. The possessed *Exorcist* girl. *Texas Chainsaw Massacre* screams. The voice terrifies me. And it's coming from me.

His hooded top billows open and underneath I see his arms tense under his vest and he lifts it again ready to release. He's strong. My bravado could only hold him for so long. He is unperturbed. He may have killed before. He grunts and effortlessly brings it crashing down with his full force. Onto the floor.

It slides across the room, echoing all around the walls like a bullet. It bounces just past my shins and into the wall behind. The child stops crying. We breathe hard. The three of us, in that little room. The squat.

'What the hell are you all doing here?' I shout. Controlled now, scolding, like a mother.

'What are we— What— This is our home! What are you doing here?' he shouts back.

'It's not… You can't just stay in a place like this. You're not safe,' I say. Unable to get to the meat of it. The preamble sounds abstract.

'From what? From people like you?' he says, his voice low.

I look around at this makeshift family home I have intruded upon. I am the interloper. They have food, a life here, it's no less civilised than my own. The climb was a nightmare but inside they've made the best of it. They are a family. They are clean. Sports wear, jeans, the youngest has ripped pyjamas, but everything is well preserved. I, however, am covered in blood, glass and other miscellaneous detritus. I look terrifying. I am the monster.

'You want the phone? Take the thing. If that's what it's about,' he says.

I feel he's about to force it into my stomach or shove it down my throat but I let it hang between us for a while. I look at it. This is the thing that brought me here. The push I needed, to come over and look for some answers. Where will it lead us? At least it's on the table. The first bargaining chip. A talking point. So where to begin?

'That's not what I came for. I came to ask you why you killed her.'

'Fuck off! I didn't do that. I didn't do nothing.'

'You've got her phone, haven't you? How did that happen?'

'It's not like she's gonna need it, is it? For fuck's sake! Who are you?' The tension is high. I'm still an intruder, in his home. He doesn't like it. I'm making him uncomfortable. Understandably. He could blow at any minute.

'So maybe it was before the police came then. The crowd dispersed and you ran in and took her phone, maybe her wallet and whatever else she's got. Or maybe you needed to hide some sort of evidence?'

'Oi, Oi. It wasn't like that. I just wanted the phone. I needed it.'

'What for?'

'My iPhone bust, what dya think?'

'And which body did you thieve your iPhone from?'

'What? I got it on contract, woman. But then I dropped the thing. Cracked the screen. Didn't kill no one. Didn't rob no one. Shut up now, you're making me tense.'

The kid giggles a bit. The whole thing now seeming ridiculous, even to a child. They can see I'm no monster. The big one softens a touch. The kid is trying to get back to sleep. As if used to these dramas. Shouting in rooms and hallways.

'Is this your kid?' I say, emboldened.

'He's my brother.'

'Where are your parents?'

'Fucking dead. After our dad died the council tried to move us to Reading. I didn't want to move there, change his school, all that shit. I got a job. Friends. So we're staying here to the last minute. I don't know who killed her, if that's what you're thinking happened. But, ain't no one getting killed over a Nokia 8210, trust.'

I summon a smirk. I was stupid to think this was a robbery or petty theft. People are desperate around here but Jean had nothing and I'm betting everyone knew it. It must've been something else. He continued:

'Let me tell you something, I see stuff around here. I saw that woman outside on that phone to the council from time to time. Spouting this and that. She had a mouth on her. She ruled this place. She wasn't afraid. I see lots of things. I saw you come out of the old lady's house.'

'I'm… I'm a doctor. I was checking her pulse for—'

'Nah, nah. Not in the day. In the night-time. The night before the night she got bumped off. Which makes me wonder. How do I know you didn't sneak in there the night after too, and kill her? And why don't I go to the police with all this?'

A pause.

'Where will you tell the police they can find you? Here?'

He sucks his teeth and sighs, he's tired of this. But I have one more try.

'You can keep the phone, I don't want it. I won't tell anyone you're here either. But I want to know who killed her,' I say.

It sounds a bit like a threat, but I've nothing to back it up with.

'Hey, how should I know? Kanye? Ghost of Tupac? Dalai Lama? Woman was old, she died.'

'I don't think so. Someone broke in somehow and killed her. Who? Give me a suggestion.'

'I don't know. And look, there are other people in these buildings. But it ain't a social club. I got no suspects for you. I don't know many of them in this place. You know your neighbour's names?'

I looked down. It's true, he's got me. I don't know my neighbours names. Just like he doesn't know his. There's Lowell. Some other names I've invented myself.

My fantasy of community. Pet names I've given a few of them. That's about it.

'Yeah, so imagine how it is when you're all lying low. You're lucky you stumbled on us, some of the others might have cut you for less. That's why you wanna get out of here and don't come back. But kill that old lady? Nah. Can't see why anybody wanna go and do that. What for?'

I say nothing. Because I don't know yet. I shake my head. I want to get out of there. So that's exactly what I do.

I notice I'm still breathing kind of hard. I pick up my bag and turn to leave. This was a big risk for exactly nothing. Forget it. We're done.

15 days till it comes. Far too late.

I'm almost out of the door and down the stairs when he says it.

'And you know what? You can tell him not to come round here any more too!' he shouts.

It stops me in my tracks. I've no idea what he's talking about. 'Who?'

'The guy that came round last time, the one who's fuckin' hand I cut open 'cos he was chasing around Nathan.' He gestures towards the boy behind him.

I stop and think. More silence. I hear the air whistle through the place.

'Who? Listen, who was this? I don't know anyone who'd come round here. Who was this guy?'

'I don't know. I gave him a good old cut though. Might have taken it into the bone. He was a big guy. You remember him, Nathe?'

The boy shuffles, awkwardly, he looks to the ground. He has a naturally happy little face, but frowns now. He looks up and speaks.

'Man with blond hair,' he says, eyes trained to the floor all the while.

I pause and consider the new information. Why would anyone come here? Other than me that is.

'Anything else you can remember about him?' I ask.

'Nah. Oh... well, he... er... he came from... what's that...? Waterway. All the names sound the same to me. Yeah, I saw him hustle back to the Waterway building, so that's where he lives, I guess. Fucking "Waterway". Bleeding all the while. All right? It's past bedtime. So. Please.'

Before I go I feel I want to ask for his name, wish him well and tell him to look after his family. That he seems like a good person and there's hope. But all those things would be platitudes and guesswork anyway. I have no idea who he is. But for what it's worth I hope they make out OK. And I hope they make it out before the bulldozers come. But they don't need my tea and sympathy. I'm embarrassed to do it but I reach into my pocket and offer them twenty quid, a tenner and two fivers.

'You take that elsewhere,' he says. 'We don't need nothing from you lot over there, woman.'

I look at him hard. It's late. 'Please, to say sorry for the late-night visit. Please.'

He frowns, reluctantly takes it and nods. It's time for me to go.

I stop at the door.

'Hey, why did you call me the other night then? Trying to scare me or what?'

'Ah yeah, sorry about that. Nathe playing around with the thing. Hit missed calls when he was trying to play snake. Didn't you, little man?'

Nathan smirks and grabs the phone and fires up his little game again and walks out of the hallway sucking his thumb.

'It's Lily. My name's Lily,' I say.

He sizes me up. Runs his tongue along his top lip. He thinks. He doesn't want to give me too much. Maybe I shouldn't have given him that. I don't know a thing about this guy.

'You can call me Chris.'

So I guess that's his name. I nod, trying to seem tough, but I'm not kidding anyone. I'm newly self-aware. I know how badly cast I am as the tough girl. It's like the lights have come on at the end of the party and I'm half naked somehow. I nod again. And get out of there.

I manage to negotiate the stairs with little mishap on the way down. Outside, I take out my notebook. I write 'blond hair, injury to the hand, male, 5′ 11″ at least'. I've got a description. It's something. Just enough to go twitching.

I look about the estate as I head towards the road. I'm not planning on coming back. But I'm not afraid of it here any more either. This is my estate and no one can do anything about that. I own it. And I'm going to find this guy. Then I'm going to stop him screwing up my neighbourhood. But first I'm going to take off my piss-soaked clothes. And have a shower.

Something approaches from the distance behind me. I turn to face it, chest out, raising myself rather than shirking. I've learnt a thing or two in the past few days.

It growls, pants and comes to me. Terrence. Where have you been all this time my friend?

I look in his dark eyes for a second, then I grab his collar and take us both home.

14 days till it comes. 7 p.m.

Various – Various – Waterway Apartments – Various – Various – Sleeping, hiding, laughing, eating, cooking, cleaning, crying, reading, watching movies, exercise – 16 degrees – All the shapes and sizes.

I took the day off today to keep my eyes open. Trained on Waterway. My bum's gone a bit numb. I was sat here all of yesterday too. Waiting for something. Making notes in my book. Getting more specific. Headings and subheadings. Graphs and charts. Crisp, white paper stuck to walls. My art teacher would be proud.

Research. Waiting for my man to show his face.

Aiden thought it was a good idea to skip work as I 'looked tired' and 'smelt a bit funny'. But he has no idea about what I got up to the other night. Perhaps he wouldn't want to know. No interest even. He feels very far away at the moment, does he care about me at all any more? He's got stories of his own he's working away on. He doesn't have time, it's a fragile commodity.

It's slipping away from us all. With every hour that goes by, finding Jean's killer becomes statistically more unlikely.

He barely blinked when I told him I was looking after a girl from work's dog for a while. Even though he knows I don't have any friends at work any more. And the building rules on animals are sketchy, but tend towards a 'hmm, no thanks'. He didn't consider how suddenly and mysteriously Terrence appeared one night. Or that I hate dogs. His mind is elsewhere. On spies and espionage. On eighties politics and Cold War secrets. Bow tie cameras and exploding cufflinks. He hibernates inside his mind and taps away at the keys. Tip tap tip tap, clatter clatter clatter, tip tap tip tap, tip tap tap.

I only ventured outside once today to get supplies from the corner shop: milk, cereal, assorted tins, pitta bread, Gouda, the nice toilet paper, carrot soup, pomegranate juice, miscellaneous vegetables, my top-three favourite types of biscuits. Essentials for holing up for a while. On the way back, just outside our building, I saw Lowell. Coming down the footpath. Jogging home from his lunch-time trip to the climbing wall. He still had his gloves on to demonstrate this to anyone watching. He works from home sometimes. I waved, he did too. As he got closer it seemed like he was limping. This made me nervous.

'Hi, Lil. How are you? I think I might have pulled something. Think I overdid it a bit.'

My worst fears were realised.

'Oh, I thought something was up. Anyway, must get off.'

'Sorry, Lil, didn't someone say you used to be a nurse or something?'

This was exactly what I didn't want. Chinese whispers travel fast.

'Doctor, actually. Used to be. I… trained. For… a year or so. Then I packed it all in. For my market research… stuff. You could be talking to Dr. Gullick right now. Imagine. Ha.'

That sounded at least vaguely feasible.

'Would you mind taking a little look? Sorry to bother you.'

Deeper and deeper.

'Course. Where's it hurt?'

He pointed, I nodded. I bent down and put a hand on his thigh. In the open air. I held it tightly. I squeezed. My hand rose a touch. Under his shorts. I breathed in and thought demonstrably, then looked up as if the answer is in the sky somewhere.

'How's that feel?' I said. His leg hair against my palm.

'Tight,' he said, grimacing.

I hummed to myself in agreement with some phantom theory of my own invention. It's a big muscle, the thigh one. One of the biggest, maybe. I don't know. I ran my hand all around it. Front and back. Foraging. I needed to get out of this. Aiden could be watching. I didn't want him to see me like this. I didn't want him thinking I'm taking my practice any more seriously. The door to the building was just there.

I punched the leg softly for no reason. I looked up at him. His pupils shrank a fraction.

'Ice it. Bag of peas. Whatever. Give it a good ice. Ice it up. Gotta dash.'

I ran off before he could say anything else. I didn't want to be out there. I had to stop doing that. A bead of sweat dropped from my head as I climbed the stairs. I hadn't realised I was sweating. I got straight back to my hide and took a deep breath. I examined my paperwork. My research. My findings.

I have a grid now. There are thirty-seven flats in Waterway, all built with glorious balconies that either look at the reservoir face on or from the side. Nine flats on each of the first four floors and the penthouse on top. From my vantage point – the bedroom window, with my elbows on the carpet and the blind low to stay undetected – not one of them can escape my gaze.

That is if they don't have their blinds up. Which many of them have. I've been to see the onsite estate agent and figured out that flats three, twenty-two and twenty-five are unoccupied and are for sale. An awkward conversation with the concierge, which involved him slowly staring at me to try to figure out why exactly I needed to know all this, informed me that one, nine, ten, twelve, sixteen and thirty are owned and unoccupied. I will mark them on my grid with the abbreviation 'Un'. The other abbreviation ('NS') refers to No Sighting. As in, their blind is up, I've seen into the apartment itself, but I haven't seen anybody in there. Yet.

Thinking of 'getting another one' was what I came up with 'and wanted to know more about the demographic of the buildings'. That's how I squeezed the intel out of the concierge. I mean, as if I could afford another one of these places. Please.

I put my new information into my spreadsheet. All of this could come to nothing, of course, if the killer has scarpered already. On a plane to foreign climes. But this is all I have at the moment. Everyone needs a project. Me more than most. Terrence licks his lips and puts his head in my lap as I make a grid:

1	2	3	4	5	6	7	8	9
Hannay	BLIND	(NS)	Rebecca	BLIND	Anthony	Un	Marnie+	Un

10	11	12	13	14	15	16	17	18
Un	BLIND	Un	(NS)	Kim	Iris and Gil	Un	Julie and Paul	BLIND

19	20	21	22	23	24	25	26	27
T and M	(NS)	Janet and Tippi	UFS	Ingrid	David K	UFS	(NS)	Joseph

28	29	30	31	32	33	34	35	36	
(NS)	James and Stew	Un	Jonny and Lina	(NS)	Smiths	(NS)	BLI	East Asian Family	37 Gregory

I'm going to go into more detail at this point, so stay with me and refer back to the grid whenever you need. I do need your thoughts on this so try to pay attention. But. spoiler alert! You don't need to remember every name. I haven't narrowed them down yet. Don't worry. Let it blow over you like a warm breeze. Just stay cool and stay with me. OK, here goes:

After previous documented sightings in the previous weeks, I can be pretty certain that Joseph, Hannay, Ingrid, David Kentley, Kim, Anthony, Rebecca and Gregory live alone. I had thought that there would be more couples in the buildings, I predicted they would be the predominant demographic, but 'single working professionals' I was told by the concierge are 'quite prevalent' in the newbuilds and that is well borne out by the findings you see here.

It is also a demographic that is too young to have any children who would be large enough to fit the criteria of the murderer. Approximately forty-eight is my predicted top age, with the lowest being Anthony, who I believe to be a nineteen-year-old student, with cash in the family. Mr and Mrs Smith are a Japanese postgraduate couple, possibly both in the field of medicine.

I will also keep a look out for girlfriends, boyfriends and everything else of that type, but it would seem rather gauche to commit a murder when staying over. Not many people feel that at home. It was eight months before I chanced even leaving a toothbrush and slippers at Aiden's old flat.

Marnie, you will find, has a plus next to her as she is a recent sighting and I believe there could be a partner, I will give it three more days studying her behaviour before I file this possibility under 'unlikely'. All of this means I'm close to extinguishing the option of any extras being our culprit.

Having obtained a good set of floor plans from the local estate agent, again on the pretence that I might be 'looking to get another one', I can confirm that the single people are in one-beds, so I'm discounting the possibility of rarely seen room-mates. It's amazing what information you can easily rustle up if they're constantly trying to flog these places.

We are then left with five people who haven't yet opened their blinds. Five very private people or lucky holidaymakers. I have seen frequent nudity in the other flats, as they are dominated by glass fronts, so a desire for privacy borne of not wanting to literally 'expose themselves' to their neighbours is not an impossibility. It's also recently been the weekend so I don't discount small sojourns to the coast or abroad.

Similarly, there are seven 'no sightings'. I am hoping the holiday situation or the 'away on business' scenario resolves itself with the 'no sightings' too. I need the last few worm their way out of the woodwork and allow me to fill in the rest of my grid sooner rather than later.

So why don't we cut to the chase and start the friendly game of Guess Who killed their elderly neighbour?

Male, tall, blond hair, scarred hand.

Extracting the women, who sidestep our first criteria by virtue of avoiding that troublesome Y chromosome, who count for twelve of the twenty-three inhabitants, it leaves us with eleven males.

Gregory, Tony and Mr Smith are on the short side, standing at five foot nine or below so let's discount them straight away.

Remember the kid described him as a big guy. Hannay is the oldest at around fifty (probable divorcee). His age is something that would have, in all likelihood, been commented on by Nathan and his brother, but I understand this point is debatable. While he is blond, he is also slight, so if they meant build by the comment 'big guy' then that also counts him out.

Importantly, and we're getting down to the nitty-gritty here, Anthony, James, Stewart and Paul could under no reasonable conditions be considered to be fair haired.

So, that leaves Joseph, David Kentley and Jonny.

Jonny is a big bloke, he could pick you up and throw you over his shoulder on a night out, despite protestations, with considerable ease. He also stalks around his tiny flat like a wild beast. Slamming his fridge and Skyping with intent. Not that his aggressive Skype technique represents the perfect profile of a murderer, but it is necessary to consider anything that could be helpful at this stage. The problem with him is that he is, technically speaking, ginger rather than blond. But so few people are what I would term '1989 Jason Donovan blond' that I think it is necessary to widen the search as far as ginger to allow for the dark night and the fleeting nature of the encounter.

David Kentley is fair-haired. He is a touch slight and a tad effeminate but this does not discount the possibility that he is a murderer. Norman Bates, anyone? He is as precise as they come, foodie and solitary. He would prefer an early night with a herbal beverage and a new Ottolenghi recipe over anything else. Last night, he also watched a horror film, one of those torpid Hollywood-remake ones, which doesn't speak much for his taste. A diseased mind, perhaps?

Then there is Joseph. There have been few sightings of him in his natural habitat. In fact, just a single but very clear one of him doing squats. My first recorded bona-fide sighting in fact! He also jogs around the area very frequently and at 6.45 every weekend meticulously cleans his racing bike using water from the fountain. This leads to some contention with the overly officious concierge. But it is always calmly handled with good humour by Joseph, which I think is to be regarded as a feather in his cap in this day and age. When the aggravation of the rush hour seems to be hitting fever pitch. When you bump into stranger on the Piccadilly Line sometimes and they give you a look like they want to tear you limb from limb. We're an angry breed these days. There really are too many of us in this city.

The boys said the attack was just a couple of weeks ago and that they cut him quite deeply so the task now is to have a good look at their hands. Something by no means impossible with these binoculars and at this distance. In fact, unfortunately, I have already examined David Kentley's hands while he made a salad. And they are very much pristine. Which I think concludes our need for him in our investigations.

Joseph and Jonny, however, have proved more elusive and I will be staying here this evening with the express purpose of filling in the other gaps in this grid and to get a better look at the hands on these guys.

Terrence stirs and goes for a wander around the house. I call to Aiden. 'Can you put out his food, Aid?' but nothing doing. I'll do it myself.

I walk to the kitchen and feed him the same dry stuff I saw in Jean's cupboards, which you can get from the little shop next to the café. I stare him in his stupid, lovely, little face:

'What happened to your mummy, eh? What happened to her?'

He snorts and runs back to the bedroom.

My phone vibrates, a text. I sigh. I want to be left alone. It's from Phil. As if your messages weren't enough, threatening to come over uninvited. Now I have another nuisance caller. I shouldn't have given him my number, he actually uses it. Sends me funny messages, as if we're proper mates. With emojis and everything. But it's not from him. It's from Jean.

I flinch. I seemed to have developed a nervous disposition. But it's no real shock at this point. The old ladies telecoms activities have really gone up since her death. Impressive. Here she comes again. She just won't go away.

Part Five: Birding

13 days till it comes. 8.30 a.m.

I shouldn't have let them keep the damn phone but I didn't want it. Neither of us fancied handing it in to the police and getting tangled up with them. I didn't want to have to destroy it either. That would be the sort of thing a guilty person would do. Someone with something to hide. I don't want to start looking like that.

There were few clues that could be gleaned from Jean's Nokia 8210. When punching in my number I'd already noted I was only the fourth entry in her phone. The other three read:

GAS

ELECTRIC

BASTARDS (COUNCIL)

I wonder how her family got in touch with her, or if they ever did. She only had calls from those three numbers in her call history, and she was the sort of woman that thought texting was the devil's work.

She had one single, unopened text from the gas company. I opened it. I'm nosey I guess. They were asking her to set up an 'online billing system'. It was from 2013.

They were barking up the wrong tree. I don't think Jean bothered joining the Internet Age. I found all this out in a matter of seconds without her ever knowing, but that's just the way I am. I've always been like that. I look at things and see a lot. We all do really, we make a thousand snap judgements about a person as soon as we meet them. Some we're not even aware of.

A neuroscientist recently found that we're only consciously aware of about two per cent of the information our unconscious body and brain uses to react to new scenarios. A million little ways to survive we'll never even know about. I don't want to blow my own trumpet but I bet I'm more conscious than most. I was known for it at school. 'Stats', the other kids called me, because if people mentioned something in class I could recall it exactly. By date, even. I could tell you exactly how many times Mr Baker used the words 'Anderson Shelter' in the first History lesson of term many months later. Fourteen, I think it was.

I am a catalogue of useless information. A hard drive of statistics and old nonsense that won't go in the trash can. I guess that's why I like birds. And people – at least from a distance. I see their distinguishing marks and in an instant I take it all in and I don't forget it. Then they're mine, in a way. Beautiful things, committed to memory, mine to keep for ever. So don't give me your phone even for a moment, who knows what secrets I'll discover.

They've got my number. That was stupid, I've left myself open, I don't know these kids. If they're dangerous or what. Now they're calling the tune. I don't want to be dragged around by their whims. I've got work to do. I suppose it's good that what's left of Jean's pay-as-you-go texts are being put to good use. But there's something eerie that hits me every time I see her number. That little, mysterious electronic envelope icon stares at me threateningly. Even though I know it's them. I open the message and take a look.

'Tomorrow. The Z Café. 8.30. Thompson,' it read.

I don't know whether they're trying to help or if they need something, but maybe I owe it to them to turn up and meet them at least. It's public too. Should they try anything funny. The only thing I know about those kids is that Jean said to be wary of anyone hiding out in those buildings. But I'm curious, to a fault. So, at 8.30, I rush downstairs and past the fountain to the café and shop, and I head inside.

They're nowhere to be seen so I order a latte from the nice Greek guy who owns the place and take a seat at the back. The Polish waitress with the constantly perplexed expression slams my drink and its accompanying tiny biscuit down in front of me. Around the corner, a group of kids can be heard playing distorted hip hop from their smart phones. One of them has a 'Hoverboard'. It's not the sort of 'Hoverboard' I was promised would exist one day. It dribbles along as dynamically as a faulty Stannah Stairlift. But he seems proud enough to dick around on it in a crowded café, to the delight of the rest of his gang. The perplexed waitress has asked them to turn it down many times but the last time they told her in no uncertain terms to 'fuck off'. These are not like the boys I met in the squat. These are bad kids.

I say kids, they're probably in their early twenties but God knows what they do with themselves. They don't look like they're part of the workforce. There is not a management consultant or postman between them. Their grey tracksuits, like Babygros, seem to have granted them eternal youth. Boom boom boom da boom. Their phones blare away.

There are three other patrons in the main body of the restaurant as I wait anxiously, uncomfortably. It's the figure I've cut most frequently since this all started. A trendy type, sips at a fruit juice and surveys his laptop so intensely, as if he would climb inside and swim around inside if that were possible and permissible. A couple eat breakfast in silence, perfectly content, their minds a thousand miles away on some Far Eastern beach, yoga types.

The last is an older guy who leans in to me, kindly allowing me to sample his stale breath. His face stays there; it would be menacing if he wasn't so frail. Despite his age he is fashionably dressed, however it's unclear whether this is by fortune or design. Maybe he has accidentally come into fashion recently, his angular face peering in at me, his blue-striped jacket hoisted to the elbows.

'Yes?' I offer.

'Are you the lady that's looking around?'

'Who wants to know?' Immediately giving myself away, which wasn't my intention.

'Right. I was having a word with the boys. Round at Alaska House. They said you were following a few things up after Jean popped off.'

'OK. Let's say that's me then. What do you want?'

'Just to pass on some information, love, thought maybe I could help out. I was speaking to them. Last night. Asked them to put us in touch when I heard you was… looking around,' he rasped, in hushed lullaby tones.

'And why… why is that necessary Mr… Thompson?' The name from the text.

'That's right.' He smiled, trying to look as legit as he could.

We size each other up. The other patrons in their own worlds.

'You see, lovely, I'm the guy that lives right above Jean. Right there. Bang.'

He points to number fifty-one. I don't know how much to trust him but I decide to listen. What harm can that do? He goes on.

'I was checking on all the racket you made with the boys that night. I realise it was me you were looking for.'

A cold shiver runs down my body. I'm unprepared to meet her killer. I punch out some sounds, remembering I'm in a public place.

'So you…' The words 'killed her' catch in my mouth and refuse to come out.

'Ah, no. No, no. Sorry about that, love. No, I didn't do her over. Ha. No, no,' he says, artlessly. He sniffs, still sniggering. That seemed to really tickle him. Then he finally gets on with it. 'But I saw someone what did. Would you like to know more?'

'Yes. Yes, all right, what do you want, money?'

'No, love, nothing like that. Doing my civic duty, ain't I?'

I'm all ears. I'd been starting to think the thing was a wild fantasy. I dived in head first and at moments of weakness I thought I was doing something unfounded, unasked for, reckless. I'd like someone to tell me I'm not so ridiculous.

'It was who the kids thought it was, I reckon. The

bloke. Er… bigish. That's the same bloke I saw coming out of her flat.'

'Fair hair?'

'Yes. That's right. He's your man.'

A beat. I stare at him. If this is true then a picture is emerging.

'The same guy that confronted the kids. The… scar on his hand?'

'Wouldn't know about that. Didn't get that close. Wouldn't dare. But he has a way about him. He hangs about. You know what I mean?'

I don't. Not really. But this is exactly what I wanted to hear. Is it too good to be true? Is he feeding me exactly what I want? What could he possibly want in return if not money? I'm not sure whether him turning it down made me trust him more or less. He holds my hand over the table and continues. His weathered green eyes and quivering mouth look right at me. He's one of those men who produce too much saliva, so every so often he sucks some of it back in from the corners of his mouth.

'Over six foot. Fair hair. Always heads back to that building. The, errr… the, err…'

'Waterway Apartments?'

'No. No, not that one.'

'Not that one?' Shit. It will be back to the drawing board if that's true. If he can be trusted.

'What's the one opposite the Riverview Apartments?'

'Waterway Apartments. I promise you. That's what it's called.'

'No. No it's not. Oh, hang on. Maybe…' He draws in the air and his fingers rise like he's conducting an unseen orchestra, trying to get a sense of something. He shifts in his seat, holding his head, closing his eyes and then finally he snaps his fingers. Then he shouts, excitedly, like he's had some scientific Eureka moment to do with dark matter. 'Yes! That's it. Waterway. I'm sorry, love. That's it!'

I breathe again, I am on the right path. I knew it, I felt it. I want to hug him. But I'm not sure I should get quite that close.

He continues: 'Yes. I heard a noise, reckon he broke in through her back window. Then not long after, he was brazen enough to come out of her front door. If I trusted the police as far as I could throw them, or they trusted me, that's what I'd tell them, Scouts' honour. Then I saw him walk away back to his building, all casual like. I tell you what, he was in and out of there in less than five minutes I'd say. He didn't hang about. You wouldn't credit it, would you, that it could all happen that quick? He knew what he needed to do. So he did it. No big drama about it. The things some people do these days. And why? I dunno. You'd scarcely believe it.'

But I did believe it. I like him now too. He was straight up.

'OK, lovely. I do hate to ask but thinking about it… if you did have a tenner that would in fact go an awful long way for me.' Hang dog look.

With some reservations I handed it over. Hoping for all I was worth that this wasn't all about the money. That what he said was true.

Boom boom boom de boom. The gang's music rose again as I stood to leave. Without thinking, I took a detour to where they were standing.

I'm not sure what I'm doing. They look up at me and I look back.

'Yeah, what the fuck do you want? Who rattled your cage?'

Maybe I was emboldened by the news I'd just heard. Maybe I simply snapped, but next I did something that seems strange to me. Somewhere in the Venn diagram of brave and stupid. I pull my foot back and kick the chair out from underneath the lad with the 'Hoverboard'. His arse hits the floor. It feels very satisfying.

My fists are clenched and I'm shouting, pointing at each of them. I stamp my feet, reading them the Riot Act. They're too stunned to move as I bring my fist down on a table next to one of them and then take a step towards another. I lean down to eyeball him, take a deep breath and keep shouting. Snarling. In his face.

I watch myself. Not quite believing it's me that's doing this. Hardly hearing the words that are coming out of me. It's as if I'm standing next to myself, looking up at me in amazement. Whose is this voice and where does it come from? A couple of them grab their bags and leave. But that doesn't sate me. I keep on at them. It's not quite heroic. I must look like a wild animal. I shout and snarl. Turning the air blue. Giving all I've got.

People change. What a strange thing I'm becoming.

12 days till it comes. 4 p.m.

RW – *Turdus iliacus* – Inner city – Good vis, wind light, 16 deg – 2 flock – Healthy colouring, strong dark chequers against a rich white breast, male – 14 cm approx. – Shy, twitchy.

The redwings are early. Very early. It's getting a little darker in the mornings. A bit colder at night. But I wouldn't have expected to see one until early November.

But there he is. The noble redwing. A true thrush. Staring back at me. He can't stay still. He probably feels a bit out of place. In plain sight. Perched on a tree. He seems somehow nervous. Is he lost? He can feel my eyes on him, I think. That's what I think. He knows. He knows how close I am.

I haven't done any work for about fifteen minutes. I'm sure they've noticed. Maybe I'm on strike, I haven't decided yet. But my arms are folded and I'm leaning back in my seat. Brazenly watching the world go by. Not a single fuck given.

Watching the light play against the leaves. Examining the redwings. Making rare use of my office window.

I wonder whether I've had my hand up for the last ten minutes. I've been miles away; I wonder what my body's doing. Do you ever have these thoughts or is it just me? You pan back for a second. Become hyper-aware of your body. Get out of your head and think some left-field thoughts.

Like, if I just got up now and threw my table over and then blew a raspberry, would anyone do anything? Would they just carry on? If I got some scissors and threw them at Deborah, my boss, right now, would she tear off her shirt and fight me? What if I just went 'mahhhhhhhh', quietly, in a dull monotone until I ran out of breath, and then started again, and kept doing that for an hour, what would everyone do?

Do you ever have these kind of thoughts? Maybe it's just me. It's just me, isn't it? Oh, I am so bored. I want to get back to my flat. Back to my watching. To try to find this guy. Instead I'm just sitting. Here.

I turn my eyes to Phil. He said he'd been watching me. At the Tube. That time. So now I'm going to get my own back. Have a good look at him. Try to work him out. I'm good at that. Working people out. I think I am anyway.

His bottom lip sticks out. He's not got an underbite or anything. He just does that when he's concentrating. He sniffs. Scratches his nose. His mouth turns into a frown and the space between his eyebrows crinkles as he taps away at his computer, concentrating. He's ordering stationery today.

He asked, 'Anyone want anything, stationery-wise?'

A voice said, 'Big bag of Mars bars?'

A single laugh came from somewhere.

Followed only by the tap-tap of nearby laptop percussion.

'No, stationery wise,' he said.

And the clock ticked on.

Yes, he's ordering stationery today. But he's making it look like he's putting up a firewall to protect government secrets. He's trying to radiate demonstrative intelligence and import. It's not working.

He sweeps back his hair and pushes up his glasses. Plain black frames. Then he looks up. Catching my eye. And stays there. Me looking at him while he looks at me while I look at him. He is expressionless. Impressive. I'm good at watching and being impassive. I practised most of my young life. But he's doing very well. I can sense he's thinking about smiling. It's telegraphed in the space between his cheekbones and eyes. But he doesn't. It's like he's trying to intimidate me. In the workplace.

People don't generally look at each other. Not in the eye. Certainly not like this. Not holding this kind of gaze. It makes people uncomfortable. Not just the people involved either. Do a sociological experiment. Get two people to stare at each other and see what happens to the air in the room. See how it changes. Get a thermometer out, see the temperature rise. And watch everyone tense up. Everyone in the room. They'll kind of half cringe. Watch them. Their fists will gently clench. Readying themselves for trouble. It's challenging. Threatening. It's primitive human instinct. We are all animals, after all.

But Phil doesn't get nervous. Not today anyway. He keeps looking at me. As I look at him. He can't help himself. How extraordinary.

'How you getting on with the strategy for the HR Directors training objectives?' Deborah says, floating the words malignantly in my direction. Somehow smug.

It makes me drop my gaze. I lose. I lose to Phil. I hate that. I look back at my screen. She waits for an answer.

'Shut the fuck up,' I say. It just comes out. Very quickly. As if in a single word.

'Sorry?' she says. Smiling, because she doesn't know what else to do.

'Yeah. Good,' I say.

Her head shakes and she goes back to whatever the hell she's doing. Unsure if what she thinks has just happened has actually happened.

'Good,' she says. Now fully resolved that she must have been imagining it.

I'm going to have to watch myself. My impulse control is getting very weak. The gap between think and do is almost nothing with me at the moment. I'm going to have to watch that.

Out of the corner of my eye, I notice Phil is still watching. He doesn't even crack a smile. He hasn't moved a muscle. He's so still. I can sense him looking. But I don't want to let him know I'm aware of him. I don't want to let him know that I know that he's watching. But I know. Oh yes. Because I'm watching him.

I think about the girl on the Missing poster again.

His index finger rises to his lips. And he breathes.

9 days till it comes.

The Situationalists say there is no such thing as personality. I'll tell you what I mean by that. In the late sixties, after much work had been done on analysing personality, by the pre-eminent psychologists of the day, Walter Mischel posited the theory that our personality was completely defined by situation. He wasn't alone, many joined him in this belief.

Yes, our levels of intelligence remain constant. We look the same no matter who we are talking to, but fundamentally, they believed, we are more a product of the situation we are being put in, right at that moment, than anything else.

One could be seen as an entirely different person with one's mother, for instance, than with a work colleague. Our choices would be different, the way we sit, maybe even the way we breathe. So, the Situationalists argued, can we then really be said to have anything approaching a consistent personality? They believed not.

Five days ago, as the man child with the 'Hoverboard' lay on his arse and the lad with the phone stood up to me, fists clenched by his sides, his face scrunched to its full level of meanness, I felt like a different person.

Maybe the situation took over and dictated what was to happen next. His brow pushing down over his eyes almost, his jaw fully tightened, he wanted to go for me, tear into me. But he didn't. This little bruiser let the situation get the better of him. He knew that with enough witnesses and people knowing he was a local lad he wouldn't be hard to find. So he just sat back down, and turned his music off.

The other patrons looked on. Their morning busted open by my outburst. They smiled as I left, but I don't know whether they were just as scared of me as they were of the gang. It wasn't like anyone was breaking into spontaneous applause.

I grabbed my bag, paid and left. Thompson was gone by that point, he shuffled off as soon as he got his money. I strode back. Adrenaline up, head held high. And felt their eyes on me as I walked to the entrance to my flat.

After that kind of thing you really wish you could storm away out into the world and walk off the tension of the moment for a while. I'd certainly have looked more heroic if I had walked off into the sunset, rather than a matter of twenty paces to where my electronic key fob let me into the hallway. Through which I could still see the onlookers in the Z Café watching me go. Thinking, who is she? What on earth does she want? Where the hell did she come from?

Well, now they knew, just upstairs actually. What was it people say about shitting on your own doorstep? That low profile I'd been planning to keep hasn't come to fruition yet.

The last few days have helped. I haven't come perilously close to any dust-ups. I haven't wandered into any abandoned buildings. Nor have I met any new friends from the neighbourhood. No, I haven't spoken to anyone in fact. Not even at work. I've kept my eyes locked on my screen. Giving nothing away.

I've kept myself to myself and waited till I could get back to my spot and keep my eyes peeled. I've barely even spoken to Aiden. We communicate in sighs and grunts, and if you're thinking that's some sign that we know each other so well that we've got beyond language, that we're somehow post all that, in a good way, well it's not that. We're strangers. Ghosts to each other. Hardly aware of one another's presence in rooms.

That feeling you have, the way the air changes when you know someone has entered the room behind you, we don't have that. I'm deaf to his heartbeat and he's deep under. His mind is in another place. He's fallen further into his book and hasn't got any time for me or any of the living world for that matter.

I wonder sometimes whether our indifference will turn into hostility. I think perhaps one night it did. But it was in the dark. In the sleeping hours, the magic ones between three and five. I can't be sure if I imagined it. In my slumber.

When I woke. In the dark. I felt his weight on me. He had his thighs either side of my body. Holding me down. He was muttering to himself. He must've been dreaming. Must've been. Though it was almost pitch black, some light spilt in under the blind and showed me his face. Crumpled with anger. And his knuckles.

He pulled his arm back, fist clenched into a tight ball.

His wrist, tight. His bones all knotted up and holding me down. I yelled for him to stop. But his hand went back and back. I'd never seen him like that before. As an aggressor. My husband. His body stretched to its full size. He looked huge and he groaned in distress as he prepared to bring his fist crashing down on me. Bearing down on me. His muttering getting louder. I yelled for him to wake up. He must've been dreaming.

Then as I closed my eyes and waited for it. Moaning, in fear, in the night-time. His other hand at the base of my neck. Then it came down. Gently tapping the pillow next to me. Like he was only playing. Then he rolled over, sighed and muttered himself back to rest.

I didn't even bring it up the next day. I didn't know how to. And he didn't. So I didn't.

He must've been dreaming. He must've been dreaming.

Right?

But dream or not. He's changing too. I don't know what's happening to him. Sometimes he scares me a little. Like Phil does.

But I'm OK. I can look after myself. I'm self-sufficient.

I've got my tip-offs and my project. My information and my grid to keep me company. Keep me out of trouble. I've had a lot of watching to do.

I'm not going to say it hasn't been frustrating. The first day was easy. Some small sightings, nothing big, but I'm resilient. I'm always thinking about tomorrow, about what might come then. About possibilities and new evidence. You need patience in the hide. You need a different mindset, you need to be hopeful and prepared because the moment something rare sticks its head out you have to be ready to see it. Otherwise, what was all the waiting for. I repeat my new mantra.

Stay awake. Stay conscious. Stay sane.

Let me fill you in a little. I've been glued to the window. No chance to even write new entries in this journal. Too busy. But now I've got a bit of breathing space. So let me get you up to speed with my last five days in the hide…

Part Six:
The Big Stay

Waiting for Jonny and Joseph's Hands

Day 1: In short, I got nothing.

No blinds came up in flats four, seven, eleven or eighteen.

I got home from work to catch Jonny, our angry Skyper, and our other main suspect, Joseph, him of the meticulously clean bike, both rear their heads, but their hands were nowhere to be seen.

Jonny's girlfriend, Lina, is away so he ordered a pizza. Joseph wandered around a little in there and read off his iPad. The whole day did not make good viewing.

My eye was drawn to Tippi and Janet for about twenty minutes when they attached a small net to their kitchen table and played a lively game of ping-pong. Janet won, 2–1 in games, in a hard-fought encounter. It was 21–17 in the decider, an excellent game, with Janet coming out the victor despite Tippi attempting to target Janet's weak backhand. They hugged afterwards. But Tippi secretly stored up a bit of resentment for another time.

Day 2: Flat 11. Blind open. Vincent.

Day two started at 7 a.m. with great success.

With one pull on the cord of his blinds Vincent revealed himself to me. Quite literally. In nothing but a thin dressing gown, which constantly billowed up and did little to preserve his modesty, he ironed his shirts, and boxer shorts would you believe. He then swiftly changed into the last pair he ironed. Hmm toasty. Momentarily giving anyone outside, who happened to be watching, a full glimpse of arse.

Vincent has a belt holster, which he slips his phone into like its a deadly weapon he owns a license to wield. Vincent talks to himself constantly. I thought he had someone else in there for a good hour, a hostage tied up next to the toilet perhaps, out of view. But no. Vincent talks to himself.

I've always thought it extraordinary how people find others talking to themselves so odd. As if people should be too private to reveal they have an inner life. Terrified what people might think if they knew they had actual thoughts. So scared of the so-called 'mad'. Of looking it themselves. Of the man muttering his shopping list to himself at the meat counter. As if every syllable could be the prelude to some indiscriminate machete based killing spree. Rather than just talking with no one else around.

Vincent is also tall, thin and kindly looking. I would buy life insurance off him in an instant. Which all could be leading to the classic 'you wouldn't think he could be a murderer' statements in the red tops, 'he was so nice, the last person you'd think would kill an OAP'. And sure, I would be willing to go along with this possibility and proceed towards level two so I can try to scope out his hands. But Vincent is an Asian gentleman. Not bleach blond either. And so I dismissed him from our enquiries immediately and watched them all go to work.

They flocked away. Some towards the overground. Some towards the Tube. Cary on his motorbike. Janet and Tippi together, a piece of toast each in some kitchen roll. Mr Smith went underneath the building to get into his Volvo and drove off to who knows where. But I stayed here. Birding.

The evening session brought nothing from Jonny and Joseph, both returning late. Joseph having done some serious overtime. Jonny having done some serious drinking. Neither standing still long enough in the darkness for me to catch sight of their hands. Alas.

I rolled into bed, kissed Aiden on his cold cheek and hit the sack.

Day 3: Flat 4. Alfred; Flat 7. Liz and Dicky.

The morning brought great joys. First a removal van with a glut of boxes arrived. I breathed in with the excitement of it all. The grip around my binoculars tightened and I awaited which building they were heading to.

In seconds a team of burly blokes jumped out and started unloading the van. They were like a cross between an army and a synchronised swimming team. They grabbed the brown boxes of various sizes, passed them to each other and headed towards Waterway. Yes!

Behind the van, three figures stepped out of a Merc and followed in behind, it was difficult to see who's who. Difficult to make judgements. I needed to identify the resident.

They settled inside flat four and there was a clutch of biceps and hands putting things into place. An hour later, the room was fully assembled by the team and two well-dressed parents, the older figures from the Merc, jumped in the car and drove off into the distance. All shorts and sunglasses, as if off to a yacht in Monaco. Maybe they were.

They were all gone but one. Their son.

Inside, the skinny boy surveyed his surroundings, glancing every so often at his smartphone before flicking on the television. I'm calling him Alfred. That's a name that could come back into fashion, you never know.

Alfred is twenty-one, saturnine, dark and slight. Welcome to the neighbourhood, my boy. Your first home, all funded by Mum and Dad. There is nothing imposing about him. How unthreatening. What they call 'gentrification' is at the end of it all. How unimpressive and easy it looks. All he represents is another cross on my grid. And the disturbing possibility that someone may have moved out shortly after Jean's murder.

It's a slim possibility. That anyone would kill and immediately sell up shop. That would be a hell of a swift move and a beast of a story to get to the bottom of. Quite a way to leave the neighbourhood with a bang. But if I don't find that bandaged hand then it's going to start to feel a lot more possible. But I decided to ignore that avenue for now and stay positive.

Just a few hours later, the sound of a rolling suitcase announced the arrival back off holiday of Liz and Dicky. Three weeks in Turkey I'd say by the look of their tans. You lucky lot. A lot has happened since you went away. They are in their mid-thirties and Dicky's are the most pristine gentleman's hands I've ever seen. Not a day's physical labour in his life. I bet he runs a successful start-up that's gifted him with long luxurious holidays at the back end of August when London is at its best anyway. I wouldn't want to be anywhere else but here at this time of year. They can keep their holidays. I wouldn't miss this for the world.

I've seen them before come to think of it. They go running together on Saturday mornings. They're happy. They're humdrum. They're of no use to me.

Stay awake. Stay conscious. Stay sane.

Only one flat to go now. One blind left to rise. Two pairs of hands to see.

Day 4: A complete shut-out.

Cary came home with a Vespa.

Gregory in the penthouse attached his feet to a metal bar, which he hung from upside down. He then failed manfully to do six consecutive upside down sit-ups. He failed to do this for around forty-five minutes. Every so often letting himself down to allow the blood to flow back around his body. He shook himself off. Before trying, and failing, again.

Day 5: Jonny's hands.

Yesterday, I got lucky. It was the day the window cleaners are supposed to come and do the big windows. But some sort of 'technical issue' meant they wouldn't be around till next week.

In their absence, a man like Jonny must step up to the plate and take on the task himself. Squeegee in hand, bucket at his feet, he leant around to try to give it a good go in the early evening. Lina looked on asking him to 'be careful'. As he leant from the balcony, precariously. She needn't have worried. I was watching too, to catch him if he fell.

I watched and waited. Then there they were. I couldn't believe it. But it was unmistakable. Undeniable. Despite being covered in suds and water.

Two clean hands. Nothing to see there.

I'm losing time.

Today.

Revelations – Resolutions – Waterway Apartments – Good vis, strong breezes, 12 deg – Flocks and flocks – The men – Various heights – Ready to reveal.

Awake. Conscious. Sane. All in equal measure.

This is my sixth day on the watch, I've slept as little as possible. I've stuck to my task. I tell myself I've done everything I could do.

My head droops. I see the world through a brownish gauze. I think I do need to get some proper sleep at some point.

Today is a Sunday and what I thought would be my best day for sightings. You know, Sunday. Not an excursion day. Not a work day. A stay in the house day.

Joseph has done just that. Not venturing out enough for me to see him cleaning that bike. He hasn't done that since Jean was killed. Not since the boys said someone came around their way and got cut for their trouble.

Maybe that's just coincidence. Or maybe he is hiding something. In his nest.

A tree partially obscures my view of Joseph and it irks me. This is probably why I haven't seen more of him already and I'd considered finding another vantage point. Behind the tree perhaps. But now he's my prime suspect I think it's probably best not to rile the man. I can't get too close. I can't give myself away. This man could be dangerous.

He's been pottering around in there doing God knows what all day. Then I lose him. I think I saw a flash of his shorts from his bedroom window so perhaps he's going for a run. I consider putting on my trainers and vest and giving chase. I'm not fast. By no means am I fast. But if I got close enough even for a second that would be enough to see his hands. But I haven't run in months and don't often do sightings without binoculars. The naked eye can be so exposing.

You're always better to stay where you are and let them come to you. That's the philosophy. If you've got a decent enough view that is. I stare at my trainers, wondering whether that would be the stupid or smart move. I don't feel like running. But that might have to be the way it goes.

Fortunately, I'm saved from any undue exercise when he comes tearing around on his bike. This is what I wanted. Full visibility. And no chance of me having to break into a sweat.

He removes a small sponge from his saddlebag and dips it into the fountain. This is it. Cleaning time. Back to the old routine.

Stay awake. Stay conscious. Stay sane.

One hand is in the water, the other is by his side, just out of view. He pulls it out, it's obscured by the sponge. He rubs the bike down methodically. Now he crouches and rubs it along the frame. It glistens in the sunlight and obscures my view. I can't see.

This is frustrating. I pull up the blind a bit, revealing myself more to the outside world. I'm taking a chance, but I have to. I need a better look. It's so close. He must be nearly finished. I can't miss this open goal. I take a chance. I leave my apparatus behind. And go solo. I go out onto the balcony.

I focus in on the fountain, as if lost in thought, serene. When in fact I'm desperately trying to stay calm. It's all a subterfuge. For his benefit. So he doesn't think I've got my eye on him. I'm pretending to be merely an ordinary person on an ordinary Sunday. Not someone scouting for a killer.

He possibly sees me. Senses me. I'm not sure. I stay still. He's so close. Close enough for the naked eye, but his hands keep moving. Then he stops. Wipes them dry and stands.

His right hand is clean. So is his left. No bandage, nothing. I see it. As clear as day. If that was my smoking gun, I'm going to have to think again. No cut hands anywhere in Waterway Apartments. It's a washout.

No tells. No giveaways. This leaves the whole grid open. Everyone back in play. Dammit.

Just then. For the first time. The blind of flat eighteen shoots up and there stands a man. Tall, blond, a plaster cast on his right hand. I stare up at the sky as a flock of sparrows passes overhead. It distracted me for a second. But I've seen it.

I gasp and want to turn to go inside. But my feet are rooted there like concrete blocks. He sees the birds too. Then he sees me. My face. Or seems to. His face is... pensive. Not quite blank, but tough to read. Or maybe he's just too far away to judge. He stands and looks in my direction for a second. And I at him. Me, unmoved. I've got him.

There seems to be an understanding between us. An electricity. No binoculars any more. Nothing for either of us to hide behind. The molecules in the air move silently between us.

Then, he turns and casually steps back, away from the window.

9 days till it comes. Evening.

WM – Waterway Apartments – Good vis, last of the light nights, 13 deg – Singular – Thick dark brow, almost Greek, died-blond plumage – Navy-blue suit and matching tie – 6′ 3″ – A model of control, coiled rage.

It's so hard to conceal ecstasy. When you have that piece of news you want to tell everyone but can't. I skip around the flat, trying to compose myself. Terrence runs around my feet, excited, he knows something's up. He feels vibrations off me. Feels it in the air. I don't want Aiden to suspect anything. But then dogs are experts in human behaviour. I don't think you could say the same of Aid.

I head to the bathroom and sit on top of the seat. I do this at work sometimes when I just need a break from the mundanity of it all. For now, I need to stay calm and stick to the facts.

Noises in the hallway. Footsteps. I can tell from the quality of step that's Lowell coming home.

The man in flat eighteen – Mr Brenner I'm going to call him – fits the bill completely. I named him after the character Rod Taylor played in *The Birds*. It's only a shorthand. He needed a name so I gave him one I'd remember. But Hitchcock's Brenner was the hero of the piece, always saving Tippi Hedren's character Melanie from gulls, crows and everything else. In fact, the Brenner home was constantly under attack from the birds. But my Mr Brenner isn't under attack. He's just under close watch.

My Mr Brenner is shifty. I can understand some level of privacy, but he seems rigorous about keeping his blinds down. He could've been away on holiday or something like that, of course. I can't quite tell for sure.

But I can tell a few things. Because he's had his blinds open for a luxurious three hours of watching time.

His home is studiously arranged. A large oak bookshelf reveals a taste for modern pop science books and other non-fiction. The angle of the flat means I can't see the entire room, which frustrates me. But I can see a samurai sword in there and an arty wildlife shot of a lion. Framed. I remember reading that an obsession with predatory animals is an indicator of a psychopath. I meditate on this.

Perhaps he had no motive. Just a psychopath. Or maybe he did have a motive, I just haven't figured it out yet. But whatever the finer details, I imagine killing people off is that much easier if you are a psychopath. The danger doesn't touch the sides. You feel neither great highs nor crushing lows. You're more pragmatic about what needs to be done. Not hampered by unhelpful fears or worries. Unemotional.

I can sympathise with him at this moment. I'm tired and hazy. I see him through a bleary-eyed film. The psychopath in the flat over the road.

He disturbed a couple of things so simply threw it away. A poker. A porcelain monkey. He's pragmatic. He was in and out in five minutes, Thompson said. Cool, efficient, unemotional. Psychopath. A definite possibility.

Then there's his arm. I didn't expect the cast. Perhaps they cut him so deep they chipped or broke a bone. It could be an arm guard or support. Or, he could've applied it himself. Allowing him to hide the knife wound and tell anyone that asks that his injury is something more benign. Repetitive strain from tapping away on his computer. Torn ligaments while playing squash. Broken bone incurred when cycling. Anything that doesn't involve a large unexplained gash to the forearm. That makes sense.

I try to get a better look at the cast, but my apparatus isn't good enough to see if it's set tight to his arm or removable.

There doesn't seem to be a Mrs Brenner. Not yet anyway. I wonder what his home life is like. I wonder if he has friends. Whether he went to a good university.

Not that any of it matters so much. I've got him and I'm not going to let him get away. But this is just the beginning. Now I have to prove it. Now I've got to get close enough to find something incriminating before I turn him over to the police. Something good. Something big time. I need to gift wrap him for them. I need something concrete. And something that doesn't make me look more crazy than he is. I'll have to keep the tip-offs from squatters and night visits to the victim to myself. I won't tell them that, of course not, no way. I don't want them laughing at me again. I hated that. I don't know what I'd do if they did that again.

There are movements in there. He gets a call. He paces around, smiling at first. Then a tightening of the features.

His eyes widen, he rubs the top of his head. Then his left hand reaches his left temple and strokes up and down. A silent movie of a troubled man thinking.

It's unclear what he does for a living. It's a Sunday so it's not a work clothes day. But I can usually have a pretty good guess at occupation from the look of someone on any old day. Whether they're in their work costumes or not. I'm not boasting or anything. But I'm mostly right.

Maybe he's an estate agent, not a slimy one. One with one of those offices with a bike in the window. That tries to convince you they're really more of a boutique affair. More like a local art gallery. Rather than a chain company set up to extract yet more money from the housing market.

Or maybe he's a a structural engineer. He has a smooth air about him, like he gives orders and has a secretary named Adrienne. But he also looks genuinely capable. Skilled labour. Some style, some substance. Respected in the workplace.

He's shouting at the guy on the other end of the phone. He's pacing around so he's difficult to lip-read. Every so often he turns his back away and then I lose even the thread of the dumb show.

He turns back. I see his mouth. It looks like he was expecting the call to be good news. But it isn't. I think someone is telling him that something is trickier than they thought it would be. Brenner didn't expect this.

'What? Why?' he says – I can make that out. Then a disagreement. Proper drama. He gesticulates wildly, he's pissed off. I even catch him saying 'yes, I'm pissed off'. He mouths more expletives. I won't repeat them here. He moves towards the wall, resting his head and his fist against it. He's still talking, angry. His mouth moving a mile a minute.

Then he breaks away swiftly, walking towards a samurai sword mounted on the wall next to him. He picks it up. He runs his palm along the handle. I had a friend at university with a samurai sword. I always thought it was a lame collector's item.

Then he turns his back to me. Still holding the weapon. I wish I could hear inside. Tap his phone perhaps. Then we would be getting into serious territory. Terrence licks his lips and puts his head in my lap again. I stroke his head. Brenner runs his hand along his murderous little toy.

Then he seems calmed somehow. Perhaps by something his friend on the other end of the phone has said to him. He listens. This could be it and I'm missing it all. The vital piece of evidence I need. To know for sure he did it. If I got it on tape, for instance. If I had the equipment. That could be all they'd need to convict. Right? I'm so close. I see that now.

What I need is to see or hear something incriminating. Not even cold, hard evidence for now. Not Exhibit 'A'. Just something good enough to confirm to me that he did it and I can work with the rest. I can take that tiny morsel of evidence and spin it into something solid. Then the police will take over.

I won't tell the fuzz I've been watching. Of course not. Nothing like that. I'll tell them I've overheard or caught a glimpse of him doing just some little thing. I'll let them assume the rest. Then once they have him in custody, his fingerprints, then they'll fill it all in. They can't bungle it from there surely. Once they've got him in their sights. They're not that incompetent.

A thought hits me. I could even call them now. Tell

the police I happened to see a local man at Jean's place that night. Pin it on him and see if it sticks. I can ring in on that number on the sign outside Alaska House. I could tell a little white lie. Put him at the scene and let them do the rest. I could make it all happen now if I wanted to.

But no. I have to know that it's him first. For sure. For him as much as me. Fair's fair. I'll get close enough to find out either way. Then when I've got what I need, I'll get it to the police, all tied up with a bow. With no suspicion that some strange woman has been hanging around rubbernecking at the case like some kind of pariah. Then it will be done. It's as simple as that.

The call ends. His rage subsides. He takes his phone and throws it at the settee. PG anger. Then he turns and frowns. His eyes narrow and he's thinking about something. Maybe his next move. If only I'd heard that call, I'd have a good idea of what that might be. That's what I need. I need to hear inside there.

He goes back to his ornamental samurai sword. Unsheathes it. Then holds the blade in his hands. As gently as a newborn baby. It's a ceremonious act. He respects it.

Then he presses one finger against the blade. It cuts him. It's sharp. He breaks the skin. Blood flows. I can tell because he puts his finger straight into his mouth. Then he pulls it out and admires his hand. Which he holds towards him, just twenty centimetres from his face. Then it comes again. The bleeding not staunched. I catch sight of it trickling from his index finger down to his palm.

And he just looks at it. Cold. Still. Expressionless.

8 days till it comes. Single white male.

Our drinks land on the table. We're at the nearest pub to the station. He went for a white wine. I wasn't expecting that. I thought he would be a mainstream lager man. I've gone for a Bloody Mary.

You should have seen his face when I asked him if he fancied a swift one after work. It was just like Terrence's when I say 'walkies'. So eager, so bright, so much hope.

I thought maybe it would be good for me to get out of the house for a while. But that's not really why I'm here. I need Phil's help. I need a geek.

'. . . I mean, I do think there's a message to it all. You wouldn't think a movie with Adam Sandler as an East European hairdresser would have so much depth, but it's actually a great performance. Certainly one of his most fully realised characters since *The Waterboy*...'

'What are we talking about?' I zone in and zone out as always. My mind on, dare I say it, more important things.

'*You Don't Mess With the Zohan*. Oh. You've gotta see *You Don't Mess With the Zohan*, it's a classic comedy...'

'Talk to me about the sound equipment.' I cut to the chase.

'What do you wanna know?' he responds, like a cocky pro.

I had no idea how much he'd know about this kind of thing,but it makes sense. I think he still goes to the Games Workshop. Paints citadel miniatures. He said he thought about joining the TA but likes his weekends too much. He loves 'kit'. All that. It's his favourite topic. Like I said, it makes sense.

'So, say I wanted to hear what those people over there were saying to each other. Those two, right at the other end of the bar.'

'Well, you've got your bugs. Which you'd have to pre-plant—'

'That's not an option,' I say, cutting him off before he waffles on down some useless byway.

'Err, OK, you've got directional sound. You point it like an arrow at your target. You simply tune in depending on the distance, like a long wave radio and, errr… Robert's your father's brother, as they say.'

'Would it work through glass?' I say, not messing about.

He stares at me. I'm giving myself away.

'Hmm. Well. It should do. Not perfectly, but it should do. You can get the lot with the transmitter and headphones for about hundred odd quid at the spy shop. You can get anything in there. Like. In the world.'

He grins. Sweetly. Stares at me deeply. Spy equipment and Adam Sandler films may, for once, not be the only things on his mind.

'Good! That's really good. Thanks,' I say, trying to break his trance.

'Yeah. Cool. I mean, if you could plant a bug, that'd be your best—'

'No, it's not an option, Phil,' I say, firm. I know what he's like when he gets on one. I don't have time.

I suck hard through my straw. Time to get out of here. I did warn him it'd be a swift one. I need to get back home; Terrence needs walking. I realise I'm not thinking about Aiden at all any more.

'Hope you don't mind me asking—' Phil says.

'I do.' Best to cut him off early. Whatever he's pushing for.

'I just thought I'd say, I could help, with whatever your project is. I mean if you do need someone. An accomplice. Put me in the game. I'm your man.'

'No,' I say, finishing up my drink. He's barely touched his wine.

'Oh, please. I'd really, really like that. Whatever you're doing. It sounds cool. And I'm always up for a bit of mischief. Remember when I hid the stapler?' he says. Puppyish.Please don't make a scene again, I think.

'Look, Phil. It's nothing exciting. Just a little project. A *solo* project. Girl stuff. You know. It wouldn't be the kind of thing you'd be interested in.'

'Oh, come on, try me! I have night-vision goggles, for for God's sake!'

'It's really not that kind of thing,' I offer. A verbal rub on the back.

His words seem to make me feel more ridiculous. Accomplice. Mischief. This isn't a childish game. It's not Dungeons and Dragons and I don't need a sidekick. And if I did I'd pick Lowell, not him. Lowell and I. We could be a brother and sister crime-solving team. He could be my Jem. And I, his Scout. Sorry, Phil. Cruel to be kind. You don't make the cut.

I think about telling him I'm a lone wolf, but then I really would sound ridiculous. Anyway, I'm not. I've got a husband. And a dog now too. That's virtually a family.

Imagine Aid's face if I brought some bloke from work back to the house too. Like I'm collecting strays. Just a mate to play around with some headphones and a directional microphone for a bit. Then he would definitely say I'm mental. Or a child.

'Anyway, thanks for the drink. I've really got to get back,' I say.

'What? Already?' He's stung. He still has a full glass of white wine.

'You stay. Watch the football. Finish your wine.'

'I don't even like wine! I thought it'd make me look classy,' he blurts out.

It's the sort of comment that makes someone with a bag on their shoulder, half hovering between sitting and standing, momentarily place herself back on her bar stool. Purely out of sympathy. I do keep my bag firmly over my shoulder though. Symbolically.

'Phil, we'll do something another time, but I've got a lot on at the mo,' I say. Dead-end friendly. I'm trying to kill the conversation before it gets a bit emotional. Again. I'm trying really hard. But it's too late.

'Do you think about him? Your husband. When you're out having a drink with me, is that it? I'm sorry if that's it,' he says, his face slightly reddened now. I've no idea what he's talking about. I don't know whether he wants to fuck me or fight me.

'No, no. It's nothing like that. It's not weird or anything.

To have a man as a mate, I mean. It's fine, you're fine. And we are mates, aren't we?'

'Yeah. Yeah, mates,' he says with a grimace.

In another life I might have kissed him at that moment. Maybe just to make him feel better. But I'm not at university any more. Those days are gone. I'm a very married woman.

'Give me a couple of weeks. Then we'll go for a proper drink.'

'Yeah, that'd be nice, a proper drink. As mates,' he says, trying a smile.

I kiss him on the cheek and hurry off. If Brenner does anything incriminating I want to be there to see it.

He calls me back. 'Lily. You will remember to get on with the rest of your life after all this has died down, won't you?' he says, weightily. He's a strange boy.

'Yes. Of course. It's just a little project.' I don't know what else to say. I turn to go.

But he has one more thing to say.

'I didn't mean that. Listen. Er… The directional microphone might not be that effective. If it's too noisy round where you are. It can be tricky if there's noise between you and your target. Didn't you say there were building works going on round near you? You might want to think about that. Just a thought.'

I don't remember telling him that. Possibly I did. I don't remember. But he's not the sort of person I want knowing exactly where I live. Just to be on the safe side.

His advice lingers in the air as I mull over the subtext.

Fuck me or fight me. Fuck me? Or fight me.

I nod and leave.

It may not work, of course. But I'm going to give the

microphone a damn good go anyway. Despite the crunch of the building works all around me.

Despite the heavy drone.

The constant rumble.

Rumble. Rumble. Rumble. Rumble.

7 days till it comes. And here we are.

Something crashes against my window. I fall and put my back to the solid white wall. Out of plain sight. I'm breathing so hard now. Shaking. The hairs on my arm stand on end. My heart is beating out of my chest.

The glass is cracked. I daren't turn my head. But in my periphery I can see something. Pressed against my now cracked window. Don't Turn Your Head, I tell myself.

I can see something. Sliding down it. Slowly. Dreadfully.

So I breathe in through my nose. Bite down hard on my tongue.

I turn my head. And look.

Claret. Against my windowpane. Blood and something else. Oh, God.

Greying feathers mashed up against the glass. What looks like a beak too. The stocky body of a pigeon, dead, slides down and down.

I study it closely. It's horrible. It seemed to fly straight into the glass. Pigeons aren't the smartest of the avian community, but they tend to steer clear of large buildings.

The rats of the air. I look at it now and it does resemble a rat. The rat I nearly put my knife through. It might just be because the rat at Jean's door is the last thing I saw dead and bleeding. But, as I look at now, with its plump body that some humans eat, it does resemble the gristle of a rat.

Ring, ring. Ring, ring.

It's still beautiful though. It's still a beautiful creature of the air. I look closer at it and at the tiny crack its body has made in the glass. I put my finger to the glass. It only takes the tiniest crack to let the rest of the world in. To ruin everything.

This tiny bird's broken body breaks my heart. I love them so. It slides so delicately to the balcony floor.

Bang! Another one. I turn my head away and scream. Every muscle in my body contracts. I shake as I turn back and watch it slide down towards the balcony too. It struck the window higher up and to the left. This one's smaller more compact body not cracking the glass this time. Its innards dangling out of its chest. Its terrible face stares in at me. I can see the whites of his eyes. I hold my mouth and try to stop myself from being sick.

Ring, ring. Ring, ring.

I rise and move towards the phone, staying low. In case more birds decide to fling themselves unprovoked at my window.

Bang!

A third hits and falls straight back to the balcony, its body not sticking to the glass. I let out another scream as I crawl towards the phone. My chin scraping along the floor, as I stay low.

I wonder if there's any way of getting my number that I

wouldn't know about. I'm sure people can get that kind of information if they want it badly enough. Maybe someone important wants to talk to me. The police. Or Brenner. Maybe he's some sort of telecoms expert. Maybe he's decided it's time to have a word with me.

It could be anyone in the building opposite, in a way. Anyone that's seen me watching them and wants to get their own back. Wants to invade my privacy and show me how it feels.

Bang! Maybe this is my comeuppance. Bang! I scream.

Ring, ring. Ring, ring.

My hand quivers over the phone. Maybe I shouldn't answer at all. I pause to look at my window, now covered in feathers and blood. It can't be real. I close my eyes and breathe. In through my nose for fifteen, out for ten. It can't be real.

Bang! Bang! A fifth and sixth come almost from below and crash into the window. They're homing in on me. Why are they attacking me? Are they fighting back too?

Ring, ring. Ring, ring.

I have to answer. It can't be any worse than this. The noise of the two bodies sliding down the glass squeals at me as they serenely fall to where the other dead ones lie. Such a terrible sound.

I grab for the phone and get low. My breath held. My eyes closed. I pull the receiver up to my ear. And listen.

'If you or a loved one has had an accident in the past six years then you may be entitled to compensation. Please press Three if—'

I drop the handset to the floor and with it goes the disembodied voice. My hands instinctively go to my head and I begin to cry.

'...one of our advisers would be happy to speak to you and make a recommendation about the best way to...'

The disembodied voice carries on. The phone lying on the floor, staring at me. I grab for the cord that attaches it to the wall and pull hard, my face and cheeks a ruddy red. I yank it from its socket. A madwoman crashing around alone in her home. For a moment it all subsides and I hear the naked but comforting sound of my own breath. Frantic and heavy.

A growl and snarl from inside the house. I jump again. Then Terrence, hiding in the bedroom all this time, wanders in and licks my hand. I pick him up and hold him in my arms like cradling a baby. He licks my face and I almost manage a laugh.

Then he turns and tries to lick the window. He sniffs it, trying to get to the blood and feathers that lie on the other side. This makes me wipe my face. I suddenly realise he is ultimately an animal. Not my child. Who knows where his mouth has been.

I stand and go back to the window. I touch the crack but it isn't so bad, the windows are double glazed and you can't feel it on this side.

I try to look out, back to Brenner's flat where I'd seen the girl taken just moments before. Through the gap between the feathers and blood. I see that flat number eighteen – his flat – has drawn up its blinds.

I turn and make a grab for the directional microphone. I bought it earlier this morning. When things were so much calmer.

I put my headphones on and play with the dial. Just in case I can hear something in there. Inside number eighteen.

I tried listening in earlier but the rumble of the building works blocked out the distant sounds, as Phil said they might. I did have some luck before that though. I listened to some music in Alfred's flat, number four. It was like I was in there with him. Sharing the moment. The two of us. Huddled together. A team. As the world floated by. He had *The Planets* suite by Holst on for some reason. It soundtracked my morning for an hour or so. The music dipping and rising. As I watched on. Considering his bare feet on his cold wood floor.

The device works. But the delicacies of the human voice are too much for it. Particularly backed by the cacophony of the rumble of the building works, amplified further through the transmitter.

Rumble. Rumble. Crackle.

I play with the dial anyway. Just in case. Just to see whether I can hear the faintest sound of a voice through the airwaves.

Crackle. Crackle. But nothing.

As I fiddle with the dial I think I should call the police. It's time. If I saw what I really think I saw I should call right now, this is concrete. The girl in the window. The burn marks on her legs. The hand that grabbed her. This is what I wanted, something real.

But it was so dark in there. Oh. Now I'm starting to doubt seeing anything at all. No, I'm sure I did. I should call the police and tell them. But would they believe me? I don't want to look like a fool, not again.

Perhaps it's all a sordid sex game. Or maybe he'll be able to get rid of her before the police come. I'll look like the strange one. Then the police will be on to me. And he will too. I'll be the only one who'll get caught. No. None of this works.

As I play with the dial, suddenly I do get something. Noises. Voices. Nothing as long range as all the way over to Brenner's flat. But something from the space in between the buildings.

Howls. Screams of laughter. Just outside. I drop the equipment to the floor and peer down through my cracked window.

7 days till it comes. Outside.

WMs – Outside Riverview Apartments – Overcast, 10 deg – 5 flock – Adidas, Fila, Dunlop – Various heights – Chattering, twittering, boisterous.

Below, the tracksuits from the café stand there. Laughing their heads off. They wipe pigeon blood on each other's hands. Playfully. One of them has feathers all over him, he hops around for the others' amusement. Another has a bucket and they all wear gardening gloves.

My blood rises. I see red. Without putting shoes on, I grab my keys and Terrence and head down and out into the street to confront them.

I tear out of the building and I'm on them, taking them by surprise. I'm trying to intimidate as I did in the café, but my face is hot and I'm clearly flushed and upset. They've got their revenge. They've got their rise out of me. And they're revelling in it.

Terrence, however, is unwilling to give up without a fight. He snarls and barks. He wants to bite back. Eventually he does. I loose him a touch and let him chomp down on the back of one the kids tracksuits, tearing a hole in it. Which I regret letting him do, instantly.

They swarm over me, this wasn't what was supposed to happen. This wasn't the plan. I hold Terrence close and crouch down, hands over my head, readying myself for their blows. One of them tries to grab the lead, the other kicks Terrence hard in the body. One of the others at the back reaches for something in his pocket.

'Oi, you lot, what the hell are you doing?' a voice shouts from behind me.

The kid grips something tightly in his pocket. His wrist tenses and shivers. He pulls out his phone, takes a picture of me and runs off. They all scatter, laughing like jackals.

'Enjoy your birds!' they shout as they disappear around the corner.

'Get lost! Or I'll call security and you'll all be arrested,' comes the voice again. Firm and strong. Officious.

I look up through my tears. There stands Lowell and one of the concierges.

'Hey, Lil, bloody hell, let's get inside. Those little animals,' Lowell says.

I'm so pleased to see him. I hug him deeply, pressing my whole body against him. He holds me up and takes me back inside the building.

The concierge talks about pressing charges and excellent CCTV cameras, but I don't want that. I may ordinarily. But not at this point. I'm already struggling to lie low as it is. This isn't the time.

Inside the hallway Lowell talks to me, measured and calm. Lulling me back to reality with his reliable timbre and stature.

'Honestly, some of them that hang around here they're really… I hate to say it but they're like a kind of vermin,' he says, unusually strident. Bilious.

Rats… The rats of the air… The rats of the street.

It would sound offensive coming out of anyone else's mouth. But his tentativeness reduces everything to a delicate reproach. Besides, I know he's just trying to make me feel better.

I feel safe with him as we rise in the lift.

'I hate it when guys say what I'm about to say. Like it's your fault. But. Take care of yourself out there Lily, won't you?' he says as we reach my door.

'Well. You said it anyway,' I say. He's a gentle man. And a gentleman.

But he doesn't know what he's talking about. I can take care of myself. I've probably taken more risks in the last week than he has in a lifetime.

'Thank you though. I'm all better now,' I say.

I touch him on the arm. He does the same to me.

'If you ever need anything, I'm just beyond the partition wall.'

Who am I kidding? I fancy him rotten. Is that terrible? He's one of those excellent geeks. Not like a geek geek. Not thick glasses with a plaster in the middle. A new geek. A good one. With strong features, characterful and defined. The kind of face you want to lick and then hit with a hammer. Or maybe that's just me. I'm reading that back and it makes me sound a bit odd.

My back's against my front door now. My home is just behind me.

'Thanks.'

'I'm serious, I know everything's been a bit… whatever, recently… I know. I know.'

What does he know? Another strange boy.

'So, I'm just next door. Is what I'm saying,' he says, dependable. Twenty per cent flirtatious.

'Ahh!' he yelps, taking a sharp step back. Breaking the moment. Terrence has come to the door and has started licking his hand. It caught him off guard. We laugh. It dies down. Then he stares at me. We keep coming back to this charged little silence. We're enjoying it. Our blood's up. It feels like something could happen. Here. Between us.

'Take care then,' he says.

I nod at him deliberately. I tap him on the chest, twice. Knock. Knock.

I turn and head inside.

Christ. Now it's my turn to jump. Aiden stands behind the door. We're all a bit jumpy tonight. He's right there. He's been waiting for me.

'Hi. Where've you been?' he asks, innocently.

But I don't want to answer that.

The more apt question is, where has he been? I was so het up by everything I hadn't stopped to wonder where he was at all. I felt so totally alone. And he was here. All along.

Did he not hear me shouting? What exactly was he doing in there?

Part Seven: In My Sights

6 days till it comes. Morning.

I'm thinking about that bug. The one I got from the specialist shop when I picked up the directional microphone. I forgot to tell you about that. I told Phil that bugging wasn't an option, and it shouldn't be. But now it's on the table and I've made some plans. Put wheels in motion.

I go and rummage around for it in my washbag and then get it out and stare at it for a while. Funny little thing. Not like a creature at all, as the name would suggest – just a box as big as a fifty-pence piece – 'GSM surveillance microphone'. I stare at number eighteen. Blinds firmly closed. He's keeping his head down, bobbing around in there no doubt, but staying out of sight and camouflaged, like the Reed Warbler on the banks of the reservoir. My intermediate eyes scan hopelessly for any signs motion. Then I get a text:

'In front of shop. 5 minutes.'

I text back: 'OK.'

When I saw Aiden last night I had it out with him. Properly for once. I put the reverse on him. He wanted to know what all the racket was in the living room while he was trying to work. Wondered where I went and who was outside the door. But I turned it around. Put it all back on him where it belonged. He's the mysterious one. He's the one hiding away. I didn't hold back.

'Oh, you're a coward. I married a coward,' I said, staring at him, accusingly.

'What the hell are you talking about?' he said, the cracks showing.

'Did you not hear the phone? The birds against the window?'

'What? What birds? That phone hasn't rung since we got here.'

I stared at him for a second. Role reversal.

He was fraught. I wondered why. He was just feeling guilty, surely. He must have heard the birds. Must have heard the smack. Smack. Bang. Bang.

A pause. He ran his hand over his face. His brow furrowed. Then I advanced.

'You hid in the bedroom. Blind down. Out of sight. Didn't you? While I was in here on my own. I forgot you were even in the flat. I forget you're around any more. You're a shut-in. You're a coward. It's pathetic.' It's all out.

He took a moment. He tutted. He blew his out his cheeks.

I waited.

'Look. I'm sorry. I'll admit I've had a lot to do. I've got a deadline. I've got thousands of words to get down and only a few days left. I switch off. I'm sorry. I'm so sorry.'

He held his head and looked up at me, his eyes reddened.

We took each other in for a moment. My heart softened. Some of the old him was back. He seemed human.

Vulnerable, but in an honest way. He looked at me and I felt his presence again all of a sudden. The presence of the man I love.

'But, Lily, I didn't hear any birds. I didn't hear any phone.'

Whoosh. A plane passed overhead. It's like they're getting closer and closer.

I stared at Aid. I know the common factor in all this strange behaviour is me. But sometimes everyone does just go a bit weird for a while. Don't they? It can't all be me. How can he not have heard it?

'Come into the living room. Come on,' I ordered him.

But he didn't want to go. Something was stopping him. He forced a smile. He was reticent. Embarrassed almost.

'I've seen the windows. They're fine. They're clean. Listen I've got to stick my headphones in and do some work.'

I grabbed his hands. I pulled them in to my chest. We locked eyes. I spoke nice and calmly.

'You haven't seen the windows. You don't leave the bedroom any more. Except to go the loo. Do you? Come on,' I said, pulling him into me.

'Lily, I've seen the windows. There's nothing wrong with them.'

'Come on. I'll show you. You'll see.' I grabbed his wrist.

'What are you doing? I've got work to do. Get off,' he pleaded.

But I still had him by the wrists. He was coming with me.

He was not happy. He dug his feet in. He chanced a smile, playing pretend. Like there was not real aggression there, like we were not both clawing at each other to get our way. I dragged him, his socks slipping across the smooth wooden floor.

'Come on. Come on! Come in here and take a look.'

'Lily, no, I...'

He finally relented and we both fell into the living room. The two of us took a good look. He said nothing, as we took in the window.

'Oh, shit.'

A pause. Only the sound of our breath. A penny dropped.

'Oh, shit. It wasn't like this before. How did it get like this?'

I don't know whether he was play acting or not, but he seemed shocked. I don't think he was lying low. I think he genuinely didn't know what was going on there. The whole time it had been happening to me. His headphones were in. He was none the wiser as I crawled along, chin on the floor. As I reached for the phone. He looked at the feathers.

'The birds. I told you. Some boys from the estate pelted our flat with dead birds. God knows why. Some of them really are fucking animals,' I mumbled.

'*Eughh!* Oh, Jesus Christ. Oh, my God.' Hand to mouth, he bent over and held back a retch. He's never had a strong stomach.

Ten minutes later, for the first time in a long, long time, he was outside. Even if it was only on the balcony. He cleaned the blood and disposed of the birds. The blood formed into slime and drifted down the window. I watched him from the other side of the glass. It was like he was bathing in soft claret-coloured blood. Swimming in it.

Finally, he wiped it to the ground, soaked it up with a

sponge and some kitchen roll. Put everything into a black bin liner. And it was as good as new. As if nothing ever happened. He stepped inside. I kissed him. We went into the bedroom. And we were physical with each other for the first time in a long time. It was nice.

Maybe you didn't want to know that, but I thought you might be getting worried.

Then, in the shower, the next morning, I'm thinking about the bug and how I would get it inside number eighteen. What tricks I'd have to pull. Because that's the only way now. I have to do something.

I started to think about who I knew that might be able to break in to a building. It didn't take me long to narrow it down. I know this is stereotyping, so I did tread carefully. I sent a text to Jean's number. Now their number.

'Do you know how to pick a lock. By any chance?' it read.

Well, I suppose I didn't tread that carefully.

Ten seconds later, my phone vibrated. Quick texters these kids.

'Why? What for?' I took that as an immediate yes.

'To catch the man that did it. Need help. Will pay.'

'How much?'

A quick barter and we arranged to meet an hour later. I hardly even know the kid. Now he's on my payroll.

I dry myself off, put on black trousers, a black shirt, black shoes. I don't know whether this is going to make me less conspicuous or more. But I'm giving it a shot. Then I put the bug in my washbag, drift over to my window to see the blinds of number eighteen are shut up firmly like a mouth closed stiff, and it's then that I get his '5 minutes' text.

I haven't been in to work for a couple of days. Calling in sick. Using up my duvet days. I am an unreliable member of the workforce. But some things are more important.

It is 11 a.m. Brenner should be out at work. Everyone should be at this time. All the normal people anyway.

Going about their lives. Leaving their flats empty. Unoccupied and unguarded.

6 days till it comes. Afternoon.

He's there. We nod. Old pros. Chris is wearing dark colours, too, so I don't feel my choice of outfit is such a dick move. I give him some cash, which he pockets immediately. He doesn't seem to have anything with him. Tools. Anything like that.

When we get to the Waterway entrance we settle on a plan. You're not supposed to hold the doors open for anyone, emails go around to that effect. Saying that, there hasn't been a robbery in these flats since they've been built and they'd like to keep it that way. Problem is, this translates to the mind as 'No robberies? Oh, good, I can relax.' Which means people do tend to hold doors open for each other. They let their guard down. I've done it. It's natural. It's one thing to say 'of course, I wouldn't just let a stranger into my building' but, in actuality, it's pretty hard to pointedly slam a door in the face of a woman holding heavy shopping bags. A woman that looks like you.

The sad fact is that there is no chance anyone would hold the door open for my friend here, but every chance they will for me. That's how things generally work. In life.

You trust faces that look like yours. So say psychologists. So he stays out of sight. And I hover a bit closer, holding a bag of organic fruit and veg from the local shop. It acts as my ID card. I'm just like you. See? I go to the shops, it says. We wait.

I notice the strange woman I gave the athlete's foot cream to. She passes by on the other side of the road. I turn my face away and luckily she doesn't see me. I don't want to stop and chat. Not now.

After fifteen minutes of nothing I start to worry I'm going to get spotted, hanging around. Loitering. They don't like that around here. Everyone sane has somewhere to be.

The one problem of choosing a time of day when everyone is at work, is that everyone is at work. We just need some work-from-home-techy type. Some student perhaps. I'm not picky. But, nothing doing so far. I wander away, trying to seem casual.

Then, as if on cue, out comes Alfred, our graduate in his first flat. I switched off just at the wrong time. Sod's law. I have to hurry, I might have missed my chance, dammit.

He's almost through the door and ready to let it fall shut. I power forward at pace, rummaging in my pocket as if I definitely have my key fob somewhere, trying to seem flustered and credible. I think I'm too far away to catch his attention.

But Alfred is well trained. A good public schoolboy, I should imagine. He sees me coming with my bags. Half smiles, nothing too personable, but holds the door open and let's me through. It's a good job no one knows their neighbours any more. Not in buildings like these anyway. No one except me.

I walk in past the gleaming glass doors and then stop, playing with my bag as if I'm checking I've got everything. The washbag and bug are beneath my prop shopping. Concealed below quinoa and butternut squash. Then I count to ten and, when I turn, Chris is at the doors. I press the green release button, he nods, opens the door and we are in.

Going up the stairs, I take a look around. The decor in the hallways is different. Brown carpet, green walls, fascinating choice of colours. Against which, I suddenly realise, we stand out like a sore thumb. Like we've come as robbers to a fancy dress party. Or we're doing silver service. Or we're puppeteers.

A concierge, in his grey uniform with blue trim, with his lime green clip on tie, bundles past us. We step back out of his way. I put my arm against Chris. I'm trying to connect the two of us. Suggest he's my stepson perhaps. Not a kid I barely know, who I've employed to break in to a flat for me.

'Sorry,' the concierge murmurs. On his way to some sort of parking-based emergency.

Chris looks at me. Stares at my hand, which still touches him on the small of his back. I take it away. I smile. He doesn't. But I think somewhere in there he's pretty amused. Flat eighteen, first floor, isn't hard to find.

As I stand guard at the top of the stairs, I glance back to see how Chris is doing. He takes two long pieces of metal out of his pocket, one bent at the end. That's all it takes. I thought it might be more technical. He slides one into the lower part of the lock, and forces the other gently into the top of it, and artfully moves the bottom one around, manipulating the inner mechanics of the lock itself.

I did a research project for a lock manufacturer once. Locksmiths used to be people who created singular locks. They were inventors, rather than craftsmen who merely fitted a mass manufactured product with subtle variations. Throughout the nineteenth century people like James Sargent, Linus Yale, Sr, and Jeremiah Chubb were artisans who brought the art forward. Each lock was seen as a tiny puzzle to be solved. They would make new locks and guarantee that they could not be broken into, then their competitors would attempt to pick them, and if they succeeded in doing so they would unveil their new locking mechanism as the new industry leader.

There were national locksmithing competitions. I think somewhere they still exist. But, as time went by, the arms race between lock and key became dominated by the key. Or rather the explosive, the picklock, the gun. Locksmiths became reticent to offer guarantees on their products without them being tailormade, which of course meant great expense. So now we have arrived at an honour system again. Where once we could be sure we were safe in our homes, tucked up in bed with our valuables, the modern world works on kind of an 'please don't' system. If anyone wants to, has the apparatus, the time and inclination, they can get in anywhere. The lock is a barrier that slows you down and asks the question, 'Are you really going to do this? Because once you have there's no going back, you're a criminal.' As I'm thinking these things, I hear the turn of a handle. No going back.

Chris beckons me over and we step inside Mr Brenner's home. I won't lie to you. At this point I am very excited. Nervous too, quaking. But you can be that much more determined when you know that what you're doing is right. Maybe she's in here right now. Alive or dead. I take a look. Inside the bedroom first. I tread carefully but swiftly. He has two mid-century French bedside tables. I run my hand over one of them as I put my other hand to the sliding wardrobe.

I waver. And gulp. I'm not sure what I will find. Not sure I'm ready to see a body. A face grimacing in pain. Dead or alive. Wrists bound together. Bruises all over the body. I'm not sure I want to see any more.

'*Oi!* What you doing?'

I jump, just resisting the urge to scream. It's Chris. In a whispered shout, he continues: 'Look, gonna leavc you to it. Getting out of here. See you around.' He goes to leave.

'No, don't leave me. We need to lock it back up after, right?'

'You didn't pay for that. If I get caught here I'm fucked.' He's gone.

My hand is still on the wardrobe. I brace myself. I close my eyes. I slide it open. The horrors that lie in front of me could change everything. I wet my lips. Then open my eyes.

Tennis balls. Underwear. What looks like ten years of tax returns. Shirts. Nice shirts. I touch them. I'm not sure why. Then my eyes roll downwards and I see a green chest. It has a combination lock. I crouch down to see if it will pull open, but it doesn't. I hear a noise in the hallway. Footsteps and voices. Chris pulled the door closed but I can definitely hear someone moving around out there. I don't want to get caught here.

I pull the bug from my bag and make for a tall fern in the corner of the sitting room, thinking I might be able to stick it behind that. Staying away from the large windows so as not to make myself visible from outside. I know the things people can see from the outside.

A knock at the door. I freeze, dropping the bug, which hits the tiled floor of the kitchen part of the room and cracks. Shit. The little box is in about three pieces. I kneel down to look at it.

Knock. Knock. I slide the pieces into a tiny gap between the built-in wine cooler and the fridge. I push it further inside, into the darkness with my fingers, desperately. Then I get up and go to the door. I quietly lean in and look through the peephole.

Nothing. They have what would be better described as 'eye viewers' in these buildings. Peephole seems so humble. These are industrial size. Giving you a better view of what's outside, but distorting it a little and making everything look more hall of mirrors strange. But all I see is the hallway. Even this is a peculiar sight at this point, it reminds me that I'm not in my flat. This is not my hallway, these lime green walls are nothing like home.

I grab my stuff. I did all this for nothing. My bug is in pieces. The flat filled with nothing but nice shirts, sports equipment and a chest I didn't get to see inside. Then a figure appears, enormous in the eye viewer. A wrinkled face. I step back and hide against the wall, just in case. Even though I know you can't see in here from the other side.

Knock. Knock.

I hold my bag tight for comfort. And lean my back into the wall. I breathe in for fifteen. Then out for ten. In for fifteen. Then out for ten. I look back through the 'peephole'. Nothing. I take a breath and take my chance.

I turn the handle and am through in an instant, trying to seem casual. As if leaving my own flat. Nothing unusual. Nothing to see here. I get about five paces before an arm grabs me from behind.

'Hey, you're coming with me. Come here!'

I don't stop to check who it is. I wriggle free and head down the stairs. They're just behind me. That distorted face, I assume.

'Stop! Right now!' he shouts.

But I do get away from him and I hit the green button to release the doors and I can see the sunlight beyond the glass. I'm nearly there.

As I go through the doors and into the air, I hear the man behind me begin to slow and pant. I'm free of him. I plan to drop my bag and run. Stay away until it gets dark and then sneak back into my apartment without being seen. Then get rid of the clothes I'm wearing and lie low for a while.

But I don't do any of that. I run out into the outside world. And straight into the arms of a man in a high-vis jacket. He has a badge. He is over six foot. I've not felt this sensation since I was a kid playing games. Caught. I'm 'It'. I'm fucked. The wrinkled man arrives behind me, wheezing, his hands go to his knees.

'That's her. She's the one.' He's security for the area, I guess. I haven't seen him before. I'm not sure of my next move. I don't know whether to reveal I live here or not. Without thinking, I play the criminal. That's the thing about situations. They dictate behaviour. More than personality. If personality even exists.

I writhe. I kick. I shout.

'Get off! Get you're hands off me! Get the fuck off me!'

6 days till it comes. Evening.

WM – Airless white room – Heavy rain, 9 deg – Singular – Brown suit – 5′ 9″ – Pensive, analytical, yet somehow casual.

So now I know what it's like. Sitting at a table in a small white interview room. Not one you've volunteered to be in. The tone has changed somewhat this time.

I'm waiting for someone to come in and question me. To try to extract things from me. If you've seen a TV drama with one of these scenes in, it feels a bit like that. But warmer than you'd expect. Not emotionally. Clammy, I mean. It is resolutely summertime. A high window behind me. No double-sided mirror or anything so fancy. Just a stuffy room.

I sit on my hands and wriggle around in my seat. I wonder if they'll be two of them. I reckon one of them will come in and without saying a word he'll cuff me across the face. I'll crack and tell him everything. I wait.

I've already pieced together a few things. I didn't count

on so many cameras around the newbuild apartments. The concierge has a few screens that flick from one camera to another. The oval eye in the hallway that looks a bit like a smoke detector. Every hallway has got one. I'd seen the one in mine. Always looking at us.

If they'd seen me with my bags heading inside Waterway there'd be nothing to worry them too much there. They don't know us all by face. They wouldn't know that one's not my building. They're not that hi-tech around here. They're not that organised. We could then make our way along the hallway looking like anyone else. Nothing to worry about there either.

But as the concierge's screen flicked over to first floor of Waterway for a few seconds, we got unlucky. He saw Chris fiddling around at the door, without a key in hand. Even saw the lock-picking act itself in all probability. The cameras can turn and zoom. To see the metal rods, to capture the very moment they turned, to spy Chris's face. Not, shall we say, exactly fitting the profile of an apartment resident. Looking like what he is. A kid from the estate.

The concierge sends an ageing security guard over to see me. He sends a message to the police, who are often in the area anyway. In the daytime at least. Keeping an eye on the posh flats. Watching out for undesirables. Keeping the estate lot out of the apartment lot's drawers. A little apartheid.

They asked me where my little friend was as soon as they picked me up. Before they even shoved me into a car. They saw us in cahoots on the screen.

I wait. What's my move? They know too much for me to play the Samaritan. A neighbour, watching over the place because she saw a suspicious kid hanging around, who happened to wander in and check if everything was all right. They know too much. They've reviewed the tapes. They won't buy that.

I played dumb on the journey between the car and this plain white room. I gave them nothing. I had my fingerprints taken. Didn't say a word. I'm not good at small talk anyway. I've got inky fingers. I look at them. And wait.

The door opens and the guy walks in, barely looks up, and sits down in front of me. The same one as before. Maybe he's got lumped with me. I'm his detail. 'You keep your eye on this one from now on OK? She's a one woman crime wave this one.'

He doesn't look like police. Not that I know anything about the police. Biggish, but today, projecting efficiency despite his tired, old brown suit. He looks more like an accountant or bookkeeper. I find myself feeling a touch disappointed.

'Hello, again. OK. Well, this is a strange one,' he says, reading off some A4 sheets crudely shoved into a leather folder. He turns on a recording device. Then continues.

'September twelfth, 2015. Ms Lily Gullick. Ms Gullick… can you tell me in your own words what you were doing attempting to and indeed succeeding in gaining unlawful access to number eighteen, Waterway Apartments?'

Silence. I shift in my seat. I've been sitting here thinking about how to answer this kind of question. For a good while. But I haven't come up with much so far.

'Is this a "No comment"? I'd give you the "Anything you do say…" but you've heard all that a couple of times, right? You know the drill.'

When? On the way here? I haven't heard it before now. I haven't been arrested before. I have been here once before but I came of my own volition. I want to object but instead I sit there in silence. There's something informal about all this. But it doesn't mean I feel under any less pressure.

'Is this a "No comment"?' he repeats, robotically. Not looking at me.

I don't want to give anything away. I didn't take anything. Didn't break anything. I don't think I can laugh it off. But I could play it down. Or play it up for that matter? Up or down. Up or down?

'Let the record show that the suspect—'

'I saw something happening over there. A crime. From my window. I live right opposite. In the other building,' I blurt out.

'What sort of crime, Ms Gullick?' he asks, still mechanically.

'Well, I'd rather not say,' I say, sitting back in my chair.

He sighs. Looks around the room. Clicks his pen a couple of times.

'So how did this lead to you ending up breaking in to his apartment?' he says, a grin almost creeping in from the corners of his mouth.

I hope he's not laughing at me. I don't know what I'll do if he's laughing at me.

I shake my head a couple of times. Personality is such a funny thing. It's all situational, I think. Normal person in one room. A killer in another. It's the power of editing. Hitchcock said you could take a picture of a man just staring, then the next shot you cut to is a baby. What do we think about the man? He's a father, a protector. Then you take the same shot of a man and this time the next shot you cut to is of a dead body. Then what is the man to the audience? A murderer. Yet, he's still the same man, in each of the shots. That's the power of editing. I need to do some editing of my own.

'I'm a birdwatcher. It's a hobby. I watch them and take notes as they fly above the lake. Then last night my attention got drawn to number eighteen. I saw a man in there throttle a woman, his wife, I think. He put his hand over her mouth from behind, then he strangled her, I think.'

There. It's out. It's something. I think that went quite well.

'Right. Sorry. You've lost me a bit,' he says, stroking his jawline.

He folds his arms and thinks. His eyes flicker up and then to the side. He's not going to intimidate me. I've got a story and I'm sticking to it. He locks eyes with me for the first time. He's more of a bloodhound than I thought. His casual air masks a steeliness inside. That's his tactic, I bet.

'So, how did that lead you to break in to his house?' A reasonable question.

'Well, what should I have done?' I say, indignant, innocent.

'Hmm, call the police?' A reasonable suggestion.

'I tried you once. Nothing doing. So now it's difficult to trust you lot. If you're not going to take upstanding people seriously. I mean, no offence. But all I know about the police is from the media anyway. And the TV. Police corruption? Police cover-up? Police scandal? That's the sort of thing I hear. Fuck the police?'

I bite my lip. I'm in a police station for the first time

in my life. And I've just said 'Fuck the police.' He doesn't say anything for a while. He doesn't need to.

'No offence,' I say. And the pen goes click, click, click.

'I'm not saying we should all go around solving crimes ourselves. Vigilante justice. All that. I just didn't know if anyone would believe me. Or if you'd tell him I'd made the accusation and then I'd be in trouble with him. I thought that might be dangerous. Which I realise as I say that, sounds bit rich, given that I decided instead to... break in, which could also be seen as... dangerous. But I don't know... I was scared... for her... and me. I didn't know what to do, so that's what I did.'

I pause for breath. There were some good bits in there.

An emotional sigh rises from my chest and gets exhaled. It's a nice flourish. I'd like to thank my mother, my father, and God...

'I guess my curiosity got the better of me. Er. My curiosity got the better of me.'

He frowns and makes a note. A couple of words. In his file.

'And where's your accomplice. The one that opened the door?'

'I won't tell you that. I don't even know. He's just some kid.' I nod. Firm in my decision.

'Just a name please, Ms Gullick.'

'No. I won't tell you that. What's the matter? Are you fucking deaf?'

There goes that lack of impulse control again. I'm not sure where that came from. It was all going so well. I've never been good with authority figures.

The next thing I hear is the slamming of a door. We cut,

one swift edit and I'm behind bars. I'm not sure if it was my story or my language he objected to most.

I call home. No answer. I hear our phone ring for only the second time ever. From the other side. Then I try Aiden's mobile. It goes straight to voicemail.

He might have his headphones on, and his battery has run dry. Or he's finally left the flat, and he's somewhere out of signal. But I wouldn't have thought so.

It doesn't really matter. I won't be home tonight. I put my head on a rock-hard pillow. My body resting on a cold, firm bed. In seconds, I'm asleep.

5 days till it comes.

I'm woken up by a knock on the door. My back hurts. These beds aren't built for comfort. But I certainly slept deep. I needed to. I slept like a baby.

I originally woke up at nine. Tried Aiden again. Tried a few other numbers. Tried my second choice, then third. No answer. No answer. Left a few messages. Was led back to my room. My cell. Ha! With nothing else to do. I went back to sleep.

A voice comes through the door. 'Ms Gullick. Your husband's here to see you. He can take you home. The gentleman won't be pressing charges.'

I nod, stretch for a second, then get out of there. Like an old pro.

I'm surprised Aiden's come to meet me. I didn't think he'd leave the house. I thought he was too scared. I thought that his thoughts and fears were bigger than his love for me. But I'm even more surprised when I see that the man in front of me is not my husband.

'Right. You got everything, darling? Bag? Keys? All that?' he says, trying to play it cool. He's not really succeeding. He's sweating. He takes my bag from me for no particular reason. Then he drops it and all the contents spill out. We drop to the ground together and awkwardly pick it up around a police officer's feet. I'm not entirely sure I want to go with him. But I want to get out of here, and fast. So I don't really have a choice.

We rise. I give him a kiss in the cheek. I feel I have to. I go to hold his hand as we leave and then take it away at the last minute. Not sure whether it's necessary to play along with the ruse. I don't want to give him anything more than I need to.

Outside, we head towards his Vauxhall Astra and he finally relaxes.

'Wow. That was bloody exciting, wasn't it? Wow,' spills out of Phil's mouth. Although I'm not sure if he found it more exciting or titillating. Transgressive. Perverse. Yes. That's what it was, for him.

He wasn't my second choice. Or my third.

'Well, Lil, I don't know what you're mixed up in. But I'm glad to be of service in some way, glad to be part of it. Happy to be in the game,' he says while starting the engine. A real cheeseball.

'Did you really need to say you were my husband?' I ask.

'Hmm. I wasn't sure, didn't understand your message entirely. But I thought I would tell them that, just in case. In case I had to be "next of kin",' he says lamely, as if he's using technical information. He loves even the softest kinds of jargon. He loves code words and secrets.

'Next. Of. Kin,' he says to himself again. Apropos of nothing. He looks at me with a glint in his eyes as he says that.

'After your message I called in and they said they'd just received word that the… er… victim wasn't pressing charges. They asked if I was your husband. I said yes,' he says, fiddling with cassette tapes.

'Did you have to show them ID or anything?' I say, curious.

'Yeah, but I said you kept your maiden name, which you did, right?'

'Yes. Yes, that's right.' I say, distractedly looking out the window.

I don't remember telling him that. I know I should be grateful. But he disturbs me this morning. He seems to know a lot more about me than I thought he did.

We pull up to the apartments. He insists on walking me to my door. Aiden will be behind it. Completely unaware. Again. Oblivious to where I've spent last night. Cowering under the covers. He's becoming a very small man. It's difficult to feel respect for anyone when they show so little care. When they cower in the shadows.

I turn away from Phil. I put my key in the lock and half open the door and then stop. He still stands there. That was really his cue to leave.

'What did you do then?' he says, smiling.

'Phil. Thank you so much. It's all fine. Please go back to work.'

'No, come on. Who was the "victim"? Ha. Can't be that bad, right?'

I stare at him. I want him to go away. I take a deep, deep breath.

'I killed an old lady. Broke into her flat in the middle of the night. Took her by surprise. Bludgeoned her over the head with a piece of brick. Pushed her to the floor. Then

I left as she bled out over the linoleum. I did all that. Just for fun. Because I couldn't sleep.'

He stares, open-mouthed.

He has that look in his eye like he wants to smile. I think he loves what I've just told him. He wants in on it. I think it really does it for him. That's what I think. I wait. It's a stand-off again. I feel like he's about to admit something to me. But I wait. And he's not giving anything away. Not yet anyway.

'But she's not pressing charges so I think I should be fine,' I say, turning. Breaking the quiet.

'Ha. Good one. Cup of tea for my trouble?' he says, his hand on the door.

'I need to lie down. I need some rest,' I lie. I've had enough rest. I need to get back to watching him. Back to the drawing board. The fact that Brenner didn't want to press charges is a clear admission of guilt. I know what I saw.

'Oh, come on. I'll cheer you up. Just a quick brew.'

I try to stop him but I can't. We stagger messily into the flat. He trips on the way. Or does he push m?. The blinds are down, the bedroom door is closed. And so is the door to the living room. It's light outside but it's dark in here. In my hallway.

'Come on. I just want a bit of chat. What's wrong with that?'

I don't like it. With him in here. Me and him. Alone, perhaps. In the dark. In my private domain. I didn't ask him in. And I didn't want him in here. I reach for the hall lamp. The light flickers on.

'Ahh. Sorry. You. You scared me,' I say. He was closer to me than I thought he was. I want him where I can see him.

The light still flickers between us. Lighting only the outlines of us, in the silence.

The hall lamp's never been bright. But I think now it's broken. It's dim. It flickers. It buzzes slightly. Feels like the bulb is about to burst. I look at him. He's so comfortable with silence. With my discomfort. He breathes, heavy. He's a mouth breather. He doesn't want to go. It's like a question hangs in the air. But I don't know what that question is any more. Then he raises his hand.

'Another time, Phil. Not now. Not now,' I say. Calm as I can.

His hand rises and pushes his hair behind his ears. He looks like he wants to kiss me. He could overpower me and take one from me if he wanted, looking at him now, he's big enough. He stands rigid. Neither of us sure what comes next. Aiden must be just behind one if these doors. Surely. I force my keys in between my second and third fingers and make a fist.

'Aid, we've got a guest for a cup of tea,' I say, moving suddenly to the bedroom door and opening it.

Light spills in, the blinds are up in there and Aiden is nowhere to be seen.

Phil stares at me. He squints, his eyes adjusting to the light. He seems disturbed by me. My energy is a little frantic. Maybe I'm showing him I'm scared. My movements are urgent, like an SOS.

'Aid? Where are you, love?' I shout, opening the living room door. He's gone. He's nowhere.

Phil stares at me. Trying to work me out. Trying to work something out. Then he turns, shouting over his shoulder.

'I'm sorry. I shouldn't have come back. I shouldn't have come.'

The door slams. And he's gone too. I breathe hard. I put my fingers to my neck. My pulse is fast and strong. I close my eyes. Trying to compose myself. Willing my heart to beat steady.

Then I step into the bedroom. And stand there.

I take in the silence. The room's natural sound. The walls. Nothing here. Just absence. It unnerves and comforts in equal dosage. He's gone. They're all gone.

Then Terrence bounds in, his bowl in his mouth. Completely empty. No one fed him last night. Or this morning it looks like.

Perhaps Aiden left last night. Perhaps he's gone for ever.

4 days till it comes.

White male – Missing – Rain – Left the 2 flock – Denim shirts and cords – Fair hair – 6′ – Playful, calm, newly introverted.

I'd call his parents if they were still alive. Even with a thirty-six-year-old man, the first port of call is always Mum and Dad. I'd call his brother but I don't have a number for him. They don't speak much anyway. I doubt he'd ring him up after three years to tell him where he was going.

Last night, I made a deal with myself and I was sure it would work. I was sure that if I went to bed. Watched a couple of movies. Tried to forget about Brenner. Then Aid would be here again when I woke up. Do you get those vain wishes sometimes? The 'if I get this apple core in the bin everything is going to be OK' thought. I thought I'd wished him away with my stupid behaviour. But I thought that if I forgot about it all, pretended I didn't see what I saw. Left it alone. Resolved to leave it all alone. Then he'd come back.

So I just trained my eyes on the glazed moving pictures on my laptop, until my eyelids drew heavy and suddenly night turned to day, and when I woke, I watched some more. Waited for my headache to go away. I waited all day.

But he's still not back.

I stare at the still closed blinds of number eighteen. He's shut up shop again. I wonder if he knows it was me. That I've been in there. In his home. In his head. Seen the samurai sword up close. Seen the green metal case. Seen everything, in the flesh.

He's put his tortoise head back in his shell. And he won't be coming out any time soon.

It is definitely true that I could be behaving irrationally. I read some of this back after I sent you my first week's journal and I know how I sound. It doesn't sound good. You'll know this by now. You'll have got my first four or so weeks of entries and you'll have been judging me for a while already.

The police have probably stormed Brenner's place. Found nothing. Pegged me as a certified crazy. And moved on. In fact, what am I thinking? They've almost definitely pegged me as crazy straight away, and haven't bothered storming anything. I wouldn't believe me if I was them.

Maybe you wouldn't recognise me. My eyes are always bloodshot. I get so little sleep these days. I've changed.

I'm making a pact with myself to leave all this alone. Yes, I think that's the right thing to do. It was dark in number eighteen, after all. And I was quite far away. When I saw what I saw. I don't even know for sure that Jean's killer lives around here. The kids were pretty vague and Thompson could've been just feeding me what I wanted to hear for a bit of a money and a headfuck for all I know.

I've been giving everything the benefit of the doubt. Encouraging the worst sides of myself. But if I just add a bit of doubt, then everything feels different. And in a way that's easier. Far more manageable. I might just need a few more days off and Aid will come back. When he knows I've come to my senses, he'll come back. After giving me some room. Everything will be all right. I miss him so much.

I made a list of all he places he could be, starting with the most likely and mundane and ending with the more high concept. It went like this:

—he's gone away to research something for his book. Forgot to leave me a message. I'm so distracted and he is too. He probably thought I wouldn't notice.

—he's gone away to teach me a lesson. He'll be back later today. He's staying with his friend Tom in Anglesey. Whose number I don't have. He's always saying he should go and see him.

—he's been having an affair for years, couldn't face telling me, he's just hit the road to be with his other family. A wife, a cat and two children, in Epsom.

—he went for a ride on his motorbike finally and has been involved in some sort of crash. When he comes around he will call me. If he hasn't suffered severe amnesia and completely forgotten who I am.

—he's been kidnapped by Brenner. Or someone else. Someone with a vendetta. Someone from the neighbourhood. Someone who wants to shit me up. Soon I'll get a letter written in newspaper clippings, asking me to lay off my search or Aid will get it. Or asking for fifty thousand quid and a getaway car, which they'll use to get to the ferry. They'll start a new life in Belgium. They'll buy a vineyard. I know fifty thousand isn't much to go on. But they'll manage.

It all sounds pretty stupid.

But a version of the last one sticks in my head. I look at the building opposite. I stare at the blinds. Thinking of Aiden being stuffed into that green metal chest just behind them. The chest I saw and touched. I turn away to get a hot towel for my face. My sinuses are aching. I'm getting a lot of headaches at the moment. I need to drink more water. Get more exercise. Stay fresh. Maybe I'm ill. I think I just need some rest. But there's no time for that now.

Crackle. Crackle. White noise. A voice.

'We just need to get rid of it. We need to get rid of it now.'

Then the voice is gone. It unnerves me. I turn, look around, nothing.

Where did it come from?

Crackle. White noise and static. The same voice comes again.

'I can't have another body around here,' he growls.

The voice is coming from inside my flat. It's definitely here. It's speaking to me.

'Help me get rid,' says the voice.

I'm hearing voices. I've finally completely lost it. This is exactly what happened with Mum. Hearing things. Delusions. This was how it all started. The beginning of her demise. That led to her decision.

No. No, that's not it.

Crackle.

I turn to my washbag and pull out the receiver. It must have been left on and has kicked into gear, picking something up.

Crackle.

I play with the receiver dial. I play with the tuning and volume. I can hear him. At least I think that's him.

Crackle. Murmur.

I fiddle with the dial until he's as clear as a bell.

Murmur.

I get into my position in the hide. I don't pull down the blind but I crouch just in case. I look out. The blinds are still down. But behind them I can hear his voice. I can hear him walking around.

'They're piling up, man. What did you expect? It's a bloodbath.'

I gasp. I'm wide eyed. The bug has kicked into life just at the right moment. At last, some luck.

Between his wine cooler and the fridge. That little box in three pieces must be alive enough to pick things up.

'But it's this fucking… this fucking girl. She's been in here. Yeah, I got a call from the police, they told me some girl had been in here.'

My ears are burning. I watch on, just in case the blind rises a touch, enough for me to see inside, or for him to see me.

I keep listening. He goes on.

'Yeah, I think I know who she is. I've seen her before. She's a spooky-looking thing. Always staring. Twitching. She's got this little fucking twitch. Ha ha. Yeah. Oh, I don't know, I wouldn't fuck her. I wouldn't touch her with yours.'

I listen. His ordinary-sounding voice, spitting at my

microphone. It picks up everything. He's loud now. It's like he's in the same room as me.

'I did what you wanted, now it's time to pay up. Yeah, the student, I did her over. They can stick up all the Missing posters they like. She ain't coming back. And she ain't missing. She's around. She's in tiny little bits. She's all over the place. I've ferreted away bits of her all over the place. I've got a bit of her here now. I've got a couple of other bodies here too. A few old ladies...'

If only I could record this all somehow. Should have bought some equipment for that too. I can't believe it. I picture the gory details. He's giving me everything I need. His guilt is there for all to hear. It'd be an open and shut case. If only everyone else could hear this too.

'Next, I'm gonna shut that girl up. That little twitcher that keeps sticking her nose in where it's not wanted.'

Oh, God. I listen. He sounds so close. He must be closer to the microphone. His voice booms back at me. I hear the full depth of it. The darkness behind it. This man is a son. Maybe a brother, a friend. But also a murderer. A serial killer. On the loose. It's all situational.

'I tell you what I'm going to do. I'm going to break into her flat. Wait till she comes home. And when she does, I'm going to jump out at her... Give her a kiss on the cheek. And shout, *Surprise!* Then I'm going to... give her a big hug. That's right, that's what I'm going to do. If that's all right with you, love. That's right. I'm talking to you. What do you think about that? Hey? Well, come on. I'm talking to you.'

The blind rises and I lock eyes with him. He talks into the bug. Its pieces in his fist. He stares into me. Speaking to me directly.

'Come on then. What do ya reckon? Cat got yer tongue?'

My breath catches in my throat. I've been caught, worse than before. I feel white with shock. I'm still. I've never felt so exposed.

'Yeah, I love murdering me, darling. I murder this. I murder that. You can't stop a bloke like me. With all me murdering and such,' he says.

And with that, he throws the pieces to the ground. My sound disappears. But he still faces me from over there.

He creases up. He's laughing at me.

2 days till it comes.

I feel stupid. I've been moping around for a couple of days. Doing very little. Feeling embarrassed that I got caught red-handed. Got toyed with and humiliated.

Embarrassed by my spy equipment. Embarrassed my husband has gone away and doesn't seem to be coming back.

I've been lying on my back. Staring at the walls. I thought about calling the police but I trust them less now than I did before. They've probably been having a good old laugh at me too. I can almost hear it. In my ears. They must've told Brenner about me and my claims. Told him to check around to see if anything was missing. He gave the place the once-over and found my crudely placed 'bug'.

It was idiotic to think that I'd been able to hide it from him, that it'd come back on, all by itself. He must be having a real laugh at me now. In there. He got his own back. His practical joke couldn't have come off better. Now he's celebrating by playing sex games in there with his skinny European girlfriend.

One thing I managed to do was some Internet research. I found all this material about the missing girl. The truth is I haven't thought about her enough. Until now.

I am trying to drop all of this. Well, I did try. For a few hours. But I can't.

I can't believe how little I thought about her, her name and picture in that poster. Until now. An appeal for witnesses generally means I look the other way. I don't even give it a second thought. I was blaming everyone else for not caring about Jean's death but I'm just the same. As if 'missing' actually means 'don't worry about it' in some subconscious human language. Don't bother casting your mind over it. You probably didn't see anything. You probably don't know anything about it.

Just ten minutes Internet research told me why I should have been thinking about her a lot sooner.

She lives at number forty, Canada House. Right next to Jean. Sonya Sharma. She was soon to become a criminal barrister, had grown up in those flats, the shining light of a hard-working Asian family.

She'd recently taken on a project too. A bit like me.

She was looking into the legalities of the contract that the development company, Princeton, had secured from the government to carry out the regeneration project. I don't know the ins and outs, but something didn't seem right to her. The possibility of money changing hands, government officials with sticky fingers. Something like that. The specifics don't really matter.

What matters is that she was asking questions. Putting pressure on people. There was a petition. Talk of an inquiry. She was a strong-willed girl. Looking to buy the residents of the estate some time at the very least. She was smart.

Really smart. But just like Jean, she disappeared, and no one seems to have a clue about what happened to her.

Like Jean, her family lived abroad, India in this case. They'd moved there as they knew their lives were about to come tumbling down around their ears, the recession had caused both parents to be laid off and they weren't finding it easy to get back into the kind of decent jobs they had before. Then they were told they'd be given a meagre sum for their family home, which in under a year would be nothing but rubble. They decided to get out while the going was still relatively good. But they'd managed to buy their flat using a government scheme and their daughter had stayed behind until the bitter end to finish her pupillage as a barrister. In her family home. For as long as she could. Which turned out to be not as long as she planned.

I need to get out of here. Just for a while. I'm becoming like he was. Aiden. I've spent too long inside. I feel like natural light, the sort that goes from the sun to your face, with no glass in between, might sting my eyes and body. This isn't right. These are agoraphobic thoughts. A shut-in's manifesto.

I tear myself away from my laptop screen. Years ago I would have had to go to the library to find out all that information. About her. About the girl. I'd have to sort through the microfiche. One of my favourite words that. But the romance and drama has left the research. A few taps on a keyboard, or the touch screen, and there you are.

I drag myself down to the shop next to the café. I need coffee and bacon and bread and avocados and juice. This will make me feel normal again. A potion to bring me back to the land of the living.

The fluorescent lights bear down on me in there. They seem to buzz at me. I am detached from my fellow humans. They see me but take nothing in. My face means nothing to them.

But I know so many of them so well. It seems odd that they don't know me at all.

Alfred is in front of me in the queue, buying cereal and toilet roll. Vincent comes past looking serious, making a call, closing a deal. The Greek guy that owns the restaurant nips in and grabs some milk and winks at the girl in the shop. She nods. She'll put that on his tab.

The girl bleeps through Alfred's essentials and smiles a 'Hello' towards me. She's worked here for six months. One hundred and seventy-eight days to be exact. She does five days a week, but three are days (7 till 3.30) and two are evenings (3.30 till midnight). I remember when she ran through some eggs, spinach, tomatoes and a chocolate milkshake for me on her first day. That's how I know all this. I made a note of it.

She's good. She's good at her job. She's got better.

She's efficient. She has a place to be. She seems happy.

She serves Alf, then me. I smile, try to resemble a normal person. Try to look at her and smile. Try not to frown with the corners of my mouth. Even though they feel weighted down. Try not to stare at her hands and analyse them, as I have been doing to everyone this last week, just in case. I try not to give anything away. I try not to crack.

I get out of there as quick as possible. They can tell. They know I'm not normal. They know my husband has left me. They know I'm an impression of a human being. People must see I've broken down the million tiny things people do unconsciously to survive and I'm doing them one by one, carefully stacking them on top of each other, aware of everything, micromanaging myself into submission, pushing the cogs and turning the wheels by hand to push myself through the day. I open the door and nearly scream.

She stands just behind it. A spooked look on her face. She pauses. She's worse than before. She looks bad. I'm sure she's thinking the same about me. She wants to chat.

'Hello, Doctor,' says the woman who couldn't sleep.

'Hello, Sandra,' I say, remembering her name in the nick of time.

'Terrible about that lady, wasn't it? Terrible business. Dead,' she says, eyeballing me.

'Is that right? How awful. Anyway I must get on,' I say.

'First the student. Then her. Who's next? Ha,' she chatters.

'I wouldn't know. I wouldn't know anything about that,' I say, it coming out sounding far more guiltily than I intended.

'The student's the funny one, of course.' She holds my gaze. Trapping me.

'What do you mean?' I urge, interested now.

'Well, I'm not saying they're related. The crimes. But the signs do both point to murder. To me anyway. And she was so active. In the community, I mean. But then, she did also have that boyfriend of course! You'd see him around. I think he was from over this side,' she babbles, almost excitedly. Letting me in.

'Really. Who was that?'

'Oh, some fella. Ordinary looking. Nice chap,' she says, guileless.

'Maybe someone should go and talk to him? Maybe he knows something,' I proffer.

'Well, maybe. All I know is he lived in one of these buildings. Fair hair. That's about it,' she says, wanting to continue the conversation. But out of ammo.

But I'm wary of her. She unnerves me. She's not the sort of role model I need at the moment.

'Well, have you told the police this?' I say, starting to move.

'Oh yes, Doctor. But they don't believe me. I tell them all sorts. They never listen. They nod and smile. But they don't even write things down any more. I don't know what's wrong with them, I don't know what they think is wrong with me. But, don't worry, I've told them,' she says, touching my forearm.

I remember that's pretty much how the police treated me too. I have a horrible thought. When they said I'd 'been there before', I really hope they weren't confusing me with Sandra. Not to be rude. But she's a good fifteen years older than me. Everyone must be able to tell that. Not being vain, but come on. And she's slightly more nervous of disposition, I'd say. Like a startled woodland creature. But it would make some sense, I suppose. Because I hadn't 'been there before'. I'm sure I hadn't. I'm sure.

I pull away and make my excuses. I'm trying not to let her in. She's just a disturbed woman, I tell myself. Maybe that makes two of us.

'Nice to see you, Sandra,' I offer.

'Bye, Doctor,' she says, a bit louder than necessary.

Sandra thinks they're connected. I never really thought about that. Only in passing. Only in jest. Not seriously. I thought Brenner was getting his own back, laughing at me for thinking he was some sort of murderer, a normal bloke laughing it up at the ridiculousness of it all. I thought he was riffing. Thought it was a skit. But maybe he wanted me to hear. Maybe everything he murmured was true. He was whispering his secrets, just for me. Taunting me. For sport. Because he knows now they'll never believe a word I say. Just like they don't believe a word Sandra says. So he can do what he wants. Right in front of my face. It's all part of the pleasure of it.

How many kills does it take to make a serial killer?

Sonya, the student. Jean. The girl at the window. Aiden.

Sandra thinks there's a serial killer on the loose. And now I do too.

1 day till it comes.

It's 11 a.m. I'm going back over to the estate. Going to see Chris. He thinks I'm stupid for wanting to go back in there. He's already told me that. Thinks we'll get caught again. If that happens, he says, it's more trouble for him than me. Not that he's been caught before. He's kept his record clean. But someone of his description seems to get in a lot more trouble for things like this than someone of my description. People tend to press charges. And he can't have that. He's got his brother to think about.

So I'm going to get a crash course in lock-picking. He says I can learn everything I need to know in one hour, with these kind of locks anyway. It's scary when you think about it. It only takes someone desperate enough to take a chance. I'm going to take a chance.

We got unlucky last time. If the cameras hadn't flicked on at the right time, to my channel, channel me. If the concierge had had his feet up watching the TV, throwing Murray Mints into his mouth, rather than glancing at the multi-screen, we would have gotten away with it. But whether I get caught or not, I'm getting in there to find out what's going on. What's in that big green chest. To see if he's got Aiden tied up in there. Anything is possible.

I feed Terrence first. Then I take some stuff down to the recycle room. I'm a criminal but I'm still civilised. I take my washbag and wear plainer clothes this time. I push the Basement button.

It smells in here. This is the rubbish lift. The one everyone uses when they're going down to the recycle room. It stinks, because everyone uses it for this. And everyone uses it for this, because it stinks.

The door opens and I head into the underground car park, which leads to the recycle room. It's always dark in there. The whirring of generators dips and rises in the background, you wouldn't want to stay down here too long. That noise, almost calming in small doses, would really get to you after a while.

I was stuck down there between doors for half an hour once, a while ago. Not pleasant. A concierge had to come and get me out. I tried Aiden but he went to voicemail, as is the theme.

I step into the recycle room. I have company. An imposing-looking guy. The door closes behind me. He turns.

It's Lowell, sorting out his plastics from his disposables. It's funny I never think of him as imposing. It's difficult to see someone objectively once you know them intimately. Not that I know him that intimately.

His glass is in one bag. Some food in another. Several bags for life, to conserve the atmosphere. Some stuff for the clothes bin in a hessian Waitrose bag. Crossing the t's and dotting the i's. As per.

'Hey, Lil, you took me by surprise there,' he says, turning.

'Sorry, didn't mean to sneak up on you. What you up to?'

'Nothing. Up to nothing actually. Really,' he says, shiftily. Like he could be up to something.

'Shouldn't you be at work?' I say, realising the time.

He probably takes days off whenever he wants. I bet he gets so far ahead of himself the boss probably says, 'You know what, Lowell, I know you won't like this, but take the rest of the week off, you've earned it,' He's that reliable.

'Ah, Lil. Can I tell you something. I'm not proud of it. Can I?'

He suddenly seems different. Situationalism. His old confidence gone. Evaporated. He winces. Breathes in.

'You see, well. I lost my job. Careless thing to lose, I know,' he says, ruefully. But trying to make light of it.

'Oh, Lowell, I'm so sorry. Sorry, mate.' I lunge in.

We hug. Long one. I haven't had one of these since the night with Jean. He nestles his head into me. I didn't think he'd be a head-nestling kind of guy. I didn't think he could let himself go so much.

'Actually, it's worse than that. There's more,' he says, deadened.

'Go on.'

'I lost two jobs. How bad does that suck, huh? First my own little company went bust, went totally under, lost two contracts in a damn week. Suddenly, no one wanted our software, so that was that. Then, they were downsizing at my nine to five. I'd only been there ten months. I defected from another company. So not much of a pay-off. That'll teach me, huh?' he mutters, almost tearing up. Which is pretty out of the blue.

'Oh fucking hell, I'm sorry.' I pull back and look at him.

Lowell will be fine, surely. It's strange to see him so weak. It could be the making of him. The vulnerability that could turn him from captain of the chess club to someone with a bit of heart. He's attractive like this. But I think that's just me. He doesn't seem to be embracing it. He's changed, hurt. I wonder how long ago all this happened. I think I've seen him around in the days for a while. When I'm not at work. He always seems to be there.

'Ah, you know. It's not so bad. I've got plenty to be getting on with,' he says.

The lights go out. They're on a timer. This little room wasn't built for standing and talking so if you don't open the door every three minutes the lights go out.

We stand in silence for a moment. I don't know why. It seems to last for ages. This black silence. Then I laugh.

Which is intended to break the tension. But that doesn't happen. We fall into silence again. I can smell him. A dark scent, strong. I hear his steady breath. I want to tell him about Aiden going missing. Maybe I should've a long time ago. I should've told someone. But also, I don't. I don't want to think about Aiden at all.

He leans into me. Grabs my arms. Holds me.

'There you are,' he says, soft and low. It's nice.

Then slowly he brings his face towards mine. Gradually. So unhurried. My breathing changes. And so does his. It's so close I can feel it on my mouth.

Then his lips touch mine. My weight goes forward and I press myself against him. He pushes his tongue softly into my mouth just for a moment. I grab for his arm but get nothing. He touches the back of my neck and pulls back a touch. He pulls away. Then he kisses me again. I haven't been kissed for a very, very long time. My forehead touches his in the darkness. My hand lifts towards him. I try to delicately touch his face. To stroke the skin all along his right cheekbone.

Then he moves me out of the way. I hear his footsteps. He's rummaging around. He's behind me and I don't know where he is. I feel exposed. Five minutes in a closet in the dark with a strange man. He moves again suddenly. I hear his feet across the floor. I move my body towards his.

The lights come on. His face flickers back into view. He speaks.

'There we go Lil. Nice to see you,' he says, cuing me.

I laugh nervously. We ignore everything. But we both know. It's charged. It's exciting. And we'll always have it. Even if it goes nowhere. Even if that's it. He's got me, even more than I thought he had.

I grab my bag and leave him in there. I turn before leaving.

'You're going to be OK though, yeah?' I say.

'Yeah. Yeah, of course,' he says, unsure. Shooting for sure but falling short.

'Well, if you need anything. I'm just beyond the wall,' I say.

I smile. He attempts one too. He winks. Smiles. Looks at the ground. Coy, but still masculine. He pulls it off.

I sling my bag over my shoulder.

I'm a bad wife. I may never have been the best.

But now I'm bad.

1 day till it comes. 2 p.m.

One of the many benefits of living in a largely abandoned building, like the one Chris lives in, is the amount of unopened doors that line the empty corridors.

First of all it makes for a good aesthetic, haunting, in a concrete dystopian kind of way. Communist. Brutalist. And each door is a little possibility. You could bust into them if you wanted to. Swim around in someone's old life. Whatever's left of it. That would be exciting. Particularly if you're anything like me. And I know you're at least a bit like me.

But the most useful thing, for me, is the amount of locks to practise on. Chris has the perfect set-up for a lock-picking training school. It wasn't easy at first, you need to feel it, get a sense for it. The first one I tried I thought was never going to open. I'd passed into that sulky give-up phase. It was never going to happen. I told him I picked a tricky one. Then he tried the same one and he was in virtually straight away.

The old locks, he says, the ones for the flats on the

estate, are very low quality. Worse than the locks down our end. But they're good to practise on.

I broke a rod clean in half in one of the locks. He charged me for that.

'Delicate,' he said. 'It's a delicate thing.'

Click. Click. Click. Click. Click.

I've opened five now. My time's getting faster, I'm feeling it. I'm virtually ready. He's a good teacher. He could do this for a living. It's possible he does.

I head back down the bare staircase. Past the graffiti that threatened me when I entered the building for the first time. It looks kind of harmless to me at this point. I lift myself out of the hatch and walk briskly down to Waterway and hover. Waiting for someone to let me in.

Lunchtime brings better luck than last time and Mrs Smith, back home for a salad (I think she has her own design store in Stoke Newington) lets me in breezily. All smiles, I keep my head down and don't say a thing. Her face falls a bit, but it's a tiny moment, nothing that she'll remember. I'm used to being painfully nice. Usually. A real people pleaser. But I don't have time for that nowadays. Certainly not today.

I ready the rods in my pocket, no one on the stairs today, more luck. I might not have that much time. I'm hurrying but trying not to seem so to the naked eye. Or the electronic one. Which I pass underneath, on my way along the corridor to number eighteen.

My black baseball capped head drifting under it for anyone happening to watch. If the concierge screen flicks over to my channel. The cap is my one concession, my one piece of disguise, to throw them off if only for a few seconds. I might need those seconds. I am a serial offender after all. They know my face. There's probably a picture of me up in the concierge office.

I stick one rod into the bottom of the lock and ease the other into the top. It looks slightly forced from the last time, maybe that will make it easier. Maybe I'll slip into a groove and the lock will virtually slide itself open.

But it's trickier than I thought. I've just done five in a row in the estate, but this lock's harder, it's taking a bit more nuance to catch the pins inside. There are five in there you have to lift up. I've been at the door for quite a while now. Which anyone watching would notice.

I try not to force it. My arm is becoming stiffer, more desperate, but I try to keep it calm, keep my actions still and not let the tension ruin everything. I imagine her in there, the girl at the window. Gagged and bound at the foot of the bed. A dog bowl at her feet for her to lap water out of. To keep her alive. I picture Aiden in another room, his throat partially cut, tied up and bleeding out. Every second may count. The lock isn't giving me anything, but I keep at it. I hear a moaning from inside. I want to press my ear to the door, but there's no time. I drop the wrench rod, the one that goes into the bottom of the lock, and bend down to pick it up. I hear something behind me. I picture a bag next to Aiden, an orange bin bag with the student in there chopped up. A mess of limbs and it's leaking. It oozes over the laminate wood flooring, touching Aiden's bare ankles. He knows when Brenner comes home, he's next. He probably thinks the rattle of the lock is him coming back now. He could be bleeding. Every second counts. I hear the moaning.

I push the wrench rod back into the lock, ease the top one back in too and feel the slightest lift, the tiniest pop.

I lift the pins, turn the wrench rod, and it opens. I step inside. Controlling my breathing. Footsteps in the corridor. A passer-by, security or police. No time to wonder. I survey the room. The blinds are down. The moaning comes from the bedroom. Where I saw the chest. I should have brought a hammer and lever to wedge it open. I look around for anything that could assist me. Nothing in the hallway.

I try his bathroom. Hotel soaps – he travels a lot – otherwise it's very much like mine. It's all situational. He has a quinoa moisturiser. A sonic toothbrush. Like me. But he is different to me. He has something to hide. But worse than what I'm hiding. The moaning rises.

I think about the samurai sword. But then think better of it. It's better at cutting into skin and bones than anything else. That's what it's made for. In a drawer below his sink I find a hammer.

I brace myself behind the bedroom door. There's definitely a girl in there. I've come to save her. This is it.

I push it open, hammer held high and announce myself into the room. She screams. He shouts. A flurry of sheets and activity. Their breathing stays heavy. I'm not sure what he was doing to her. But it wasn't so violent. I stand, in his bedroom, a hammer in my hand.

'What the fucking hell are you doing?' he shouts. He stands, naked. I see everything. 'Get the fuck out of here, you mad fucking bitch!'

He's enraged and a little scared too. I would be, if someone broke in to my home. While I was at it. My mind a thousand miles away from home security. She covers herself. But I see most of her. I just stand there. Hammer aloft. She seems to recognise me suddenly. From when I pointed my fingers at her, my pretend gun, from across the way, from my lair. She pipes up. I just stand there.

'Do you know this woman, Rich? Are you shagging her or something?'

'Do you really think… look at her for fuck's sake. She's fucking mad. Get the fuck out, you fucking weirdo.'

I drop the hammer. Everyone jumps as the noise echoes around the room. I get out of there. As the door closes behind me, I hear his muffled explanations.

'I didn't want to tell you because I thought it would freak you out. But some woman, *that* fucking woman, broke in here the other day, she's a nutcase.'

I pause, then hustle down the hallway. Maybe I can get away. Maybe it'll be OK. But it's not likely. I deserve to be caught. I deserve to be locked away. She didn't look hurt. I saw the whole of her. She had no bruises. No burn mark. Nothing. It's not right. She's the same woman. Smooth, tanned skin, distinctive. But there's not a mark on her, they couldn't have cleared up in just a few days. It's not possible.

But I saw them through my binoculars. I had her in my sights. But they're playing tricks on me. They must be. I hear a shout as I get to the end of the hallway.

'Hey, come back, get back here,' he shouts.

I don't want to do that. I don't trust him. I still see him as the man from before. As Brenner. He's imposing. He shouts again.

'Come on. Just come a bit closer so we can talk.' He's calmer.

'I'm sorry, I'm so sorry. I'm seeing things. I must be.' I stop at the end of the corridor.

'Just come here. Come a bit closer. So we can talk.'

I do. I give in. I'm broken. I'll give him whatever he wants. I just don't want him to shout. I hope he doesn't shout. I move closer still.

'There. Just there. What's your name?' He eyes me, seriously.

'It's…'

'Lily, isn't it? Yeah, Lily,' he says, gentle.

'Yes, yes,' I mumble, only just holding back hot tears.

'Just come a little closer. I don't want the neighbours to hear.'

'I'm so, so sorry.'

He's calm with me. Careful. Like he doesn't want to scare away the tiny bird. But I'm not sure what he wants to do with the bird. When he's got it.

'Look. Listen to me. I'm sorry. I didn't know how to react. To all this. It's not a normal situation. I didn't mean… but it's not. Normal, I mean. Is it?' he says, exuding comfort and mercy.

'No, no,' I say, contrite.

He leans back against his door frame. He looks inside. Nods to tell her it's all OK. Then looks back at me.

'Lily, the police told me I should press charges. Even if you were… Even if they thought you might be…'

'Mad?'

'No, harmless. But I didn't want to. And then I found that thing. That ruddy thing under my fridge. I thought you knew it was all a laugh by then. I was having a laugh with you. I know that doesn't seem… normal either.'

Suddenly he's like the boy next door.

'Lily. I'm not going to press charges, or anything like that, because I think this is partly my fault and clearly you're... I mean you're a... not thinking straight. But that's OK.' He's making excuses for me now.

'Thank you, thank you.' I sound pathetic. I dry my eyes on the sleeves of my top. My body turns.

'But, Lily, I do want you to get help. Or... I think maybe you should see someone. After this kind of incident. Because it's not a fucking... small thing, is it? So please, do that for me, OK?' he says with a hint of steel.

My mouth tuts as I open it. It's dry. I nearly shrug but don't want to seem indifferent, I want to seem resolved. I am resolved. I hold my head up. We stand there. There is some understanding between us.

He's waiting for me, I think. Waiting for me to tell him I'll do that. That's what he wants. But I don't know if I want to give him everything he wants.

I think of my mum. I give him a long look.

The Day It Comes.

My doorbell goes. It's 8.30 a.m., but it didn't wake me. I was awake already and looking at the ceiling. I got a call from Deborah, my boss, at eight, asking if I wanted to 'make my time off a bit more official'. She says she'd noticed a change in me. A withdrawal. She also says she 'knows and understands'. Everyone seems to 'know' and 'understand'.

She wants to put me on a one-month sabbatical for 'mental-health issues'. Apparently, my behaviour has been erratic for a while. Something about unresponsiveness. She guardedly mentions a few 'incidents'. I don't remember any of them.

She's gentle and kindly on the phone. It makes it all the more humiliating. I want to tell her, 'Oh, fuck off.' Tell her to shove her job. But I doubt that would help to convince her I'm not out of my tiny mind. I want to tell her I'm moving on to bigger and better things. Better job, more pay and respect. But I'm not. So I don't.

A month off on full pay. It's a gift. What to do with

it, what to do. I'm thinking all these things when the doorbell rings.

I leap up. It must be Aiden, forgotten his keys perhaps. Finally home. Everything fine. People don't often ring the doorbell. They just knock.

We used to ring the doorbell when we first moved in though. As a joke, even though we had our keys. Then it'd be him. Or it'd be me. We'd put on some funny voice and say, 'Oh, hi, I'm Nigel, the account manager, and I wanted to test whether the doorbells were in full operational order.' It's probably that. It's probably him.

Two men stand at the door. Neither of them Aiden. One of them is the police detective from before. The other is more burly looking and in the appropriate uniform. Our man from before still looks like a bookkeeper. He's the one that speaks.

'Ms Gullick, we have a couple of things we need to talk to you about,' he says, less laissez-faire than in our previous encounter.

'OK. I'm all ears. Fire away.'

'I think this is the sort of thing that would be better handled at the station. If you'd like to come with us?'

I think it's a question but it doesn't sound like one. It sounds like an order. I go with them. Perhaps Brenner or Rich didn't come so good on his promise. Arsehole. He probably called them up and told them everything. I may need a better story. I may need a lawyer.

It's only when I'm in that chair again, in that little white room, that I start to think about Aiden. I should tell them about him but I doubt that's the norm. 'Ooh, while I'm here, my husband's been missing for five days. Yes, I should've mentioned that earlier perhaps, but there we are, any chance of having a look?'

No. Best to keep it close to my chest. Best to keep it all close to my chest. This must all be down to 'Rich'. Not proving good on his word. I can handle the rap for a bit of breaking and entering. I'll break down maybe. They'll buy that. But the bookkeeper doesn't want to talk about that. He doesn't even mention it in passing. He wants to talk about something else.

'Can you tell me what your relationship is to the recently deceased Jean Taylor of forty-one, Canada House?'

The tape is on. It whirs in the background. What is this? The other policeman leans in.

'I've seen her around. I'd heard that she died. There was a commotion outside her flat the morning she was found. That's it.'

They listen. Giving nothing away. Then a slight smile from each.

'I'd seen her picture in the *Guardian* – she wrote an article in it. We were on nodding terms. I… I saw the sign up saying they were appealing for witnesses. Do you think there was… foul play?'

There are those two words again. Infantile in my mouth.

'So… you've never been inside her residence?' says the bookkeeper.

I mull it over. What to do, what do. Don't give it away.

'No. Never,' I say, firm. I smile for a moment. At one of them. Then the other. Resolved. Then a thought hits me. It's worth a try.

'Have there been any developments? In the case? I've

been very much hoping that someone would get to the bottom of it.'

Listen to me. Even I think I sound suspicious. Unnatural.

'There may have been. But leave the questions to us.'

Air again. You could drive a bus through these pauses.

'Nothing else for us? Ms Gullick?'

They weren't keen on the Brenner story, it got me nowhere. But I could tell them everything. That would be one way to go. I could tell them about the tall fair-haired man. About my three corroborating witnesses, which I sourced myself. About the suggestion that he, or someone like him, had been spotted with Sonya. That he may even have been her boyfriend. I could tell them about Aiden. And my binoculars. I could tell them everything. But I don't. I smile ruefully. I tell them nothing.

'That's funny, because after we took your fingerprints the other day we got a match on a set of prints that were taken inside her flat. She was a lonely woman. Only two sets of prints in there. Yours. And hers. How do you explain that?'

Now I do have a choice. Not a good one. Something. Or nothing.

'No comment.' It sounds more guilty coming out of my mouth than I thought it would.

'Then we've got the fact that you broke into another neighbour's flat the other day.'

Just the once. He didn't mention the second time. He didn't mention the hammer. Perhaps Rich was as good as his word.

'We've even got eyewitness reports detailing you hanging around the estate just nights before she was killed. And on subsequent nights afterwards.'

'I live quite nearby. I sometimes cut through that way. Who—'

'But what worries me most, Ms Gullick, is that we followed up a report of a doctor arriving at the scene before we did. A doctor that fits your description, when we looked into it. We've got a frequent but not entirely reliable witness who described the doctor as looking very much like yourself.'

The air goes cold. The muscles in my face slacken. A shiver shoots down me.

'You're not a doctor are you? Ms Gullick?'

'No comment.'

'We just wondered whether Jean Taylor thought you were one. Because, maybe, you told her you were. You might've used that authority to get into her flat. Mightn't you? That's at least feasible isn't? From our point of view.'

I'm pinned. I am a bug under a glass.

'I don't know what you're talking about.'

'Don't go anywhere, Ms Gullick. You are a suspect in the murder of Jean Taylor. Stay close. Only the guilty people run. It's a cliché, I know. But it's a perfectly good one.'

Part Eight: The Woman on the Fourth

The day it comes. Afternoon.

They taxi me back home. My head is pounding. I think there's something seriously wrong with my sinuses. I'm pained. I used to get migraines as a kid, maybe it's that. I don't know. It might also have something to do with being what seems like the only suspect in a murder inquiry.

Everyone seems to be watching. Talking about me. From some disturbed woman who I once gave athlete's foot cream to, out of the goodness of my heart, to the possible psychopath over the road. And all sorts of other assorted faces, watching from high windows. I'm not the only one who was watching.

A friendly face greets me as I step out of the car and slam the door. Lowell jogs up in sportswear. He has a skinnier frame than I would have thought. Broad shoulders, exposed in a white vest. Jogging back from climbing, I imagine – he has his gloves on. To remind people of his masculinity. Keeping fit in the afternoon. A privilege of only the self-employed or the unemployed.

'You OK, Lil? Mind me asking what's up?' he says, eyeing the police car as it pulls away.

I should be embarrassed but I'm way past that at this point. At least he's shared things with me too. We can be partners in the doldrums. Shame twins. I'm just happy to see a friendly face. I give him a hug. He's warm. Clammy. Then I pull away.

'Oh, it's…' I say hesitantly, turning towards the building entrance.

'Go on,' he says, eagerly, a bit nervous at what I might say.

'I'm just helping them with their inquiries,' I say, casually.

He holds his hips. Squints in the sun. Takes a sip from his water bottle.

'Wow. About… about what? Do you mind me… er…' He trails off.

For the first time in a long time, I feel enabled. Tough. I have a secret. Everyone wants to know what I'm into. I'm into some serious shit.

'Tell you what. Do you fancy a cup of tea?'

He's inside. My base level of tidiness has kept me afloat. There are old newspapers scattered about. Unwashed dishes and cups. A few. I notice them as if they've just appeared. But other than that it's pretty good. It's funny how strangers make you look at yourself with fresh eyes. But I'm doing OK. Keeping my head above water.

He leans on the arm of my sofa, demonstrating that he's not staying long. Or, most likely, embarrassed to be sweating a bit in a half-stranger's living room. It's strange to be an intruder when you're not at your best. I told him he could shower first but he was keen to hear my story. He kicks it off. He gets right into it.

'Is it about the break-in?'

'Which break-in?' I say, meeting his gaze.

'Hmm?'

He pauses. He's sweating. But then he has just been running. 'I heard there was a break-in. In the other building?' he says.

'Oh, you heard about that. Yeah. I think I heard that too.'

Suddenly I feel like I hold all the cards. It's novel. Thrilling.

'No, no. It wasn't about that,' I say, looking away.

He gets up and paces around the room. A sudden need to dominate the space. He stalks around like an animal. He looks funny. Maybe he's nervous, it's got a bit real for him I think. Not sure how to help. Unsure where we go next.

'It's a funny story really,' I say, helping him out.

He stops and stares. Beat. Beat. The tension is palpable. I guess he's worried about me. It's understandable.

'They seem to think I know something about that old lady. The one that died.'

'Oh, right. Right.'

I leave him hanging. I'm enjoying this, I don't know I why.

'So, Lil. Do you? Know anything about it?'

'No, no. I just knew her a bit. To nod to. That's it.'

'OK. I guess they'll take anything they can get.'

'And I went to her house. One night. Kind of late.'

'Right. Did you?' he mumbles.

He sips his tea for the first time. It looks kind of small in his hand. A toy cup. He is taller than I remember. Bigger in sportswear.

'Yeah. I just went to say hello. I'd seen her in the paper.

There was a story about her. Wanted to check she was all right. I was being a good neighbour.'

'And you were just telling the police that,' he says, presumptuous.

'No. I didn't tell the police that.'

'Then… what did you tell them?'

Another sip.

'Nothing. Didn't want to look like I was part of anything I wasn't. Didn't want to be bothered by them. So I said nothing.'

He leans against the sofa again, finishes his tea in another gulp. 'That's probably for the best.'

'Yeah, I'd say so.'

He isn't asking where Aiden is. A strange man is in my flat. Trying to dominate the space. Not asking where the man of the house is.

'You did the right thing. Save yourself a lot of bother. Right?'

The transatlantic tone in his voice comes through strongly. It's cute when he uses words and idioms he's picked up from here. Like when he says 'bother', 'rubbish' or 'cup o' tea'. He probably doesn't now how subtly but beautifully alien they are in his mouth. These tiny imitations and replicas of the real thing.

I'm expecting him to chip off. But he's still lingering. He's concerned. Maybe about me. Maybe he wants to help but doesn't know how. He's not going anywhere. He's got something to say. The noise of the diggers rises.

Rumble. Rumble. Rumble. Rumble.

'I'm in a bit of bother at moment,' he says. There he goes again, being borderline adorable. But his tone has changed. He stands. 'See, I bought a couple of those flats. The new ones? Before my twin sackings. Ha.'

I consider this for a second. Twice a year they break ground on a new building. After the wrecking ball hits an old one, within a few months they can clear the ground and start work in earnest on the new project. Canada House is scheduled to be dust within two years. If you root around on Princeton Homes website, you'll find there's a building called Aqua View ready go up and it will open in the first quarter of 2019. Things happen fast after they break ground. That work involves diggers and foremen. But it also involves graphic designers, computer-generated images of proposed idyllic landscapes. Plus parties. Lots of them. Pimm's and Prosecco flows. Current owners can often be seen there thinking about putting down a deposit for another flat. Just a little investment. Where else is there to put your money these days, huh? Initially they get you to put down a small amount. A few grand. Then twenty more around six months later. Six months after that they'll need sixty more and so on. And so on. The longer you can stay in the game the more chance you have of 'flipping it on' for big rewards from Far East investors or some such. But you wouldn't want to default, you wouldn't want to take on too much. You could lose the whole thing.

'I actually went in for three, Lil. I've got payments I need to make. And soon.'

He has a habit of falling on his feet. I'm sure he'll work something out. He'll find a way. He's one of those guys. But three!

'Ooh. You'll work it out. You're one of those guys.'

'Yeah. Yeah, I'm sure it'll be fine. Long as they hold their value. I'll be fine.'

'Why did you get three? If you… don't mind me…'

'Things were good. Very good. Then they got not so good. I overdid it a bit. Why does anything crash? Over-spending. Not that I'm going to crash. Ha.'

He makes a move. He offers to wash up his cup and I take it off him and put it on the side. We're suddenly awkward with each other. I think he thinks we overshared. We've got to know each other far better these last few weeks. It's all happened so fast. Possibly too fast.

But we're still buddies. He'll be OK in a moment. It's good to share the load.

'Well, I'll get going. Any news. Any… thing? I'm always here.'

'I know.'

'And stay away from those cops. Seriously. Whatever's going on around here, I think we need to stay out of it. Keep it on the down low. Know what I mean? After all, you know, nobody likes a squealer,' he says. Kind of dorky.

I stand and walk him to the door. I don't know why. It's not a big flat. Just one bedroom. For the two of us. He has two bedrooms. Just for the one of him. Perhaps he likes to stretch out. Or maybe he's just greedy.

'I wish Aiden was around to say hi.'

He stops. Looks at me. Almost as if he knows. 'Yeah. How are you doing with all that?'

'Oh yeah, it's really tough. Him not being here.' I smile.

He frowns. Confused at something. He has a startled look. 'Yeah, tough. How long has he been gone now?'

He looks at me meaningfully. He's coming on a bit strong. He puts his hand on mine, what's his game?

'About five days.'

'It feels like that, huh?'

'No, it is that. But don't worry. He'll be back. His bike's gone. So he must have gone out in that.'

His mind is doing mental long division. He softly punches his hand.

'Didn't they… wasn't it written off? In the… crash?'

Now I'm doing it too. My eyes moving from side to side. My feet shuffle. I'm outside myself. 'I'm sorry. Did you hear about a crash? I didn't hear about a crash.'

'You told me about it yourself.'

'I'm sorry, what?'

Is this a game? Does he know something I don't? Is he playing with me?

'Just after you moved in. The wet night. A car came at him on the blindside. They didn't see each other.'

I feel faint. It's all I can do to keep myself standing upright.

'What are you talking about?' I manage to utter.

My knees turn to jelly. I lean on the hall table, to stop myself from hitting the ground.

'Oh, Lil. Oh, man. You need to sit down for a second.'

The day it comes. Evening.

My knees buckled.

When I come to, I am in bed. A cold flannel on my forehead. The first thing I see is him. Leaning over me. His face filling my field of vision. He starts off in a blur, like a nightmare, then comes into focus. I am pleased he is here. So at least someone is here. But I have some questions to ask. I try to handle it with calm and grace. But I don't think I handle it with calm and grace.

'What are you doing in here?' I say.

'You fainted. You were… There's some things you need to… hear.'

'What the fuck is wrong with you? Do you think I don't know what you're doing?' I attack straight away. Attack is the best from of defence.

I watch his face for weaknesses. For a smile or smirk. For a tell, a look to the side, the sign of a liar. I've done a lot of lying recently. And I've been played with a lot too.

The police, 'Rich', Lowell. What's he trying to pull? What's in it for him?

'Lil, your husband died five months ago. In a bike crash.

I remember seeing you a few hours after it all happened. You'd had to go and identify the body. You'd got a call. It was sudden. He didn't suffer. He didn't feel a thing, you said. It was just like that.' He clicks his fingers. 'I came around to talk about it. I've been here, in your living room, talking to you about all this. Before.'

I look down. I blink. I can't take it all in. He fills the silence.

'You said you'd been seeing someone about it. Then a month or so later, you told me you stopped seeing someone about it.'

I'm angry. A fury that rises deep from within. I can't stop it.

'Do you think I don't know my own mind? I... I know my own mind. What's happened to him? Do you know where he is? Where he really is?'

'Lil, I think I should go.'

'Yeah, go. Get the fuck out,' I shout. I'm so angry with him. I almost can't control myself.

'But you need to see someone. You told me you still had the number. Just in case. In case you needed to see her again, you said...'

'Are you trying to get someone to put me away? Is that it? The way they put my mum away?'

'It's not like that. I... I think I should go. You just need a little help. Don't be alone with this. I don't know what the protocol is... but I'm going to give you some time. I'm just beyond the wall.'

I'm not sure if that's a threat or a promise. I don't know what to make of any of it.

'Here. Here's my mobile number too. Just in case.

Wherever you are. If you need anything. I'll be on call. Promise,' he says, examining me.

'OK. Whatever you say. OK.' I yield.

He lets himself out. And I'm alone. I've felt this loneliness before. But not for a long time. I think. It's a particular type. A particular feeling. It's got its own shade and colour. Yes. I've felt it before. In my flesh.

I search my drawers for clues. I don't know what I'm looking for really. I turn the house over. A scrap of paper falls out of a Daphne du Maurier book I read months ago. On it is a written a number. I don't recognise it. It's a London number, above it is written 'Helen'. I touch the ink, the words, running my finger along them as if they might disappear under my touch. It is my handwriting, but I don't remember ever writing it. I don't know any Helen.

I check through my wardrobe, frantic. Looking for a memory that might unlock things. Once and for all. That might prove or disprove. My theory.

I touch his clothes, still nestling in his drawer, ironed and neat. Still warm from his body, surely. I notice the grids and charts on my walls, a madwoman's cove, think how they must look to Lowell, the only one I've let in here. His discomfort makes sense now.

I see my room like a stranger, like a detective or anthropologist, I touch the words, my forefinger feels the pencil-indented lines of my grid. The numbers and names. The cross-references. The coloured pins stuck hard into the charts, piercing them and sticking into my walls. The brown string that runs from one name to the other, the links, the clues. The inside of my head exposed for all to see. The quirks of a fantasist. I seem so transparent from a distance.

I run my hands through his jumpers, high in the wardrobe, I can barely reach them. They too feel warm. I hold my ear to them. I rub my face against them, my features feeling every thread. His smell is here, so close. It must be a trick. It's impossible, he was just here. I'm sure of it. He's so close. Between two jumpers I find a note. Blue pen on crisp, white paper again. A number, and beneath it, 'Helen'.

I throw open his drawers now. His private things. The ones you're jealous and guilty if you rifle through. I tear them apart.

I find the boring stuff, the proofs of him. His accounts, receipts, proof of life. He was here. He was just here. His passport photo stares back at me. No smile. He looks right into me. I jump back. My hands to my face, warm tears fall to the carpet that holds me. In my cell. That stops me falling through to the cell below. That keeps the others in their cells around me from seeing me. From touching me. I am the tiny cell on an Excel spreadsheet. On a long empty page, with endless unfilled entries, so alone.

I grab for the files at the bottom of his side of the wardrobe. They lie next to his shoes. His Converse, his Nike, his Doc Martens, all worn in.

In these files are his writings. The unpublished words of his book. Of his most recent novel. I grab them, throwing them around the room. The pages swirling through the air throughout the room. Pages and pages. Meticulously arranged by date. The room is covered in them. They're still filed by number. Every one. He never let himself go. He kept everything just so. Here they are. The pages he wrote. The pages and pages. He'd print them out at the end of the week. He said it didn't feel real when it was only on the screen. He said he couldn't judge it.

Here they are. The words he wrote. Proof. Not just his things, but his words, time coded. I go back to the start. I smile now. It was them that were playing tricks on me. Them. Everyone else. I can trust myself. I know my own mind.

February. Here's all the writing he did in February.

An introduction. The words: 'Russian'; 'Camera'; 'Kudos'; 'Splash'; 'Snow'; 'Feet'; 'Painting'; 'Ardour'; 'Beautiful'. Beautiful, the words he wrote. Him flooding back to me. I know he was here, I saw him, I spoke to him. I held him. Kissed his cheek. We made love. Only a week ago. My breathing slows. I calm and think about my next move. I continue through the pages, by date, here they are. His words.

I empty all the files and put them in a big pile. I go through it chronologically. February leads into March. His words, flooding my room. I skim them all to take them in. To breathe him in again.

I wonder when he will come home. No one could take him away. He rides on his motorcycle so free. He's broken free of this room. That's what he's done. Maybe he finished his book. Then went out to ride and see where he ended up. To celebrate. He's a free spirit. He'll be back soon. When he's done whatever he's doing.

No one could hurt him. I said he was weak. But he's not, he's strong. He's free. He rides into the cold night air, I can picture him.

April comes. I read his April words. Week by week. Dated day by day. The many words he wrote. Prolific.

Each one a little victory. How smooth he rode. Nothing could stop him, nothing could slow him down. He was a professional. That rarest of things. An artist. I never knew how much. I never realised how strong he was. I picture him on the motorcycle. In the rain.

May. We're closer and closer. Chapters sixteen and seventeen and eighteen and nineteen go by. Everything he wrote. There's so much. He's done so well. And there's so much more within these files. My hands are heavy with paper. His little life, that I'm holding. His heart in my hands. His life and blood. It's all here. The proof that they're lying. I saw him writing them, right in front of me, and here they are. Adjectives, nouns, adverbs, scattered across my room. Weeks of them. There's so many of them. And so many to come. My hands are still filled with reams of pages.

I charge through them. The words rushing at me each time. Then nothing. A blank one. I stop. May twenty-first. Then nothing.

I go to the next one. It's blank, but I stare at it like it couldn't be fuller. Like it holds something hidden within it. I study it for clues. For codes. There's nothing there. I go to the next one.

I stare. Nothing there. No words! The next is blank too.

Another blank. Another blank. Another blank.

I flick ten ahead. My breathing getting heavier. A plane passes over head. Whoosh! They come so close.

There's nothing, no more. No more words. That's it.

The rest of the heavy pile is blank. But I saw him write the words. Whoosh! Another plane passes, so close it could have taken the roof off.

I want to go to the window to look. Did it crash? Has the plane landed in the lake?

No more words. It's impossible. I saw him write them. Whoosh!

All sounds disappear. I put my had to my ears. The ringing in them gets louder and higher pitched. I fall back into the pages. That cover my room. They flood the place. They smother me. I clutch the paper with my fists. My ears deaf to everything. I don't hear my body writhing in them. Because the ringing stings my ears, like I've been next to an explosion.

I wait for them to recover. But they're not doing it. It's impossible.

I bite down hard on my lip. Nearly drawing blood. My chest lifts to the sky. Then it comes. Then it comes.

The day it comes. One minute later.

My body shakes. Uncontrollably. It's not me doing it. It can't be. It's like foreign bodies, invisible bodies, have stalked into my room and have hold of me. Shadows that have me by every muscle and limb and are shaking me. Every sinew shakes. It's a horrible sight. An exorcism. But I close my eyes. I don't see a thing. My skull hits the carpet. I can't do a thing about it. I can't stop.

Then my hearing returns. Slowly, the shaking subsides, the fit passes and my body stops. But I can't move. I tell my arms to lift me up. I tell my spine to drag itself from the floor. I tell my feet to at least give me a sign that they are still there. But they all say nothing back. I am catatonic. I am still. There has never been, in my life, anything as terrifying as this.

I hope my heart can beat by itself. I hope my organs can pump. The millions of things that keep us alive, that you take for granted.

My breath still works. I feel it, across my lips. My lungs pushing along, automatically. Everything else is still. Except my eyes. They turn and look at another note to my right.

I see that number again. I see the name: 'Helen'. There's another that rests on my chest, a yellow Post-it. Same number again. My writing. 'Helen'. I stare at it, in wonder.

It's so hard to describe the feelings you have in this state. When you can't move a muscle. Like every bright thought has a dimmer on it. A black cloud hanging over it and casting every memory into a shade. I try to switch my mind off. I would try to sleep but feel I might swallow my tongue. And anyway, I'm far too afraid for that.

I think about images and things. I think about Aiden. On his bike. Riding in the dark. It feels like a nightmare or a threat or a fear.

But it's a memory.

I remember getting a phone call on my mobile. An unknown number. I don't usually answer those so I reject the call. They try again; I reject it. I'm at work. Bored and busy. They try again; I answer it.

'Yes,' I say loudly, the entire open-plan office turns.

'Ms Gullick of forty-nine, Riverview Apartments?'

'Yes. What?'

'I think you might need to sit down.'

I am sitting down but I don't want to be in the office, so I go outside for this. I go into the corridor, out of earshot of my co-workers, who seemed to sense something. With their prying eyes and ears.

'Yes. Go on. I'm sitting,' I lie. I'm standing staring out of the window in the corridor. People from other offices pass. There's no privacy here. It's one of those buildings.

'Your husband has been in an accident. In the early hours of this morning, around 6.45 a.m., he was involved in a collision.'

There was another car involved. And a lorry. Heavy rain.

He had an early meeting. Something about his new book, somewhere out of town. Sussex or Oxford. Hampshire or Hertfordshire. I don't remember.

In the hallway, people pass by me. Going from office to office. Almost nudging me as they go past. I stare out of the window. A flock of starlings swoop and fly into the clouded skies.

I go down to hear the story from the local police. They are kind. They are trained in this. I am not. I'm scared of them, tentative and nervous. But I can't summon the right feelings. Not on cue. Not even when I see the body. I almost feel like there's something wrong with me. But then I dismiss that thought. My mind locks it away somewhere. And I just look.

I get in a car and it takes me home. I watch the world go by me as I look out of the passenger window. Nothing has stopped. Everyone goes about their day. The world still keeps going on. I pass by a park and people sip coffee on a bench in the rain. An old couple. They fascinate me.

I'm given some numbers to call. A checklist. I make some appointments for myself. I do this blankly. Matter of fact. The tears don't come. Someone has sapped all the energy from my body. It's like some husk is making the calls for me.

Then I call his brother. A couple of friends of his. His agent. His brother cries down the phone so hard. I listen to it. Interested. But unmoved. For the first time I feel the slightest guilt at this. But that quickly passes.

At home, I look at his clothes and consider what to do with them. He's only just gone. I look at his jumpers, hanging in the wardrobe. I look at his files, his passport, his personal effects. I iron some shirts of his. Methodically. I hang them up. Then I sit down. And that is that.

In time, I'm forced to talk about it. That's the advice I get. I tell lots of people. People I'd lost touch with because I had Aiden. He took up all of my time, we did everything with each other and for each other. He was my best friend. I didn't need anyone else. Even they cry. I ring up old friends from work I hardly see any more. I ring up cousin Sarah in Devon. I listen to it down the phone. It doesn't touch the sides.

I remember telling Lowell. I do. I remember it now. In the hallway. He came inside. He's been here before. He hugged me. I didn't soften or move a muscle. I didn't really know him then. I hardly know him now, but even less then. I'd practically just moved in. He left.

I want to phone you, Dad. But I'm so stubborn. I'm still cross with you. Every message and voicemail I ignore is a little punishment for saying those words to me. For comparing me so perfectly to her and all her faults with one dismissive phrase. Every time you call. 'You Know Who'. You. It's another bit of the marathon. Leaving it to ring out or hitting the 'reject' button. Another feat of endurance. And it makes me feel good.

So I started a journal. To meet you halfway. So I could control the narrative. Have things my way without you undermining me. Or 'trying to help', you'd say. Of course. Well, maybe. But this way you don't get a chance. It's just me and the page and I dispense justice my way and I can have things how I want them.

I blame you. As I remember the light shining past you in the hide. We said nothing. Just watched the birds go by. And never talked about it. About her. About how we felt about it all. We never cried together. We never did any of that.

I don't know whose fault that is really. But there we are. I do blame you. And maybe that's unfair. Maybe I'm being unfair. But that's how I'm being. That's me. Here I am.

I sent you my dispatches week by week. I must have sent you five by now. And every time, you call. You say you'll come over whether I like it or not. And in between the calls, you text. But I'm not ready yet.

I have another thought. It might be daydream. It might be an imagining. I picture myself in there, with the student. In her place. Sonya. She has a chest infection, she's had it for weeks, she says. She doesn't know if it's from all the dust and muck that's around from the demolition of the buildings. She can't seem to shake it off and she's wondering if it's something she should be worried about. She's heard about me. She's heard about Dr Gullick. She wants me to look her over.

I put my hand to her chest and feel her heartbeat. She looks afraid. Of me. Of what I might say. And do. I touch her skin. I look at the glasses case next to her hipster fruit bowl. Her handsome bookcase. Her humble little cactus. I tell her to breathe in and out. In and out. I tell her to cough. Which makes her cough more still. Deep and rasping. And going on and on. What a cough she has. She leans into my hand, which I manage to keep firmly against her chest all the while. Feeling the mechanism quake beneath her thorax. The fascinating feeling of the ribcage dipping and rising. And the echoes of everything beneath. I click my tongue and look at her. She looks quite, quite afraid. I hold my breath and look her in the eye. Right in it. Before telling her to inhale some steam. And that everything will be fine.

I'm still stiff as a board. It's a daydream that feels like a memory. But it can't be a memory. It can't be. I'd remember. It's just a funny drifting thought. One of those strange imaginings that visit us all in the day. Maybe they're all I have now.

So here we are. Now I'm still. Frozen still in my bedroom. Unable to move a thing. It feels like it's been hours.

My fingers wriggle. I've been telling them to for a few minutes now and they finally submit. The pins and needles are so painful in my elbow, I don't know whether to laugh or scream. My legs flop around as if they're not part of my body. I punch them for a bit, but they're dead. Then gradually they thaw and come back to life.

I lift my body and feel the air around me. It's thick, so I open a window. My brain is telling me I've had a shock. But my body is just glad to be alive. I jump up and down a couple of times. I'm free. I'm so relieved. I duck under the blind, lift it over me like a sheet and open a window so I can put my head out of it. And let the air flow over me.

I suck in the cold outside. Then after a few seconds, I lift the material back over my head and step backwards into the dark of my room. I'm still for a moment. Then I pull the cord to raise the blind, just a touch, just enough to get some light in. But not enough to see the windows of the other apartments. I feel that would be dangerous. I'm not ready for that yet. I hear my own footsteps echo off the tiles and around the kitchen. I am alone. For the first time I feel fully alone.

I grab at the Post-it note stuck to my shirt. I'm going to use the home phone. It's a novelty. I type in the numbers. The numbers above the word 'Helen'.

The day it comes. Evening.

Jack Snipe – *Scolopaci, Lymnocryptes Minimus* – Wetlands – Overcast, 10 deg – 3 flock – 22 cm – Two pale, lateral crown-strips, healthy dark plumage – Foraging

I look out the window. I allow the phone to ring, the receiver to my ear. It went on for what seemed like an age. I stood and waited. Come on, pick up. I considered what was beyond my blinds. What was going on out there. But I stopped those thoughts in their tracks. I need to stop looking out there. Keep the shutters down. Cut off the impulse before it all starts again. I waited for someone to pick up.

'Hello,' the voice came back.

Not for the first time, I told my body to do something and the body kicked back. I ordered my brain to talk, but the words refused to come out. Speak.

'Hello,' the voice came again.

I put the phone down. I don't know whether I thought

I didn't need Helen or I was afraid to speak to her. My body was making decisions on pure impulse.

I feared her bringing a bit too much reality with her. I'd had too many shocks for one day already. Enough was enough. So many epiphanies. It's all come at me so hard.

I see Aiden's laptop on the floor. Where it's always been really. Him tapping away on it, an imagining. I touch the bathroom door; he used to hide behind doors sometimes, in my mind. I look at the bed sheets I slept next to him in. And didn't.

For so long he was never here. I touched myself and imagined we were making love. I grasped the air and made myself believe it was his body. I could smell him here, on the pillows. When the scent would die I'd spray his aftershave around again to keep his ghost close. To convince myself.

I recollect the conversations I had with blank walls. Imagining he was talking back. My imaginary friend. I pictured him cleaning the blood off the windows. The blood and water appearing to run down his body. As I envisaged him on that rainy night. After the collision. As his body lay on the tarmac and the rain came down on him. Almost serene. I am back in the living room. I lie on the sofa. And meditate on the lies I've told myself to keep going every day.

Then there's a knock at the door. My body tells me to ignore it. Whether it be police, a friend, or foe. My instinct says put your head under the covers and wait for it all to go away. Go back to bed. Wait for another day.

But the knock comes again. I could chance the enlarged eye viewer. My flat's fish eye lens. If my home were a camera.

But I'd rather not know. If I count to fifteen and breathe through my nose. I breathe out for ten through my mouth. Do that three times. Then by the time I've finished they'll have given up and go home. In for fifteen. Out for ten.

Knock. Knock.

They'll have to go and get a search order to get in. They'll have to get a battering ram. I'll stack up all my furniture. I'll make a barricade. I'll clog it up. I won't go quietly. I'm sticking here. Not answering, they can't make me.

In for fifteen. Out for ten.

Knock. A single knock. Solitary. My mind is cast back somewhere. A special knock. Just one was all it needed, for me to know it was them. Our secret knock. I'd knock once back, to let them know my tempest was over. Whenever I had a tiny storm inside my head. I breathe in the memory. They knew to leave me alone. Then they would knock just once to check I was OK. To check I was ready to come out.

I return a single knock. One rap from my knuckles to the wood. I wait. Nothing. Then I remember to count to ten. That's how it went – four, five, six, seven, eight, nine. Then knock. Knock. Two slow ones, with a full gasp of air in between them. Then I'd make my choice to be seen. If that's what I wanted. If I was ready. That's how it used to work. I remember how this goes.

I don't bother with the peephole. I close my eyes. And open the door. I open my eyes. Gently, like a newborn baby, as if for the first time. And there he is. He's back.

There you are. Dad.

We stand and look at each other. I want to hug you.

You seem to want to hug me too. I don't know. I think you do, you'd have to tell me.

But instead we stare. You outside, me inside. A precipice between us. It's only been a year. But you look a fair bit older. I hope you don't mind me saying. I know you've not been well. Your sinuses, like mine, go on the blink quite heavy sometimes. It gets worse as you get older, you told me. Things that were little pains, stick around and get worse. They're there to stay. They don't shift so easy as when you're young. Maybe they'll be the death of me, you said. You do look older. You're an old man now. It's taken some time away from you to see it. But you're still handsome. Objectively. Still Dad.

Then a creeping fear comes over me. I feel like I want to say 'sorry'. Or even 'I'm so sorry'. For not letting you into my life. My feelings. I wrote you a letter. The day Aiden died. Because I couldn't face the phone call. Because I was so angry and stubborn. I wanted to keep you out. I thought maybe it would hurt a little less if I did that. If I decided to resent the little things. Or maybe I was afraid someone kind might say something nice that would make it feel even worse. But it didn't work. I'm still afraid. And now I'm ashamed too.

You step inside. We still don't say anything. You have a suit on. You always like to travel formal. I assume you've just stepped off the plane. The dark-suited man. The expat. Already lightly tanned.

I imagine you've set up somewhere not far from a beach. Maybe near a cliff. A place to yourself. People to nod to, but not to speak to. Solitude. A bridge club on Tuesdays at most, if they do that over there. Then you sit in the sun drinking gin. Father's ruin. Somewhere you can watch the birds. I imagine it all. I don't need to ask. I don't need to know the details.

I'm so afraid at what you're going to say next that I myself can't speak. I show you the bedroom, wordlessly. Aiden's papers are strewn everywhere. The bed is a mess. Binoculars out of their case. Grounds for a grounding. You say nothing. Then the bathroom. Spacious and modern, tidy enough. A bath that I once pictured myself crying into, but never did.

Then the living room and kitchen. Strewn with charts and paraphernalia. I'm not so ashamed. This is where I am. Best to be honest about it. Best to wear it. Wherever you go, that's where you are. I don't want you to speak now. For a while it hurt me to delay the inevitable. Your judgement. I quickly make a wish that perhaps we can stay in silence like this for ever. I feel like you're about to speak. I don't want to hear it. Inside, I tremble.

Then you hug me. It catches me off guard. And warms me.

'Oh, Lily Anna. I love you so.'

And inside I let it all go and I weep with relief that you're here. But, in reality, my tears carry on gripping tightly. I can't quite speak yet.

'I got the journal. I read it. Every word,' you say.

'What did you think? Did I tempt you back with English garden birds?' I mutter.

'No. No, I had to come. Because of how far away you'd got. From how things really are.'

The same thing that happened to Mum. I read your implication. Your careful steps half warm me, half make me nauseous. I don't need any more silence and careful talk from Dad. I want you to make it better. I wonder why you aren't making it better. I remember now that you used to. You always did.

'I thought you were going to be OK. I thought it would be safe to leave you. I thought it wouldn't happen to you,' you say.

You're talking about a particular incident. I'll spell it out for you. A period of a few months in particular when Mum had wild delusions and spells of forgetting who we all were. She thought I was the neighbour's child. Who came around for toast and jam. *That,* I remember. That hurt. That was the beginning of the end of it all.

'That's unfair. That's so unfair, Dad. Of course it was safe to leave me. I've always done things alone. Why wouldn't I be OK? Why wouldn't it be safe,' I say, raising my voice.

'That's what I said. Don't misunderstand me. There were little echoes from you. Eccentricities. But nothing more. Then this trigger. Aiden, you see, triggered it all. I see that now. I'm sorry. I am. So sorry. I shouldn't have gone away. I think in some ways you never… dealt with Mum… dying. I should've talked to you more about it. I should've made sure… you were OK.'

I thought this was what I wanted. All this time. Now I don't even know why you're apologising. I know it's me.

From the moment you walked in. Maybe for my whole life that's what I've wanted. A sorry, from someone. For Mum being the way she was. And then going the way she did. Maybe we should've talked about it. But it's not like we didn't spend time with each other. We always did. Always. You made time for us to be together. Even if in silence. Us and the birds.

But when you say sorry it means so little. Because you don't have to be sorry for anything. You're my dad. And you've done so much for me. I couldn't wish for anything else, I know that now. I say it here because it's hard to say it to your face. But thank you.

But anyway, you do say sorry. For what it's worth. And it's strange, getting what you want sometimes. The earth doesn't shift on its axis. Everything is just the same. Like after a death. A butterfly flaps its wings and the world does fuck all.

But something has changed. My dad is back.

'Are you going to offer me tea? Do you have Lady Grey?' you say.

'Yes. Take a seat. You must be tired.'

We play pretend. Act like it's not awkward that I have refused to answer your calls, avoided you encroaching on my new reality. We're well practised in pretend.

'Lily. Lily Anna. It's so good to see you.'

Your words warm me. You're even warmer than I remember.

'Lily Anna. You're so smart. So smart when you're all together. But I've told you. If you have any illusions. If you have even the smallest hint that they're coming on then you must call me right away. Then we can sort it out together.'

Then we really do talk. Maybe for the first time ever. About Mum. And us. We talk. As adults and equals. I won't bore you with the details. You were there. We talk of Mum before she was ill. My earliest memories. We talk of Aiden and make some plans for how I move forward.

We talk of the birds. We tidy up. A good deep tidy like we used to do every Sunday. Until everything is almost as good as new. I know you know all of this, Dad. I know you were there. But it's important to remember the tidying up. Because this journal has become a record. A kind of timepiece and apology. I'm writing this down as a record now. I'm just trying to make sure this all sticks in my mind. If I ever happen to relapse again.

Then I fill you in about the past few pages of my journal. The ones I didn't send you yet. The seven days when it really got real. I tell you about it all.

I tell you about the search for the blond-haired man. Your face turns. You look at me, gravely.

28 September. 9 a.m.

We sleep on it. You on the fold-out sofa. The next morning we're awoken by the home phone. Its ringing is not such a novelty at this point. I hurry to it. You're probably tired from the flight. You look well though, lying there contently as my eyes wander over you. For a second, I admire the impression the continental sun has made on your complexion.

I don't want you disturbed, you need your rest. Your head sleeps sound on the pillow. So I dash to the phone. I pick it up and take it into the bedroom. Waiting for the recorded voice to ask me about PPI. Or an accident claim.

'Ms Gullick?'

I wait. It's not recorded. They need a response.

'Yes. Yes, that's me,' I say.

'I have Helen on the line for you. Are you free to speak?'

I consider the choices. I suppose I am. I'm not sure who Helen is but I have an inkling now.

'Yes. I suppose I am. How did you get this number?'

But that voice is gone. Hold music takes its place. I raise the blinds and look out. Rich's blinds are closed, luckily. I won't bother with any of that. I've promised. Not unless Dad says it's OK.

People are going about their days. There is a small festival on at the other side of the lake. They do them every so often. I think it's part of their remit. To bring the two sides of the complex together. The apartments and the estate. There's face painting. Jerk-chicken wraps. People kayak on the reservoir. It's for the children mostly. But most people show their face. Whatever their age. The hold music ends.

'Hello, Lily.'

'Helen?'

'Yes. We received a call from your number. Don't be alarmed. We tend to do that. We know it's hard to call and harder still to speak sometimes. We like to reach out and give people a helping hand. Tell me. Please. How are you? I've been wondering.'

Her voice is warm and smooth. If it was a colour it would be a fresh, light blue. I remember thinking this as I sat in a chair in her office for the first time. When I was a therapy virgin. Her voice drifting over me like a breeze, making everything gradually more manageable. Her voice is a safe place.

'I'm not great actually. Not great.'

'Well, that's OK. You must tell me everything on Monday. Can you come in and see me Monday. Just be gentle with yourself over the weekend and come and see me then.'

'Yes. It's far worse than before. Something's happened.'

'That's OK. Just tell me something. You don't have to

tell me everything, but tell me something now,' she says, so calm and bright.

Soon I'm giving her the outline. The delusions. Far more vivid than before, I tell her. Full-blown. Then I tell her what I saw in the other apartments. How I'm not sure if any of it is real or not. But it feels real. Realer than Aiden.

I tell her I don't want anyone to tell me it isn't real. I'm afraid of that. Because they don't know for sure either. And I don't want the rug pulled out from under my feet again.

I'm not sure if this sounds clear and reasonable. But that's what I'm aiming for.

She has a suggestion. She sets me some homework. She always liked to do that. Back to school. She says she likes the fact I've kept a journal and I must number the days within it. The days running up to my fit. Count them down. To when it came. Yesterday. When I shook so hard. Then couldn't move at all. It's a useful middle point. We have to see what led up to it. Become comfortable with it. Then work on what comes after, she says. This will help, she says. I'll be able to refer back to it and she will too. We can look at it together. And use it as a reference.

So I do. I rearrange it a bit. So it doesn't look entirely how I sent it to you. So it's in the best shape for her purposes. I read back everything I've said. It's my project for today. Turning my journal into a record, as I've been told to do. I skim it and try not go too deep, not yet. I don't want to get confused, I still could be a bit fragile, I don't know.

But if I can just get through a couple more days. Then it'll be Monday and Helen can start putting things right again. Helen who sits me down and lets me talk in her office. A couple more days to stay on the straight and narrow. Then I can start getting fine again.

You get up and I make breakfast. I still feel so much better addressing this all to you. Though it feels funny now you're here.

We have eggs Florentine. I make it so well. I feel good. Healthy. Today is Saturday and the late September sunshine pours in through my windows. I pull back the door to the balcony and let the air in. I see my neighbours at the other side of the lake. Dots in the distance. Almost too far even for binoculars.

I think about bringing it all up. Everything. But you do it for me.

'I know what you think you saw, Lily. I want you to consider that it was another illusion. I'm not going to push the fact. But I think we can agree that it is quite likely.'

I eat on. Chewing on my toast. I don't completely disagree. Because I don't completely disagree. I would think the same if I were him.

'But, Lily, I think there is one thing we could do, which might really help. Other people aren't our enemies. Of course, you know this.'

'Hmm. Yes, Dad. I do know that.'

'They can help us get things clear. Cross-referencing. That sort of thing. You understand?'

'Yes, Dad. I understand.'

'Well, if you don't mind, and I really won't push it, not if you'll feel ashamed, but if you don't mind, I think we should talk to a few of them. The people. From your story.'

He looks at me in the eye. Then continues: 'The lady

that thinks you're a doctor. The boys with the contraption too.'

'The "Hoverboard". It's an electronic gliding device.'

'Yes, even them. Chris and Nathan. If we can find them. Your neighbour.'

'Lowell.'

'Yes, him. And I think that, after that, things should become just a bit clearer. One way or the other. We'll see what they say. So. What do you think?'

I think I want to say no. I want to disobey my daddy. It could be mortifying. Poking around with that lot, Dad in tow. Them thinking I'm even more mental than before. Asking them if what I know happened with them actually happened. Getting it all down for third-party analysis. An independent adjudicator. My dad.

They'll all just stare at me, with their prying eyes. It won't make me feel any better. We won't find out any more. About Jean. Or me. So I don't want to do it. I don't want to. I want to ask him not to make me. To beg on my knees. To plead with him not to make me do it. But I feel I have to do as he says. Because Dad's come all the way from France. And I feel like owe it to him now.

Dad knows best. I'm going to have to get used to trusting other people, at least for a while. More than myself.

Part Nine: The Tick Hunter

28 September. 12 p.m. The Bad Kids.

A dreadlocked older man plays an acoustic guitar at the local fair. A pretty, brown-skinned girl sings, her voice so clear and smooth. There is the smell of barbecue in the air. A modern dance group are scheduled to do a performance later. This is how Hackney borders has a good time. We are searching for familiar faces.

I've left Terrence at home. I feel bad keeping him inside so much recently but it'll be fine once it all blows over. I'll be a proper good mummy. But I don't want people to notice he's Jean's dog. People might get funny. I don't know.

At least you know Terrence is real. You have the ocular proof.

You know that Jean died, was probably killed. You believe that, I think.

You don't know that I'm a suspect. I couldn't quite tell you that.

But you would know I didn't do it. At least, I think you would know that. I think that's what you'd assume.

It's strange out here. Everyone looks so happy. Wired.

I'm not sure what they're so happy about. I guess everyone loves a get-together. I didn't think we had this much community spirit around here.

Don't read into this that I'm being snide. I'm not being snide, it's just that everything seems alien at the moment. I haven't been outside for a while. There's a dizzying amount of people. Children run around on reins near my feet, their parents follow not long after. Others drink cans of cider on the margins, near the water.

But it's safe and sweet. It feels like a community. I think about the family Aiden and I planned to have. I get lost in that thought for a while. I look at children in pink sunglasses and maritime T-Shirts as they pass by.

I see the 'Hoverboard' from a mile off. The bad boys, in the distance. I don't want to tell you this is where we should start. Because it might not be the friendliest place to begin. But I want to get them over with.

I tug on your arm and point. We amble over through the crowds. Past kids with faces painted like tigers. Past tofu stands and book clubs looking for new members.

They're kicking a log. Far too old to still be amused by causing minor mischief to nature. Burning ants with magnifying glasses. Stamping on rats, killing pigeons.

But then, they're probably into harder stuff than that too. Stuff I haven't seen yet. I tread carefully with them. They aren't the sort of kids to be messed with. Last time they saw me it didn't end so well.

'Hey. Hello? Excuse me?' I say, to the gang of them. I try to seem small, insignificant, to cut a different figure than I did at the café. They probably wouldn't get nasty here. But who knows?

'Hey. Look, I wanted to say sorry.'

I don't want to say that actually. But it'll break the ice.

'Sorry, what, love?' one says. Head freshly shaved into an undercut.

'I saw you in the café. I wanted to apologise for my outburst. That's all.'

'Sorry. Don't know what you're talking about. But whatevers.'

They're on their best behaviour. I could push them a bit. Get a rise out of them. Get a bit of the old them back. But I don't. I play nice.

'It's all right. Come on. I just wanted to say, whatever you lot threw at my window, I've disposed of it. Of them. Let's leave it now. I'm sorry. Have a good day.'

One of them laughs. It's not rude though. They seem changed. They smile at each other. Playing innocent. This must be how they stay out of trouble. Out of prison or worse. They play it as sweet as punch. I could take a few lessons from them in my attitude to authority figures.

'Sorry, love. You're thinking of someone else, I reckon. But have a nice day. You enjoy yourself. All the best.'

I turn to Dad. He knows I can't have imagined that. Surely. The birds against the window might seem a push. But I remember cleaning them off my windows. I did all that. I remember that now. I can almost taste the blood in my mouth from the smell of them.

I turn back to them. I don't want any trouble.

I probably shouldn't even be out here. But then I'm not sure how to behave these days. I've never been the suspect in a murder trial before.

I stare at them. They smile back. One of them goes to light a cigarette. The other gestures that there are kids around so it's best not to. Tells him to put his fag back in his packet. The other agrees, affably. They turn and smile at me again.

'See you about, love. All the best.'

There's not the faintest touch of malice about them. I hear their words and could read passive aggression into them in another mouth, but he isn't offering that. He's playing it straight down the line.

I smile back. They win. 'Yep. Sorry. Must be someone else. Have a nice day,' I say.

I get a look from you. Don't say it.

'They seem like nice boys.' You say it.

'Don't start.'

'What?'

We wander towards the estate. I've got some more people to see.

'Of course, they didn't want to let on, did they? Dad? They're criminals. They attacked me. They don't want anyone to know the sort of things that they get up. Do they? Dad?'

'Of course, love. I understand. Just keep calm. We'll talk about it after.'

I'm losing your faith already. But I want to see Chris. He trusts me. He knows I'm not imagining it.

28 September. 12.45 p.m. Nathan.

We're standing outside. The place is grubby but doesn't seem as scary as it once was. You grew up on an estate and have seen far worse than this before. In the fifties. You wait, patiently, like dads do.

Dads are used to waiting. In cars to pick up their children. For their bosses to get back to them about reports they've written. By the phone for telephone calls in the olden days. They're professional waiters, they're used to it. Waiting gets easier as you get older. The theory of relativity in a nutshell.

I'm calling Chris on the mobile. But it's ringing out.

You survey it all. It doesn't look so scary to you. Not anything like I described. But then it's daylight. It looks deserted and harmless. No mysteries here. But then you haven't seen inside. I'd invite you in myself but I don't think it's a trip you'd appreciate. It wasn't the smoothest of rides the first time. Plus, the grate I pulled off its hinges isn't loose any more. It's been put firmly back on. Just as it was before. By who I don't know.

It rings out. The answerphone picks up but it's not

Jean's voice any more. They've changed it to that generic recorded voice that blithely reads the phone number out. Things are being placed back to how they were. Stones turned over are being kicked back to where they were before I found them. Things are conspiring to make me look unreliable. But it's not me that's being unreliable. It's them.

No answer again. I call again.

'Come on, Lil, doesn't look like there's anyone in there.'

'There is. I promise you. Some of the kids have broken back in there. They're leaving it right up to the wire. Staying till the bulldozers come. There's signs up about when it's going to be knocked down. So they know exactly how long they've got. They've got their own little community in there.'

'I read that part, Lil. I know what you said. Let's just leave it for a while and come back later, shall we? They could be out.'

'No, *they're in there*.'

I stand back and look up at their windows. I put my hands either side of my mouth. I use my makeshift megaphone.

'Oi! Come out. Chris! Boys! It's me. Come on!'

'Lil. Let's try later, shall we? I'm not saying they're not there.'

You put your hand on my shoulder securely and try to lead me off. I break free.

'Boys! It's me. Caroo! Caroo!' I shout. Pishing.

'Come on, Lil,' you say, chasing me around a bit.

For a moment it's like when I was six and you were in your forties. Chasing me around the garden. Playing funny games. The two of us.

I shout again. 'Caroo! Caroo!' I shout.

Then I see something. In the window, one of the metal grates opens on a hinge and closes again in a second. It glints in the light. Its rusty green momentarily sparkles against the sun's rays.

'Dad! Did you see it. Something's up there. Did you see?'

'No, I didn't see anything. Come on you.'

'No, I saw it. I saw it move. They're up there. I *saw* them.'

But you don't believe me. It's so frustrating. I can't talk you round. If you were here the first time you would have seen everything, but you weren't. If you were just looking up at the right time then you would've seen that, just then, but you weren't. But I did. I saw it.

'Oh, come on!' I shout again. But there's nothing doing.

Chris isn't showing his face but I know he's up there. He's gone quiet on me too. Making me look bad. Showing me up in front of my dad. I hear the noise of a football being bounced behind me. It's Nathan, the baby. The ball is almost as big as him. I suppose he's just about old enough to go out and play on his own. Here he is, I've got him.

'Nathan.' He doesn't turn. I thought he'd turn. Instinctively if nothing else. Even if he was trying to keep his head down. These kids learn early to play it cool, it seems. These kids are natural actors.

He bounces his ball and walks on. Away from the building. The place where I know he lives. He's a savvy, clever thing. But he's not going to outsmart me that easily. His little arms pumping away, as he throws the orange football down and kicks it along.

'Come on, Nathan, it's me, remember,' I say, running up to him.

He stares at me. No recognition flickering across his face. He rubs his head. Not scared. Confused by the strange lady.

'What? Nah. I don't know you,' he says.

Then he's off, away from the building, he'll loop round and stay away long enough. Until we're gone and he can make sure you aren't from the council.

He needs to make sure he doesn't give it away. For his brother. And the rest of them in there. Or they'll be out on their arse or moved on to who knows where. He's been taught well. I try to follow, but he runs off, kicking the ball. Me, a crazy lady, again.

'Nathan. Oh. Oh, come on!' I say. My fingers lace around the top of my head, pulling gently at my hair in frustration.

I give up. I turn and smile ruefully to you. 'Dad. I promise. I'm not mad. I promise you.'

'Come on. Let's go back home for a while.'

I turn back to the building.

Quiet, undisturbed.

As if there's nothing to see inside but old bricks ready to be knocked down.

28 September. 1.10 p.m. Sandra.

We pass the Z Café, then the shop, in silence.

I'm in partial shock. I can't believe what's happening. Then a face I don't want to see. It's like she waits for me around here. She can't help my cause, surely.

'Hello, Doctor. Is this your boyfriend?' she says.

'Ha, no. This is... a colleague,' I say.

I don't feel like telling her you're my dad. I don't know why. I don't want her knowing anything personal about me.

I wish she wasn't my only friend. This isn't the kind of company I need. She'll only make me look bad. You are silent. You know all about the doctor thing, but you were never good at make-believe. You pretend to be interested in something on your shoe and then stare over at the fair on the other side of the lake until this goes away. I hope it goes away soon too.

'Ah, anyway, Doctor, lovely day. See you soon,' she says, brightly.

I stop her. Maybe she's not so bad. Maybe she can give me something. The smallest glimmer of credibility.

'Hang on just a moment. Do you remember that night I gave you something for your rash? Do you remember that night?'

'I think you took a look at me. Yes. You did. But you didn't give me anything, Doctor,' she says, falteringly.

'No, I did, Sandra, didn't I? I couldn't give you any pills. But I did give you a cream.'

She stares at you. I just want one thing to go right. One thing to be exactly as I said it. She smiles at you. Swallows. Then at me.

'No, that would be malpractice, Doctor, I'd think. Giving me medicine without a prescription. Out of hours. And you wouldn't do anything like that. You told me to go back to bed and it'd be better in the morning.'

'I came to your flat. I spoke to you in there.'

'No, no. You didn't. That wouldn't be proper. And you are always such a good doctor, Doctor.'

She smiles at you. As if she's giving me the perfect recommendation. She must think you're my superior or something. I close my eyes. You place your hand flat between my shoulder blades. A gentle 'calm down'.

I want to grab her and shout. I want to lift her up by the lapels and say, 'Come on, woman! Just be normal for a second! Tell it like it was. Exactly like it was, with nothing added or taken away.' But I doubt that'd make things any better.

Dad, you were proving a real turn-off when it came to calling a spade a spade. People mistrusted you. Then mistrusted me. I'm not blaming you. But this was all built on words from behind doors. Secrets in hallways and nods in the street.

What did you expect? That it would all be easy? That

they'd all just come out in overwhelming support of me? No. It was never going to work like that.

'Look, Sandra. I don't want to put you on the spot. But I was just telling my dad about the student's boyfriend.'

More silence. She shuffles from side to side.

'You remember. You'd seen the missing girl going out with a man from the apartments from time to time. Isn't that right?'

She looks at me, wide-eyed and desperate. At you, then at me, pleadingly. Not sure what the right answer is.

'Did I say that?' she says.

'Yes, you did.'

I'm showing the strain now. Flushed. I'm trying not to lose control. But it's hard. So hard when everyone around you is making you look bad and not playing fair.

'Oh, well, I say a lot of things, Doctor. You don't want to pay any attention to me. I really should be seeing a doctor regularly. You understand? On account of my funny ideas. Don't listen to me. No. Don't listen to me.'

She disappears around a corner. I am usurped as the strangest person in our latest encounter. Sandra walks along, talking to herself, looking like one of those people. I hope that's not what I look like to anyone, I think, despite myself. I shouldn't have pushed so hard. You squeeze my hand. There's a man waving at me. Coming from the other side of the lake. A tall thin man. Older. I'm fearful now. Afraid of what might happen next.

28 September. 1.40 p.m. Thompson.

'There she is! The love of my life,' he shouts.

I wonder if he's on something. Jesus Christ, I've been hanging with a motley crew. He's as long and frayed as a piece of string. A can of Strongbow in his hand. He's the life of the party. He's coming towards me. Like an old friend, apparently.

I wonder what you thought at that moment, Dad. This was not my rebound. No matter how far things go. No matter how low I stoop. It'd never get that bad.

'Lucy, innit?' he says, standing far too close to me.

'Lily.'

'Lucy, that's right. Is this your old dad?'

You smile. So do I, at least he acknowledges me. At least he knows who I am. And doesn't think you're my fancy man. He slaps you on the back a bit too hard.

'Coming over? Want a whizz on the bouncy castle? A go on it, I mean, not an actual widdle,' he garbles.

It's a flurry of consonants; I'm not absolutely sure what he's on about. He sways a touch like a sail in the wind.

'No, we had a good look. Very nice. Everyone's over there.'

'Yep. Everyone's there. I usually keep myself to myself as you know, Becky, but I'm over there. Havin' a laugh. Get some courage down me and I'm anybody's.'

I size him up. I'm thinking it might be better to do this when he's sober. Then you speak.

'I think Lily said that you'd met her in the café?'

He pauses. Puts his hand to his head. Breathes. 'Yeah, Yeah. That's right. It's where we first met. I remember it. Over a hot cappuccino, how could I forget?'

He says 'cappuccino' with rich exoticism, as if he's saying caviar or Zanzibar. I take over.

'I was telling Dad about that bloke that you saw. Heading back to the apartments on the night before the night Jean was killed.'

I tried to keep it conversational but suddenly the words hit the floor like a dead weight. They seemed to echo around the place. If I didn't know better I'd say every face at the fair turned to stare at us. I was with the drunkest man in North London and I was the one feeling gauche.

'Don't know what you're talking about, darling.'

You nod. Just as you thought, I guess.

Hands go firmly into pockets. There's a patience about you still. I see all the times you were patient with me, laid out before me in one physicality.

You stare at him. For a moment I think you're enjoying it. For a moment I think you might hit him in the stomach, stand over him and ask him what he really knows. But I barge in before that.

'No, come on.'

'No, you come on, darling.'

'This is my dad. He's not going to tell. He's not police or anything. I was telling him about it all. He wants to help. You wanted to talk in the café, right?'

He changes, an anger makes his jaw stiffen, and he leans in to me. You, rightfully, are immediately on your guard.

'Yeah, well, careless talk costs lives all right? Whatever I did or didn't say can be between us, but I'm not going to start shooting my mouth off in broad daylight for you. You believe what you want to believe anyway, you do. I can tell. You make it up as you go along, sunshine, don't you? Don't you!?'

A peculiar feeling hits the pit of my stomach. His yellowing teeth confront me. His odd aspect. I'm not sure if it's his breath that's intoxicating me or the shock of all this, but things shake in my vision. I feel as if I'm at sea. My ears ring. I could throttle him as I stare at his mouth. I follow the corners of his chapped lips as they move and rise into a smile.

'Oh, sorry, love! I'm only messing around with you. I'm only having a laugh. Come here, gimme a squeeze, I'm sorry.'

He hugs me. There's nothing I can do about it.

Despite myself, I smile because he's going to spill the beans.

'Come on then. The guy. The suit. Blond hair?' I say.

'Yeah, yeah. All that. We talked about it in the coffee shop. I said I saw the fella coming back to Riverview Apartments, after it happened. I saw him.'

I beam at you. You don't know whether it's a big thing. It doesn't feel like a big thing. To you. But it is to me. It's the mother lode. The big one. It matters. Then I consider what he's just said.

'You mean Waterway Apartments. Right? Over the way there.' I point to the building opposite mine. The one where Brenner lives. I'm not calling him Rich any more. He's definitely a Brenner.

'No, no, no. Look. I'm not entirely sure which. I'm getting myself all turned around now. But I promise you, he's in one of these two. For definite.'

It could be the one over the road. Or he could be in my building. That's what he's saying. Shit.

'No, no, no, you said to me specifically. I asked you to think. To make sure. And then you said it was definitely Waterway.'

'Well, I was trying be definitive, wasn't I? Look, I'm not fucking with you. Pardon my French. I can't say which for sure which. I've got myself confused. But he's definitely in one of these two.'

'And you're sure about this, Mr Thompson?' you say.

'Yes, my friend. Absolutely doubtless. Bandage on his hand. Blond hair. He's a wrong 'un. He's in one of these two. Trust me. Now, bon voyage, the main band's just come on the main stage and I'm feeling some dancing coming on. Good luck, darling precious!' he says, heading back towards the fair.

My mind spins. I was so sure my grid contained all possibilities. But now I have to open myself up to the possibility that there are a lot more faces about to join the party.

And the worst part is. The one place you can't see. In a place like this. Is to the side of you. To see what next door is up to. Binoculars can't help you. It's your blind side.

I've had enough of being outside. I can feel their eyes again. I can feel I'm running out of time.

He may be drunk and hopeless, and today has hardly been a ringing endorsement of my sanity, all told, but I think he knows what he saw. Don't ask me why. I trust my sources. Trust is always the best place to start.

But it does mean it still could be Brenner. I think he tried to shame me into thinking it wasn't him. He tried to dominate me. But no matter what anyone says, I'm not ruling him out.

I still feel like I'm so close. In fact, I'm sure of it.

I just need to convince you of that.

28 September. 3 p.m. My saviour.

I've mentioned before that people wander through this place like ghosts. Here one minute, gone the next.

As intimately acquainted as I've become with the people opposite, I don't know the ones around me at all. The ones I share the air with. And a roof. Under which the killer may reside.

But Lowell does know them, he's my link. He goes to meetings. He liaises with the concierge. He's building rep or something of that ilk. Some kind of supervisor. He knows everyone. I know he can help.

So when you go out to get some fresh air and walk Terrence, perhaps to get a break from me for a while, I go to knock on his door. I've never done this before. I've never even seen the inside of his flat. We're getting much closer now. I knock.

'Yes?' he says, from behind the closed door.

'It's Lily,' I say. Trying not to seem flirtatious. Despite our earlier encounter. I don't want him to think I'm coming over for anything like that.

'Just a second,' he says.

As I wait, my head turns to the cool clean hallway window, its straight lines and smooth face cleaned just this morning. From there you can see downstairs to the entrance outside. I see a man in a flat cap entering the building. I could swear it's Brenner, but I doubt myself. Everyone's making me feel like I don't know anything any more. He couldn't have a fob to this building. Could he? Maybe he's managed to get one. Maybe he's coming for me. My fists clench. I need him to open the door. I bite my bottom lip. I'm about to shout for Lowell again when the door opens.

'Hi,' he says. Standing there. Strangely formal. A long coat and a red scarf. It is getting nippier sadly, but this seems a bit excessive. These are winter clothes. But he does look nice all dressed up. He's a perfect Watson, Samwise, Cosmo, Goose, Jem, Hastings.

'I need to come in now,' I say, urgently.

'I was just heading out,' he says. I suppose his clothes told me that. But if that is Brenner I need to get inside, just in case, and fast. Dad is out. And I don't want to be home alone. Not today.

'Please, I need to talk about some things.'

He doesn't look keen, but I'm pressing hard, not giving him a choice. I feel like I hear someone coming upstairs. I'm agitated and he can see that.

'Of course. Come on. Come in,' he says, with an easy charm.

The door closes and I'm inside. I'm not going to mention Brenner yet, he might think I'm being silly. I want to find a few things out first. I'll only let him in if he seems pliable.

Momentarily, I'm struck with flat envy. It's a higher

spec than ours. More room. He has all mod cons. A well-stocked kitchen with a marble top, a huge fridge with an ample separate freezer. I only have a little fridge with a tiny compartment at the top, only big enough for some frozen peas. It's weird what makes you feel belittled sometimes.

It smells a bit in here though. Which makes me feel a bit better. I don't know what of. I think it's just of man. I also notice he has a suitcase out. In the living room. Maybe he's going on holiday. I think about asking but there's no time for small talk.

'How often do you have those meetings. About matters within the building. All that? How often?' I say, locking eyes with him.

'Er… once a month. They're no big deal. Got something to bring up? You can come along?' he says, attempting to make this a normal conversation.

'Yeah. I might have. I might have.' I hear my heart beat in my ears as I speak. Brenner could be just outside.

I could become the building rep in his place. Get to know them, one by one. They might come to me about their problems. Suggestions about the recycle room. Requests for more bicycle racks. I could invite them in and size them up. They would come to me. I wouldn't have to go to them. But this seems like a long-term strategy.

I need to act now, before Dad loses my trust, before the next knock on the door is Brenner. Or the police again and they've tied me to Jean in some other way I didn't see coming. I try again.

'I suppose you get to know most people in the building doing that. Right?' I say, treading carefully. I don't know how much to give away yet. He seems on his guard.

'Yeah. You meet all kinds of folks. Complaints about the heating unit. That sort of jazz. Real hardcore politics,' he says, grinning.

Good old Lowell. He was born to do that sort of thing. Sorting out other people's shit. Always the one to stick his hand in the air and take the hit for everyone.

'You met anyone that seems suspicious?' I say, suddenly pointed.

I wonder how close Brenner is.

'Plenty. People keep themselves to themselves in this place until they think you can do something for them. The teachers on the second floor that can always smell mould in their flat? When no one else can, not me, not even environmental health. The Brazilian dude on the sixth that smokes a ton of weed and complains that he thinks his balcony is going to fall down when he's high? That's a knock on the door at 10 p.m. I always look forward to.'

I don't need anecdotes. I need more. And fast.

'What about the law student? From Canada House. You ever meet her?'

Lowell looks to the sky. His mouth creases. He is quiet all of a sudden. He shakes his head. Thinking. He goes to talk, then mumbles something. Another scratch of the head. Showing me he's struggling.

I guess it's difficult to remember everyone. Each building has one or two reps. There are six buildings in total, what with the new apartments and the two old estate buildings that are still there. They meet monthly. Some sort of council remit. The mirage of community. Integration.

'You know, Lil, I don't think I do remember anyone like that. No.'

What he doesn't know is that I'm going push him on the matter because my Internet research on her told me that she would've been at those meetings. One of the ways she was pushing through her views on the new buildings was through them. She was taking every chance she had to cause a fuss.

'You sure? She was causing a bit of a stir I heard. Wanted a review of what Princeton Homes were doing to the area. Trying to question their government contract? Wanted to find a way to pause the regeneration before all the old buildings were gone and it became "a nature reserve for the middle classes". I think is what she said. I read about it.'

'Hmm. Yeah,' Lowell mutters.

I think I'm jogging some memories. The little grey cells are working away in there. I continue. Maybe I'm annoying him now, but I've done my research so I may as well show him what I've got. Full disclosure.

'You know. She wanted to know exactly how many people were being rehoused in the new builds from the old blocks. They'd been promised at least thirty per cent would be. She wanted to get all the work paused. The diggers out of here. Until an investigation was mounted. Is what I heard.'

I show him my workings. I don't think he's holding out on me. Maybe it's difficult to remember everything that goes on in those meetings. But I've definitely stumbled on something here.

'You know what, yes, of course.' He clicks his fingers. Then continues. 'Little slow on the uptake there. Yes, I do. Uh huh.'

It was then I remembered that you'd be back soon,

Dad. I need to hurry him up. I don't want you to know I'm making house calls without consulting you.

I think this is making him feel interrogated somehow. Lowell is a smart guy. He knows something's up.

'I mean, I'm not the guy to ask about all this to be perfectly honest. There's a host of people there. I think they keep minutes. I mean, I think I remember her, sure. Wanted a review of a host of things to do with the building contracts. Had been working on it for a while. Uh huh. All that. It put the cat amongst the pigeons I think you could say.'

'I'll bet, weird. Way to make us feel guilty for living our lives, huh?'

'Uh huh. Right? Ha.'

I don't want to tell him any of my plans yet. I don't want to spook him. But I need to know one thing. Me and that impulse control. I have to ask.

'So, Lowell, what was the first thing you thought when you heard that girl went missing?'

He stands in the doorway. His eyes seem to plead with me to let him go. He's tired of hanging around with the mad girl. He breathes a heavy sigh and leans against the door frame. He's half in, half out of his flat.

'Which girl is this, sorry?' Slow on the uptake again. He's weary of this.

'The lawyer. Sonya? Who went missing?' I persevere.

'I didn't hear about that.'

This seems unlikely. I shake my head, speechless for a second. I don't want to show him what I'm thinking. As incurious as I was, as cut off and in my own world, I still saw the missing-poster signs, they were everywhere.

I didn't look closely because I didn't feel connected

to anyone or anything, at that point. But Lowell was as plugged in as anyone. And he knew the girl. He'd been at meetings with her. At the very least this must've come up at the most recent meeting. It'd have to. Something's going on. I'm forced to fill the pause.

'Ah, well. She did. Go missing. Funny.' Not funny ha ha, of course.

'Yeah. That's crazy. Listen, I've got to go. I won't be long.'

But I'm not letting him go. Not till Dad comes back. I can't be alone.

'No, no. Please. I want you to come and meet my father,' I plead.

'Ah. Is he over from France?'

I forgot I'd told him all about him. He has a good memory for some things.

'I'll say hi when I get back then, Lil.'

No, I want him with me. For protection. I want to keep him with me until you come back. And I don't want you to know I've been wandering around and bothering people. I need to get him in my flat. He might be my saviour.

I think about kissing him again for a second. But then my mouth opens and I go all in. 'I think someone murdered that girl. And I think that after that, he killed again. And I think I know who did it.'

His face becomes serious. A face I've never seen from him before. I'm sure he's judging me. But then, it turns out, he isn't.

'OK, I'm listening. Can you tell me how you know all this?' he says, with open body language. Ready to receive whatever I'm willing to give.

'Better than that. I can show you.'

I take his hand. We head next door.

28 September. 3.30 p.m.

'Oh, God. Fucking hell,' I whisper under my breath.

I lead him through the hallway and into my flat. I pull him in hard and lean against the wall. One of my hands on his wrist.

'What is it, Lil?' His eyes are wild now. His face ripples with concern.

'That was him. Brenner. At least that's what I call him.'

As we left Lowell's flat and headed to mine, I saw the side of Brenner's face in the hallway. He was talking to someone at the end of the hall.

'What are you saying, Lil?' Lowell says, his voice low. 'You think that guy is some sort of psychopath? Are you sure this isn't—'

'Don't. I need you to listen to me.'

'OK, but stay calm.'

I'm not sure whether he's trying to calm me down or wind me up. He's making me feel jumpy too now. That's not what I need from him. I take a step back and shake my hands. Wring them out. Trying to shake away the tension before I speak.

'He lives in the other building. I've been watching him. Watching everyone. Because I think the person that killed both of those women lives in one of these two buildings. I confronted him. Angered him. And now he's here. What's he doing here? I think he's coming for me.' It comes out without a breath. Without a thought.

'And what makes you think all this, Lil? What makes you think it's him?' he says. Holding my hand. Tender again.

I'd thought I might show him my grid. The names I've crossed off. The people I've considered. The description and the thing I'm looking for, the scar on the hand. But I don't. I think about the police and how I saw them snigger. The porcelain monkey. The poker. They seem so stupid in a vacuum. But I believe in them with all my heart.

I wonder what you'll think when you come back and catch us here with our blood up.

I wonder if Brenner's still in the hallway. I try another tack.

'Lowell. I was there. The night before the night she died. The old woman? She's the other one that was killed. And then... afterwards... I saw saw into her flat. There was a crowd around her house and I went in. Someone asked me to. And there was a porcelain figurine missing. And a weapon she used for self-defence. I think someone broke in there. In the struggle the figurine was broken and she hit him with the poker. Brenner ended up clearing up the smashed pieces and getting rid of the poker just in case it had any of his blood on it or anything like that—'

'Lily, I'm worried.' He holds my face in his hands. We're standing by my door. He has me.

'Worried about what?' I say. Biting my bottom lip and breathing.

'Have you ever had any fits? Or blackouts? Anything like that?'

This seems an odd question. I don't think he's with me. Perhaps he doesn't want to be.

'Yes. Once. Or twice. Why?' I say. My face still in his hands. Under his control.

'I'm afraid that you've been doing things. Yourself. That these are more memories than accusations. There are already things you don't remember. Versions of reality that aren't quite right.'

I'm stunned. I want to spit at him.

'I'm not saying you've done all this. I'm not saying that. Not by a long shot. But I'm worried that with you being so close to this, nd being the way you are, that's what people… that's what people might be led to think.'

The door bursts open. We turn. My head in his hands. My tears still not coming. But only just. And we're caught out.

There you stand. You've no idea what on earth is going on. Nor have I for that matter.

You're one of the world's best ignorer of things. For better or worse. I think it's a positive. I do. In some ways it's been tough for us. But in others it's been our greatest strength. You withstand whatever is thrown at you. Whatever *I* throw at you. You carry on regardless.

'It's really cool to meet you. I think I remember Lily saying you lived abroad.'

'Yes, that's right,' you say. The man of few words. Watching everything though. Taking it in. Pretending this is a normal situation as we all sit on the sofa. With everything hanging in the air, palpably.

'You over for long?' Lowell says.

'I'm not sure. Nothing in particular to do here. I'm checking in. Making sure everything's all right with my little girl,' you say.

I like you, Dad, but these pleasantries are getting in the way. Colombo never brought his dad along with him. Nor did Poirot. Or Ironside. I know I'm not a detective. But the point still stands.

I'm a great ignorer of things too. I look at Lowell, making myself forget everything he's just said to me. If I focus on that it'll tear me up from the inside. I can't believe he'd even entertain that possibility. So I just ignore it.

Then there's a lag. The kind that someone must pick up. I breathe in, ready to carry on. There are a few things the two of them need to hear. I need to bring them with me on this. But Lowell gets there first.

'I think his name's Rich. Lily. The guy you saw at the end of the corridor. And I think he's got a fob and maybe even keys. 'Cos he owns the flat at the end there. He rents it out. So I imagine he was just checking on his tenants.'

I shake my head and look at the ground. I don't care about his property portfolio. None of it makes him not a killer. It just brings him closer. Means that he's one step nearer to getting me whenever he wants to. All he needs to do is pick my lock. Like I did to his. Step inside. And snuff me out.

'Just putting Lily's mind at ease about something, Mr Gullick. Lil, he's been to a few of the meetings. I think I remember seeing him there. I think he bought himself two flats when they were being built. One to live in. One to rent out. So that's that.'

But that isn't that. It isn't that at all. He keeps pushing me and prodding me. He may not be meaning to but he is. I roll my eyes and get it out.

'Well, I suppose it's time for me to speak again and I know you both might not believe a word I say, but here it is. Lowell, I also have information that the student was seen with the man I'm looking for.'

Lowell stops, as if in freeze-frame. He's interested in this.

'So you want to know what I think? Brenner or Rich, if you must, met this girl. This upstart. At those meetings. He saw her and he liked her and hated her in equal measure. This little thing from over the council flat side. Who does she think she is? He doesn't know whether he wants fuck her or kill her.'

'Language,' you say.

Lowell, just leans and stares like he's watching a star implode.

'So he does the lot. The best of both worlds. He decides to shut this girl up. This stupid girl, who comes to his meetings and tells this capable guy what's what.'

I don't want to tell them about breaking in to his place. Don't want to tell him about the woman at the window. I'm not so sure that's what I saw at all now. That's the bit that sticks in my throat. No, I mustn't tell them that.

'He's classic alpha. I've seen him in there, roaming around like an animal. He's got a samurai sword!'

'Doesn't mean he's a murderer, for God's sake!' Dad says, uncharacteristically raising his voice.

'But there's something up with him. I know it. I can sense it!'

My thoughts are wild. I stand and flail around in the kitchen, you try to pacify me but Lowell just sits. Perhaps he thinks there's something to it. Perhaps he's just embarrassed. I want so badly for you to believe me. To come along with me on this. Both of you.

'Look. I don't know for sure about the specifics. But I know something's wrong. Brenner is my prime suspect.'

'So you're saying that this man is what?' Lowell finally pipes up. His voice is pure doubt in audio form. 'A psychopath?'

'I don't know. Maybe. A misogynist? A killer of women? Certainly. Sonya. Jean. Maybe others.' I say all this without looking at him. My nerve just about holding out.

'It's a long shot, Lil. Why would he kill that girl. Because he doesn't like her coming to his meetings? Seems a bit far-fetched,' Lowell says. Fair now. Not wanting to squash it. He indulges me just a fraction.

'Not if he thought she was a real threat somehow. To him. To his livelihood. To. His…' I trail off and look to the floor. To the laminate wood flooring that lines my flat. The same brand that lines everyone's flat in these buildings. It's simple. It's still extreme. But it's also simple.

'Lily…?' Dad says as I collect my thoughts.

'Aiden nearly bought a flat in Manchester. Do you remember, Dad?' I say.

'Yes. Yes, I think so,' you say.

'It was a few years ago. He'd sold his third book and made some decent money off it and before we decided to move into this place he thought he might get something up north, you see. As an investment. It was supposed to be part of a new development. It was going to have a load of shops, at least ten new residential buildings, restaurants, the lot, it was supposed to transform the area. Regeneration.'

'Just like here,' Lowell says. His chin resting against his fist.

'Yes. Only, the thing is, after the first two buildings went up everything stalled. Something to do with market forces. So all the work around there stopped. It was only supposed to be for a few months, a year at most, just until the building company could sort out finances and get everything moving again. But the more they waited, the less confidence anyone had that it would actually happen. So then these buildings, so popular early on, rising in value all the time, were becoming less and less valuable. Their value plummeted. Then when people's interest stopped, the knock-on effect was that if the company did get building again their rate of return on the new flats would be much lower.'

'So they pulled out?' you say.

'Yeah. The company even went bust in the end. All because of that little pause in the long-term plan. The lack of confidence it engendered. Now that area is a big hole with two very plush, but very cheap, high-rise apartment buildings in it.'

'That's the chance you take. That's what I said with this place. Twenty-five-year projects are all very well if they come to fruition. But that doesn't always happen,' says Lowell, sagely. Lost in thought and consideration.

'Yes. And if the student got this project put on hold, even for a few months, there's a good chance they'd devalue. It was a good job Aiden didn't buy that flat.

He didn't write a thing for a while after this third book. He got terrible block. Not much money coming in then. So what I'm saying is, Brenner has two of these places. They aren't cheap. Maybe his entire livelihood is tied up in them. How about that?'

As I end my oratory, we all stare down from my window towards the building entrance. Brenner is leaving, he looks around. A newspaper under his arm. We all take a step closer to the window and peer down at him. He breathes into his hands and rubs them together. It's nearly October. He turns to look around and the three of us step back in unison. Then look at each other.

'Lily,' Lowell says, with a disconcerted shake of the head. 'I think I might be with you on this.'

A little light sparks up inside me.

'At least, I'm not saying no. There could be something in it. I just don't know. But let me look into it, will you? Let me ask a few questions. Will you let me do that?'

I nod and he rises to leave. His voice is firm. But it warms me. It has hope within it. At the door he turns.

'I'm serious. Don't go to anyone with this. No one. You understand? It might be dangerous for you. If you do. So don't.'

That seemed overly stern. Heavy handed. Almost mean.

The tone changes and you feel it too. You fill your pockets with your hands. A typical sign of Dad discomfort.

'Listen, we'll talk anon. Good to meet you, Mr Gullick.'

You stride over. Bringing with you some ceremony. You stick out your hand. A man-to-man gesture. Handshakes seem funny to me. They aren't something that exist so much in my world.

Lowell stares at your hand. They don't exist much in

his either it seems. But then, he is a capable man, he does business, he does man to man. I'd imagine he has a firm handshake.

His hand clasps yours. Shakes. And I see it.

Lowell's gone. I lean against the wall by the door. Stock still. For a few moments we say nothing. Then you break the silence.

'Did you see it?' you say. Almost reluctant. Almost afraid.

'Yes, I saw it,' I say. Not moving.

You will not bring it up. You don't want to stoke the fire, so to speak. But you know what you saw. A fresh enough scar that ran from the flesh between Lowell's thumb and index finger to around the middle of his forearm on the wrist side. A hefty cut. Not made by a surgeon. Not a clean incision. But one made by something sharp.

Lowell is also six foot. A bit over that perhaps. And has blond hair. I don't know how I never saw it before.

When I replay the meeting in the hallway with the girl that night a few weeks ago, he did have a bandage then. I didn't know anything then. But he did. I think. Intermittently he wore his climbing gloves. I hardly noticed. I didn't know what I was looking for.

His arm was mostly hidden the night I saw him with a woman for the first time, his hand carefully placed on the small of her back. But I'm sure I saw it. I can see it now in my mind's eye. I don't think it's an illusion. Or a false memory.

One thing I know for sure is that you saw the scar too. Because your mood has changed. Quite dramatically.

You pace around uncomfortably. You saw it too.

You saw it too.

28 September. Evening. 6.30 p.m.

'I don't know, Lily. This could be a test, I think. Of us. You put enough things out there, some of them are going to come back and look suspicious.'

'Some of them? We're looking for man with a cut or scar on the hand and wrist. Who possibly lives in this building. Of his height and description! Earlier I questioned him and I could tell he knew the student, but he denies it.'

'Yes, but we have to be sensible. I can't give in and let you follow this sort of thing. Maybe he doesn't remember the student.'

'Doesn't remember? Everyone knows that the girl's missing. She must've come up, time and again. I can't buy that version of things.'

You turn to me, shrugging, challenging, but not chastising. I feel like you're asking me to convince you. You stand open and ready to hear me. I feel like you're giving me an 'in'. I take it. I go in hard.

'Oh, come on! I laid it all out and not even he could say a thing against it. I don't want it to be true. But did you see his face change. He was white as a sheet. It has to be him. I need to apologise to Brenner. Because we got the wrong man but the right motive.'

'So suddenly it's him. You just want a suspect.'

'Of course I want a suspect. What are you saying? Of course! Otherwise the suspect is me. Do you understand that?'

'Yes, I do,' you say, turning and looking towards the lake.

But you don't know the half of it, yet. You don't know the police think that too.

'He's a strange guy. I've seen him with a woman once. Once! The whole time I've been here. And I haven't seen her recently. Maybe he killed her too.'

'Listen to yourself. When you thought it was "Rich" it was because he was some alpha… ladies' man. Now it has to be Lowell because he's some sort of overly private outsider.' You turn, confronting me head on.

'Yes. Because they're both good profiles of a bloody murderer!'

'Ah! You're not thinking straight. You're obsessed.'

'Yes, I'm obsessed!' I shout.

Everything goes quiet. I don't know why I wasn't keeping my voice down. He's just next door. He's only beyond the partition wall. I don't think he did go out in the end. He went back to his flat. I heard him. Change of plan.

A hush. You're paranoid too. You gesture for me to keep my voice low.

I speak in hushed tones. 'Yes. I'm obsessed. But I'm in it now. There's no going back. I've been accused of murder.'

'What? By who? By the police? You didn't tell me that.'

A shiver runs down me. I was trying to hide that from

you. My last secret. I don't want to lose you now. Not when you can see I'm on to something.

'Yes, the police. They've seen me snooping around. Everyone else has been keeping their head down but I want to solve this thing. I started asking questions and now I'm a suspect.'

'You shouldn't have done that,' you whisper. 'You should've stayed out of all of this.'

'Well, it doesn't matter now, does it? I'm in. I have to see it through to the end. A woman was murdered. So, yes, I'm obsessed.'

You look at me, Dad. You don't want to take my hand on this. You knew Mum could rant and rave. Could get 'obsessed'. You know all the dangers. You've seen them all. You saw them in her. And you couldn't stop it no matter how hard you tried. You couldn't stop her ending.

The last thing you want to do is whip me up. But you also know there aren't many choices left.

'Tell me how he got that cut then? On his hand,' you say.

I smile, but cut it off in an instant. I want to show you I'm not having fun. It's not that.

'I don't know for sure. They said he was hanging around the estate. Then he tried to fight Chris and got his hand slashed for his trouble.'

Your eyes light up, Dad. You take me over to the other side of the room. The furthest point from the adjoining wall. The one I share with Lowell. You're right. It feels safer over here. We're close. Our voices so soft and low. But close enough to hear him if he makes any sudden moves in there.

'How about this? Those kids saw something. Or, at least,

he thought they did. Those pairs of eyes in the building. He thinks they saw him bump off the student. Or the old lady. So he went after them.'

'Oh, right. You're right. That could be right,' you mutter.

I'm excited, but do it all without words, the tiniest shrieks coming from my mouth as I point at you vociferously.

'Dad, do you think he could've done it? Do you think it's him?'

As you pause to consider this, taking your time, I remember that Lowell's kept a close watch on me since he saw me with the police. I remember how he changed when I told him I'd been speaking to them about Jean. The discomfort in his voice and posture. He's always been around since then. Keeping a close watch on me.

Come to think of it, maybe he's been keeping a close watch on me for a while.

'Lowell has just lost his job,' I say.

You squint a bit and rub your face. You draw a breath, taking it all in.

'But even if he's in way over his head, no money coming in, losing value on his flat isn't going to kill him, is it?'

'What about if he owns four of them?'

You look around, then move towards the kitchen cupboard. My dad, springing into action. You take a glass out but don't fill it with water. You take another and give it to me.

Then you draw up the blinds fully and take a look at the neighbourhood outside. You play everything I've told you over in your mind. Then you look at the wall that divides my flat and Lowell's. We both do. Desperate to see through it.

I've only ever seen this in films. So have you, I imagine. We don't know whether it will work. But together. We take our glasses. Place them to our ears. Push them against the crisp white wall. And listen.

Part Ten: The Hastings Rarities

28 September. 7.15 p.m.

SWM – Lowell – Riverview Apartments – No visibility, strong winds, 15 degrees – Singular – Blond hair, male – 6′ approx. – Social, dominant

Let me remind you of a few things about the Hastings Rarities.

So the story goes, George Bristow, a gunsmith and taxidermist from the Hastings area, recorded a series of sightings between 1892 and 1930, which led to an incredible twenty-nine bird species or subspecies being added to the British Birds List.

However, many years later these sightings were heavily disputed. In fact, the analyst John Nelder suggested that anything recorded within a twenty-mile radius of Hastings during that time should be literally stripped from the records and reference books. He was calling George Bristow a bare-faced liar. It was a serious business.

The upshot was that five hundred and fifty entries, relating to between eighty and ninety species, were rejected. Because, as we all know, once someone says they've seen something then imaginations tend to run wild.

Of course, George Bristow, as you well know, was discovered to be an utter fraudster. He would import stuffed birds from abroad, then record a sighting of that bird in the Hastings area, which would allow him to then sell the thing as a rare example of the species found far outside of its more usual habitat. He made a tidy profit using this method from wealthy ornithologists like Walter Rothschild.

The only twist in the tale comes with what we know now. That almost immediately after all this, nearly all of these eighty or ninety species did have confirmed bona fide sightings on these shores.

This means there are two possible morals to this story.

There's an understandable school of thought that says George Bristow did see some or maybe even all of the birds he claimed to. But the manner in which he went about it and the scale of his incredible discoveries made everyone think he was a liar.

The second moral is that some lies, even errors and guesses, do turn out to be true.

I consider telling you all this. I consider reminding you about the Hasting's Rarities. But I don't.

Instead we listen. Creaks. The occasional footstep. His shoes scuff the laminate flooring as he wanders around in there. Or is it the sound of pipes? Our ears strain for something telling.

'He's wandering around in there. He's uncomfortable,' I say, speculating.

I look at you, a glass placed to each of our ears. I feel

young. It's good to have you back. Playing with me. It's nice to have company. We're back in the hide.

'If we heard a phone call. One where he gives it all away. Hard evidence. That would be something, but...'

'I've already bugged one flat, Dad. It didn't go well.'

'Christ. Well, I'm not suggesting that. I'm not suggesting anything like that. We don't want do anything silly, Lily Anna,' you say, still being careful with me. Not stoking the fire but trying to solve a problem. Like you're rewiring a plug for me. Or bleeding a radiator, to improve the efficiency of my heating system.

'I know, Dad.'

I was so scared to tell you about all of this. I didn't know what you'd do or say. But here you are. Practical to the last. Entertaining all this, at least. On my side. My dad.

I walk around uncomfortable. I'll bet Lowell is doing the same in there. He's probably replaying our last conversation. Rolling it around like a marble in his head.

He could be listening to us too, a glass against the wall. Trying to figure out what we know. And if he's going to have to do something about it.

'Well, I do have one idea,' you say from the bedroom.

The binoculars are back in your hand and you're roaming around. Checking what you can see from window to window.

'I can't quite get a good angle,' You say, lost in the lens, adjusting the dial. Like father like daughter.

You crouch, looking for a vantage point. This seems odd to me. No matter how you twist your body, however expert you are, using old tricks or new, you can't see into the building next door. The geometry isn't right.

'What are you doing, Dad?'

'See that window, there? Sixth floor, blinds down?'

'Yes.'

'I'm getting a reflection off it. So now if I can get the right angle, I can get the outline of him in there. Shadows and light mostly, but it's better than nothing. This is just to see what we can see, you understand. Out of interest. Just to take a little look. Understand?'

'I understand.' I try to hold in my excitement but fail. My fingers twitch.

You lodge yourself up against a wall. Your right shoulder leaning into it. You get low to steady yourself. It's textbook. Like you've done it before. I wait patiently. I'm already planning my next move. I remember I have his number. He gave it to me the other day. In case I needed it. Just in case.

'There he is,' you say, coolly.

'You see him?'

'Yes. He's moving around. Steadily. Side to side,' you say, rational, without drama. Simple facts for our journal.

I imagine some strange ritual. In there. In that flat. A ritual that doesn't make a sound. A mime. A silent act in his silent flat. My bedroom backs on to his. We could be in the same bed if you took the wall away. I picture the hours I was living here. My illusions not so abstract by comparison. Because next door was him. Silently. Making things perhaps. But what? Torture implement? Weapon? Maybe he's sawing. Maybe he's sawing something up.

'I think he's ironing a shirt,' you say.

'That's not very incriminating,' I say, disappointed. 'This isn't exactly gold, Dad,' I say. Back in the hide and nothing to see. The waiting hours.

'Hang on he's coming towards the window.' You shift a bit.

'Shouldn't you get out of sight?' I pull on your arm. 'Can he see you? In the reflection?' I'm worried now. We don't want to give ourselves away. Not when we're so close. Not when he's so close.

'Not sure. I'm not quite sure.'

'Dad!' I say, snatching the binoculars off you and pulling you to the side. 'If we can see him. He can see us.'

But you're still watching. Not giving up.

'I'll just keep a lookout. With the naked eye. It's less conspicuous'

'Don't let him see you,' I warn.

'He's at the window now.'

'What's he doing?'

'He's right there.'

'Dad, careful.'

'He's closed his blind.'

I feel safer with you here. But that doesn't mean we're safe.

'Did he see you? Dad? Did he see you?'

We need to do something. I clutch my phone hard inside my pocket.

28 September. 8.55 p.m.

I've sent a text, but there's no response. Not yet. They didn't get back to me last time. They didn't even show their faces. They're hardly reliable. But I hope they come back to me this time. Because I really need them.

I was nervous to tell you about the text, so I didn't. But then I'm a master of suppression at this point. I didn't think you'd want me to do it. I didn't think you'd think it would even work. Because, come to think of it, you're not even sure the people I've texted exist.

'Check number attached. This is guy u saw. I've got him. Need him out of his flat. Plse txt him from this number. Threaten him. Tell him anything. Need ten minutes in there. Plse.'

I sent it an hour ago. I look at my phone. It obstinately refuses to bleep. I might have to send another to hurry it all up. It needs to happen tonight.

You've settled down on the sofa. Pensively pushing it all around in your mind, like a reluctant detective. I'm not sure if you're indulging me to pacify me. Or if you have a plan too. Intermittently, you glance towards the wall and then to me.

You wouldn't like the second part of the plan. You'd have several reservations. You'd think it was dangerous. You'd think it would be breaking the law. You don't want me to be caught in the wrong place at the wrong time. You wouldn't want me to get into any real trouble. I'm afraid of all these things too. But I don't think we have any other choices left. We wait.

I send another message. To hurry them up. Or just in case the last one got lost. Or in case they respond better to pleading than straightforward questions. Or maybe it's just because it makes me feel a little less helpless.

'Pls. Need to get in there. In danger otherwise. We're so close.'

I put my phone back on the glass coffee table. I check it's not on silent. Twice. I wait ten minutes. I check it again. I check the volume is up. I check I have signal. I look at Terrence. Unaware of everything. His simple face knowing neither great highs nor lows. Contentment being food in his bowl. Water in his dish.

You stroke his head. We're still in silence. Giving nothing away. Just in case Lowell's listening somehow. Or maybe we've just run out of things to say. We wait.

29 September. The small hours.

The sound of Lowell's door closing. I wake and check my phone. It's 6 a.m. Both of us have fallen asleep on the sofa. I place a blanket over you gently and put my eye to the peephole. I wait. Terrence stirs. I put my finger over my pursed lips to hush him. As if he understands. Footsteps down the hallway. We stay as quiet as mice. You just sleep and I want it to stay that way. I search around for my bag, my tools for breaking and entering already packed and ready to go.

Then more footsteps. He's coming back. More hasty this time. We wait. Terrence and I. I feel he's about to bark. I put my hand over his mouth. Holding his jaw shut. He looks at me with disdain. But stays silent. I don't want Lowell to hear a peep out of us. I don't want him to think about what we're up to at all.

He wasn't out there long. There was a noise and something opening. Some rustling around. Then he passed our door again. I see him through the enlarged peephole. He's so close I gasp. His blurred image. His face, magnified to the size of a cinema screen. Then I hear his door slam shut.

He's back in his hide. I reach for my glass. Still holding Terrence. I put my ear to it. And hold the glass to the wall.

He's searching around. I just hear rumbling. It could be anything. He could be throwing bags about. Or it could be the pipes. It could be distant diggers. Or him, searching for a knife. I can't tell.

I stand waiting. Like a musical statue. My phone bleeps. It's early for correspondence.

I reach over to cut it off. Just in case.

I read the text: 'It's done. Dunno if he'll buy it. But it's done.'

I'm not sure what took him so long but he's come through.

Something is going on in there. Is he buying it? I wonder how much he can hear through the walls. They can't be that thick In these newbuilds. I'm sure that if you pressed your ear against our flat, from the other side, and listened hard enough, you could hear us breathing.

I keep listening.

A door slams, wildly. I jump. I'm worried you'll wake, but you don't. Terrence lies down, cool as milk. Lowell's outline flashes past. I see it. I hear his feet go down the hallway. Then down the stairs. No lift for him. He's in haste. The footsteps get quieter. Dying away.

I keep looking through the peephole. Just in case.

It's time. I count down with my fingers as I get everything I need.

Ten, nine. It's a slow ten. Just to be sure he's gone. I grab my bag.

Eight, seven. I find a bone for Terrence.

Six, Five. I breathe. Let's go. Show time.

Four. A noise in the corridor.

It's an Indian family with their child in a buggy. I don't know them. I have no names for them. They could be new to the neighbourhood. Maybe off on holiday. How nice. Normal people aren't starting their day yet. Hope you have a nice time. Now get a move on. I watch as they roll along the corridor and wait for the lift.

Three, two. I resume the count. The lift pings. It opens.

One. They step inside. The sound of the lift closing.

I push open the front door and turn right. Towards Lowell's place.

My metal rods are in the keyhole. I'm patient. I'm glad you're not watching me do this. It would make me nervous. You have to look good doing everything in front of your dad. Even breaking and entering.

I'm practised by now. I keep my movements smooth. I want it to be quiet. I don't want to rouse anyone.

The sound of the lift. I get ready to pull out of the manoeuvre.

Then the lock gives and we're in. It all happens in a matter of milliseconds. I push the door open, step quickly inside and close it behind me.

I've applied gloves, just in case. I've already left fingerprints in two other flats. I resolve not to leave anything of myself behind here.

I take a look at the place. I wanted to see inside for so long. Now I've been in here twice in twenty-four hours.

Lowell is a reader. The place is covered in books. Some ordinary. Some extraordinary. Contemporary American fiction. A lot on Egypt. Some medical books. Some philosophy. Cookery books and teach yourself Spanish. I should be looking for something a bit more incriminating than a strange library history but I can't help myself. I'm curious. Old habits die hard.

I turn and open the bedroom door and start rifling through his wardrobe. I'm thorough. Lines and lines of slacks and shirts. The same slacks. The same white shirts. Order is clearly a priority. I head to the spare room.

I'm ready to hustle into his cupboard at any moment. If he comes home. I scope out the hiding places, just in case. Yes, the wardrobe would be the one if he bursts in.

I search his drawers. Lines of white underwear. Drawers and drawers of plain white socks and T-shirts. That's all.

I can't help noticing Lowell is a hoarder. There's meticulous order about the place, but his wardrobe could give the Kardashians a run for their money. Not in style but in volume; it's like he's never thrown anything away. Old shirts and jeans in the bottom of the wardrobe. A ton of them. Plus, there are tidily kept newspapers, with crosswords finished on pencil in each. Reams of them. Catalogued.

I head to the bathroom and look under the sink. Nothing. Fifty different aftershaves. A perfectly stocked male cosmetics drawer. It's as if he knew he was having guests. I wish I could keep my place so tidy.

I take the top off the toilet and take a look to see if he's stuffed anything into it, where the handle attaches to the pumping system. Inside. But there's nothing there. I haven't got long and we need my smoking gun. Blood in the hallway. Gloves thrown carelessly into the bin.

I open the bin. All I see is an empty bin liner.

He could have just taken it. The body. In fact, he could've taken it at any time. Maybe even when I saw him in the recycle room. He could've been disposing of everything right before my eyes.

I'm getting desperate. I rifle round behind books and a big oak bookshelf. I check behind his speakers and under his sofa. I check his coffee table. I give his fashionable standing lamp the once-over. Lowell has excellent taste. Scandinavian furniture. Tidy and sleek. Wood and pottery. His drawers only show an excellent selection of herbal teas and designer cutlery. I turn and hear a noise behind me.

'Ahh!' I shout. Barely concealing an all-out scream.

It's you. You must've woken up. Twigged. Stepped into the hallway and seen Lowell's door slightly open. Assumed the rest and opened it. You always said you could read me like a book.

I hold out a hand. Like you used to do to bar me from crossing the road when it was busy. It pleads to give me a couple more seconds. I turn and see the suitcase again. You go to grab me and pull me out of there. I struggle towards it. You're pulling me back with everything you have, but I'm stronger now. I break away, there's nothing you can do.

I lift it up. A dark fluid reveals itself from under the case. It languidly drips out and onto the wood laminate floor beneath.

You raise a whispered voice to try to get me out of there.

Your palm goes in front of your mouth. As I start to unzip it. It is definitely the source of the smell I noticed when last I was here. It oozes under my feet as I unzip. I'm sure it's blood. He must've had her in the freezer to try to keep the smell to a minimum. To keep it from decomposing before he decided what he was going to do with it.

As I struggle with the zip, I look at you.

It's only then that I see him behind you.

He coshes you hard on the head. Then he grabs a kitchen knife. But I see his move and grab for it too. You crawl into the corridor, blood coming from your head; it runs down the back of your neck.

I struggle with him. He's caught us red-handed. He knows we've seen everything and we have to go. He wants to dispose of us. He and I hold each other's hands. They're clasped tightly around the handle of the knife.

I lean in and bite him hard on the wrist. He drops the kitchen knife and I get past him into the corridor but he's locked the door. I turn the lock and open it as I see you make it into the bedroom and slam the door. My hand is on the handle when I feel a kick from behind me.

'Bitch!' Lowell shouts. 'Come here, you stupid bitch.'

He's got me and he's trying drag me back into the kitchen. He wants me in that freezer. He'll knock me out first. Then cut my throat. I can see it coming. But there's no time for daydreams. Whatever happens will be here soon enough. He grabs his cosh and hits me on the head with it. My adrenaline is so high I barely feel the contact against my skull, but my legs give up the fight.

He tries to hit me again but it's a glancing blow. It's messy. I get under it and knee him in the groin. He shouts.

I try to open the door again but he gets me by the throat.

He squeezes. He lifts me up and pushes me against the door. I hear my neck make sounds I'm not ordering it to make. He's strong. Every bit of him is focused in on choking the life out of me.

My eyes roll back. I feel like I glimpse bone.

Then I see him again. He nods. Yes.

He keeps me held off the ground. He looks me in the eye.

I start to lose consciousness. My last thought is about you. How I brought you here. How stupid I've been. I hope you get out of this.

I struggle and squeal. But I've got no fight left in me.

My legs, a foot off the ground, can only gently kick back. And tap his front door. That's the sound hear as I start to lose consciousness.

Tap, tap. Knock, knock.

29 September. 6.35 a.m.

Some could see this as an epitaph. I address it all to you, because you were my accomplice. You believed in me. Without you I wouldn't have made it. So this is all for you.

I do something I've never even considered next. I draw my head back. This is not imitative behaviour. I don't know where it's come from. I certainly haven't seen anyone do it before. Not in real life. I throw my head forward as I stare at his spitting, gurning face and smash my forehead into it.

I connect with his nose. Which gives in easily against my forehead. I can feel it.

It's like cracking an egg. Easy.

It's a messy blow and it hurts me too. But it hurts him more. I don't know what I'm doing really. It's all animal instinct now.

My head throbs. His festoons with blood. His hands immediately reach for his face, releasing his hold on me. I grab at the door, force myself through it and run. Then I hear it open and know he's not that far behind me.

He's so close, I can't stop. He'd be on me again before I

even got my key out. I pass my door. No time to grab my knife from my bag, the only moment in my life I actually need it. I jump down flights of stairs. I don't have a plan. I can hear him shouting but I don't listen to the words. Flecks of his blood fall from his head in between the flights of stairs and onto the ground floor carpet.

I knock on one or two doors on the ground floor as I come past, desperately hoping someone might hear the commotion and come out. It might slow him down at least. I want to get to the concierge office. That's my den. He can't get me once I'm there.

No one answers. No one stirs. Everyone keeps themselves to themselves in this place. Most of the flats aren't even occupied. The others are filled with people who wouldn't lift a finger for anyone else. Living their solitary lives. With their broadband and their Netflix. I hit the green button. And I run. Desperately. For my life.

I cut through the air. I scream and shout. As Lowell gains on me a little. Surely someone will hear the racket. A Samaritan. Or a security guard. They caught me quick enough in broad daylight. But racket means trouble. Means 'this is nothing to do with me'. Means 'I'm sure it'll blow over in the morning'. Like the noise of cats fighting or foxes having sex.

If I keep going straight towards the Concierge office he'll cut me off before I get there. He's faster than me. So I head left. Towards the dark. Towards the estate. It's the sort of choice that often doesn't end well. We're coming to his domain. Where he killed the last ones. But I've at least got a bit of a head start this way. Maybe I can lose him. In the dark.

I go past Alaska House. I want to shout. To see if

anything might come out to help me. But they may be gone by now. I remember the wrecking ball is about to bring the place down in a matter of hours. I turn to see him as the light stops and we enter the part of the estate that is only darkness. His face, red and desperate, any smile he had when I was in his lair now gone, fades into the black. And mine does too.

I kick off my shoes to mask the sound. He's behind me. Something sharp, maybe glass, crunches under my feet. But I daren't cry out. I have to keep running. Then I see a skip. Left there by the workmen. I think about how I can get to it.

'Lily! Lily!' He screams.

Guttural and raw. Deep from within him. Devilish. It terrifies me.

'Come back here you mad bitch!'

Breathe in through your nose. For fifteen. Out through your mouth. For ten. Stay calm. I feel my feet bleeding onto the concrete.

And then his hand grips my waist from behind. He gets a hold of my shirt. He has me. I feel his skin, wet with his blood. His voice echoes around the buildings. I'm sure we can be heard for miles. But no one comes.

I'm going to die here. Metres from people's homes. The million pound penthouses. To the new media middle classes in their first flats. To the people hanging on to their homes in the estates. Right in front of Canada House. With its residents with little time left on one side and it's swathes of evacuated rooms on the other. In a few days. A missing-poster sign will go up. People will walk past it. And no one will care.

He grapples me to the ground. We roll along the tarmac.

His hands go for my throat again. His left hand gets to me and starts to squeeze. I feel the tenderness and bruising around my neck. He straddles me. Holding my hands down while laying his forearm across my throat, all with his left arm. He's so much stronger than me.

I lie under him. Powerless. As he grabs his cosh with his right hand. A distant car passes and lights up his face. He seems happier. He feels like it's all over. He must've shut the student up this way. Sonya, who wanted to fuck up his life. Wanted to bankrupt this capable man. To destroy him. Well, Lowell's the pragmatic type. He solves problems.

A car comes past again. I see the cosh raised in his fist. I'll bet he used that on Jean and the student. Who then lay stuffed into the suitcase until he thought the time was right to get rid of her. I manage to get my left hand free. But he brings the cosh down.

I dodge out of the way of it. It thumps the concrete next to me with incredible force. It's a long, tough leather strap, which forms into a large ball at the top. Easy to hold. Heavily weighted. He probably read a book about one. He probably got one on ebay. It's all part of it. For him, I imagine. The gear. He's still got me.

He mumbles and I squeal. We fight. Like brother and sister. Like man and wife. He brings it up again. I see the cosh. Bloodied from your head. And God knows what else. A car comes past on the road far behind us and it's distant headlamps light him again. I grab something from my pocket.

He starts to bring it down. But I get there first. Stabbing into his side with everything I have, just under his ribs. A Princeton Homes pen. They're always giving them out.

It's lucky I picked one up. I push him off as he pulls it out of him and moans.

I run to the other side of Canada House. The deserted side. But I hear his echo. He's back up and I can't see where he is. He could be to my left or right. It sounds like there are two of them. It could be my mind playing tricks. The sound seems to get closer from either side. I feel my keys in my pocket. I don't want to use my torch and give myself away. He's still coming.

Then I see the skip. I run over and place my hands on it. I would normally be very careful about this. Who knows what's in there. But this isn't an ideal situation. I don't know how much longer I can hold him off. I need to wait for back up. I lift myself up and into it. As quietly as I can.

Then dive down into the muck. The sawdust and mattresses. The nails and wood cut offs. I try to control my breathing. I can hear him getting closer.

29 September. 6.45 a.m.

I put my cheek against the cold metal on the inside of the skip. I don't feel like crying. I don't feel like feeling sorry for myself. I feel like getting out of here alive. For a moment I think I hear distant sirens, but it could be my imagination. They may not be for me anyway. They may be going down to Green Lanes or along the Seven Sisters Road. This is London, after all.

A piece of wood pokes into my shin. It's uncomfortable but hasn't broken the skin. There is a mattress under me and I try to hold my body away from some sharp metal springs on my left. My body quivers as I try to maintain this position. There aren't many hiding places here. He would've heard my footsteps if I'd left the area. As I would have heard his.

Somewhere above me is Canada House. It strikes me how strange it is that half the building is occupied, the other half evacuated and growing mould, waiting for its executioner. Like Siamese twins – one living, one long since deceased. I smell something. Is there something leaking below me? Or bleeding? I move my left hand around and touch what feels like skin. A shiver takes over my body. I think there's someone next to me. I want to look. But I don't want to scream. I reach for my tiny torch key.

My hand feels up and I think I have their clothes. A dress. I think what I can feel is its leg. It's cold. Now I come to think of it, I think I can smell the same scent that was in Lowell's house. It must be human flesh. I try to ignore it, but that's a tough thing to do.

Don't look, I tell myself. *Don't look.* The footsteps can be heard again. Two lots. Or one? I can't tell. Keep quiet.

I have to look. I'm deep under wooden boards and a mattress so the chances are he won't see the key light. I turn my head to meet whatever this is next to me. Then I press the button. Light streams onto a face.

I screw up my eyes and try to keep my breathing slow. I put my hand to it. Who is this? The woman I saw Lowell with? Another victim? My mind races. I touch her cold face. I am so close to it. I hear the footsteps closer. Maybe they've passed by me.

It's plastic. I tap its cheek once, quietly. To make sure. It's a mannequin. It has no legs. Just a torso. A red velvet dress stretched across its body. I breathe a sigh of relief. This place is uncomfortable enough without sharing it with a dead body. I free my hand. I relax for a moment. Lean into the mattress and pull my leg away from the piece of timber and my side from the metal. I breathe a silent sigh. Then the wooden board is torn from above me.

I rise, holding the timber. What once was part of a bunk bed, I think. I smash it over the figure's head. It reels back in shock. For a moment I wonder who it is I've hit. It could be a security guard or passing stranger come to help me.

It's Lowell. I look into his eyes. I throw my makeshift

weapon at him, jump out and run, as he collects himself after my blow. If there was someone else around I don't see them now.

I run towards the derelict side of Canada House. I see a grate wrenched open and I lift myself inside. I turn and try to push the grate closed but he gets his fingers under it in time. I see him through the gap. His eyes stare at me. Inhuman now. All of my old neighbour gone. His face, a bloody mess. I slam my fist against his fingers and run.

'Fucking bitch!' he shouts.

I turn as I go up the stairs. Lighting my way with the torch. There's no going back. Only going up. There must be people just on the other side of this building, getting ready to start their day, it's nearly beginning to get light outside. I keep going up. I hear the sound of him pulling the grate open again.

I slip. My bloody feet squelch against the moss and weeds as I get back to my feet. Maybe if I can get far enough ahead of him I can hide out in one the rooms. Or maybe I can get to the roof.

'Come here! Lily!' he shouts.

This place suddenly seems like an asylum. Two people of questionable sanity chasing each in a concrete playground. I'm tiring. He sounds quite far behind me. I go up and up. On the eighth floor I open the door to the corridor and close it behind me.

I look for a stick or something to bar it with but I can't see anything. The windows are completely broken open here and the dim light trickles in. No metal slats on these windows.

Light, the smallest glimmer from the distant streetlights. Enough to for me to see the desolate space. Bits of it already knocked down. Wires peep out from in between bricks like weeds. I duck into the last room on the left and keep my back against the wall.

Then the door opens. He steps inside. Nowhere to run. I grip my key in my fist.

29 September. 6.55 a.m.

My back leans against the cold, damp wall. I shiver. Summer is over. Balcony furniture will be taken in. Barbecues, not strictly allowed anyway, will be put in storerooms. Summer clothes will go into suitcases and jumpers will get stuffed into draws. I breathe in the damp.

The footsteps are lethargic. I beg them to come closer. I can't stand the waiting. Then they seem to get further away. A pause. Silence. Outside it has begun to rain. I can hear it. See it slightly if I chance a look out of the hole next to me. What was a window. The rain drifts in, half lit. And I hear the door close.

I count to ten. He must have gone upstairs. If I can creep downstairs and out of the building fast enough I can make a break for the concierge and they can call the police. We have all we need. We have a body in a suitcase. Scars he's given us. Blood he's spilt. Mine and yours.

Nine, ten. I lift my body and go to the doorway. Smoothly, slowly, I peek out into the corridor. His hand engulfs my face and he takes me into the room. He has me now. I try to scream but I can't. Even if I could no one would hear. This is it. I've fallen into his trap. I think of you. Whether you'll have called it in already. But I don't hear any sirens any more.

He has me. He shakes his head as he holds me down. This time. For the last time. My body has given up. He bleeds, but he's not weak. He's not going to let me go. He has me right where he wants me. He could do anything. Strangling is difficult I've heard. But he might have enough in him. Or he might beat me to death with the cosh. He holds it up. I'm so scared.

I start to shake. A fit that consumes my body. He stops. He stares at me. He steps back. He's wondering whether any more violence is necessary. Whether I might expire without him having to go to the trouble of exerting himself any further. I stare at him as my body convulses. I think he might smile for a moment but he's also confused. Disgusted. His nose is broken, I think. His right nostril sags. It bleeds. He said the kids were animals. But that's exactly what he looks like.

Every bit of my body vibrates. My head bangs against the concrete floor. I might swallow my tongue. I gag. I splutter. He sees it all. Watching, fascinated. All I can do is stay alive. Hope it stops. But even when I do, he'll still be there. My body smashes against the floor. My eyes fall back in my head, just as they did last time. I close my eyes and wonder whether death will come next.

Blackness.

When I open them, it has subsided. He stands over me. I am still in the nightmare. But now I can't move. I breathe in with effort. I am catatonic again. I want to shout out but I have nothing. My key light flickers somewhere next to me, lighting us both. Me. Still. Paralysed. Him. Just looking.

'You're going to die here,' he says.

I try to speak. Blink even. I try to shout back. But I can't.

He kneels over me. He holds my face in his hands. 'You're going to die here because you couldn't control yourself.'

He touches my hair. He kisses my mouth. Salty. Blood and sweat. I lie still.

'I'm sorry. I'm really fucking sorry, Lily. But you should've stayed out of my fucking flat! What else can I do now, but this?'

He lies down next to me and speaks softly. It's like we're sharing a bed. 'You women just can't do as you're fucking told, can you? Sonya couldn't keep her mouth shut. Everyone else just quietly moved on. Let us all live here and took it. The free market. Right? But no! She couldn't do it. She had to be a bitch about it. So what could I do? Tell me. What can I do? My hands are tied.'

It's intimate. Like therapy.

'You're quiet. It's nice. It's better.'

His smile fades.

'I'm going to get what I deserve. I've worked too hard for some stupid, weak cunts to take it away from me on a technicality. Those animals around here. You know what those fucking rats are like. You hate those fucking cockroaches as much as I do, right? They can't control themselves! They disturbed me when I was trying to do a few chores over there. I could've got rid of the suitcase there… do you see? So, it's their fault you're in this mess.

Not mine! I'll have to finish a few of them off too, eventually.'

His eyes are wet. He wants forgiveness. He wants my blessing. As a friend.

'Oh, Lil. Look at you.'

He holds both my thighs. Leans over me. Looks into me. It's intimate. I'd grab him if I could. Grab his balls. Or his face and pull at the skin till I ripped something. But I can't.

'Anyone would've done the same. When put in a position like mine. You think the old neighbour would think twice? I mean, she stuck a poker in me. Look at that!'

He lifts up his shirt and there, indeed, under his ribs on the right side, the other side to where I stabbed the pen into him, is a healing scab-like mark under his ribs.

'It'll all be over so soon. This won't even hurt, I promise. You won't feel a thing.'

He rises and grips the cosh. This is it. All I can do is feel and hear.

His voice. The sound of distant cars. And rain.

'You know, I just really wish I hadn't seen you coming back from her house that night. Because then I couldn't be sure about you either. That really cut me up, I swear.'

A tear rolls down my face. It's been such a long time since I've felt that feeling. I say goodbye to you mentally. To Aiden. To this place.

'In a way, you killed her by going over there. Making me suspicious. So it's your fault too... when you think about it... we're in this together. But I forgive you. So, forgive me too?'

He grips his weapon. And raises it. I close my eyes. I close them.

'You know. I see everything round here too. Absolutely everything.'

It all happens so quickly. He breathes in to summon himself to do it. Then I reach for my key light. Grab it. And ram my key into his right eye. It sticks in firm. Like a nail into a wall. But easier. Like a golf tee into turf. He falls back. Blood leaks out from him.

His legs wriggle. I see them as I rise. I stand over him. He seems to wink at me. He winks at me, Dad. I'm not making it up. One eye a goner. The other one still staring at me. Just to let me know he's still watching.

I look. It's fascinating. But grotesque. Even I have to turn away. I hear the sirens closer now. You see, when I closed my eyes I knew I could move again. I feel so much better now.

He tries to get up, but he can't. Now he's the one that can't move. I'm not sure if he's conscious or not, but I speak anyway.

'They're going to lock you away. I'm going to find that body now, Lowell.'

I turn to go. But then I hear him speak.

I turn back, calmly. I know he can't get up. His body is in shock. He's in so much pain.

'What did you say?' I say, standing over him.

His face is half smile, half fear. From the floor. He summons what sounds like a laugh. Through the blood.

'There is no body,' he drawls. Snake-like.

His head rolls back and thuds against the floor. He passes out. I turn to leave. Fast. I have to go and get that case. I have to. I'm going back to his flat. I'm not mad. I know what I saw.

I remember my keys are in his eye. I've no time to be

tentative. I bend down and pull it out. It makes the sound of a kiss. I wipe them down as I hurry out of there.

Outside, the day has begun. The early starters get on collapsible bikes or head towards the Tube. I pass the workmen heading to Alaska House. Setting up for another demolition. I walk past the signs again. The road is blocked off. I'm reminded that today is the big one. September the twenty-ninth. The biggest demolition of them all.

I sprint into my building and back up my corridor. I try Lowell's door and it's open. Inside, you are sat up and leaning against the bed. But I pass you. Time is still of the essence. I head towards where I saw the suitcase.

The case. The case isn't there. Nor is the fluid or residue that dripped from it. It's impossible.

'Dad? Dad? Where is the case?' I say, imploringly.

'What?'

'The case, Dad. The suitcase. Did someone come and take it?'

'I don't think so,' you mutter.

It's nowhere to be seen. Someone must have taken it while you were out.

'I tried to call the police,' you say, stirring. 'But the lines are down.'

I should stop and check how you are. I want to do that. I lean down to you and check your head wound.

Then it all starts up.

Rumble. Rumble. Rumble. Rumble.

I stand. It's obvious now. Where to put a body to make sure it won't be found. To make sure it's hidden among a ton of debris. In a suitcase. And taken away on a skip and put in landfill. Like a forgotten family heirloom from a forgotten family. Like a crucifix. They're stoking up the machines. Soon the demolition will begin.

I give you my mobile phone.

'Dad. Dad! If you get out onto the balcony you should just get enough signal to call the police. Do you understand?'

'Yes. Go. Find it. Go.'

'Call the police. Tell them what happened. Tell them to come to the building site right away.'

I push the phone into your hand and run towards Alaska House.

29 September. 7.35 a.m. Sunrise.

I run fast past the slow-moving commuters. I'm the only one in a hurry this morning. I look at the estate as I go, turning everything over in my mind.

I like it here. The whole of life is here. I'd hate to have to move away. But I doubt myself and Lowell would make great neighbours if somehow he gets away with this thing. Which is looking more likely. Because I don't know for sure I'm right about this. About where the suitcase is. Not for sure.

The thought crosses my mind that I could bolt now. I know it's usually the guilty that run but I think for a moment I could come with you. Go to France and start again. Skip all this. The ramifications. The repercussions and what not. I could call off the search now and make a run for it while I still can. I've enough cash for a last-minute ticket to Calais. I could wait for you there. You could help me start a new life.

But no. I like it here. I like the trees. I like the types of people. Despite their taciturn nature. Despite the fact they're always looking at their phones. Despite the queue for the escalator. I like the variation of every day. I love this city. The big city I always dreamed of coming to when I was a kid. London breathes with people and I don't want to be pushed out of it.

Getting out of this city would be death for me anyway, so I may as well stay and fight.

Rumble. Rumble. Rumble. Rumble.

Then I see the site. The wrecking ball gearing up to start the day.

I slow down, looking for my entry point. This is a bigger site than usual. And there are more workers around than normal. But sometimes overstaffing can mean carelessness. Can mean 'someone else will deal with it'. Can mean gaps to exploit. And it's not like they're expecting a madwoman to run into a building that's about to be demolished anyway.

I stop and watch. Picking my man. I see a figure, no more than a boy, laconically carrying some cones on the west side of the building.

The rumble and crunch is about to become more defined. The ball will soon tear into brick. Instinctively, I become poised. My body ripples with excitement. I'm about to do it and no one can stop me. A feeling comes over me like when animals sense a storm. Danger is near and I'm about to run straight into it.

Rumble. Rumble. Rumble. Rumble.

I see a gap where a metal slat has been pulled open on the ground floor.

I watch. Everything that happened in there is about to be destroyed. The wallpaper. Memories of people who once lived there. I want to see it all come down. I want to bathe in the water and dust as it blows into my face. I want that now. I want it all. So I'm going to step inside.

Rumble. Rumble. Rumble. Rumble.

I see the wrecking ball roaming around, readying itself to hit. But it can't start till 8 a.m. That's the law. That gives me time. I see the boy carrying the cones drop a few and bend down to pick them up. I make a dash for it. I pass him, not too far behind him, but the noise of shouting and chaos masks my route and I make it to the opening on the ground floor and swiftly hoist myself inside.

I search the bottom floor. Using my key light. It looks like they've started work on the insides this morning, knocking down the inner walls for easier demolition. I scramble through the debris and check the corners of this open-plan floor and see nothing. I head towards the stairs and the second floor as the rumble of the machines gets louder outside.

I stumble to the second. I haven't had much sleep. I drive my body on. There isn't much time. They don't know I'm in here. Every step I take means I have to take another back. At the end of the corridor on the first floor I see a figure.

He comes to greet me. This place should've been evacuated. It's Aiden. I turn and head up to the third floor. He sprints up the stairs after me.

'Darling, come on. What are you doing, let's get out of here.'

'Shut up,' I say. I dreamed him into existence. But I want him to go away for good now.

'Please. Come on. Let's go back home and get back to normal. You can have the day off. I'll make you breakfast. Then you need to sleep,' he says.

'No, go away, Aiden. Please.'

I reach the third floor, nothing. I go towards the fourth. The shouts outside rise. The machines strike up in earnest. It's deafening being this close. Being so close to everything, to demolition. To extinction. The fourth floor has nothing. Aiden still follows.

'Vot is zee matter, darleeng? Are you tired, Lil, girl? Come on home,' he says, mocking me.

'You aren't real. You arsehole.' Now I am crying. The tears come. 'You aren't real. So… so, fuck off!'

'Baby. Lily. My Lily. Vot is da meaning of this?' he says. A pleading look on his face. He seems so fragile.

I grab him by the shirt and pull him towards me. 'I'm sorry. But I've told you. I don't want you to go. I don't want that. But that's the way it has to be. You have to leave. You have to. Now!'

I push him hard and he falls over the rail and down into the ground below. Tears fill my eyes as I reach the fifth floor and see something in the corner against the wall. I dash towards it.

It must be close to 8 a.m.

Rumble. Rumble. Rumble. Rumble.

I get close to it. It's the suitcase. I try to pick it up. I have to get it downstairs. There's no time. It's so heavy. I drag it away.

The noise is deafening. It rises and rises. And when I think it can get no louder, it somehow does. I reach for the zip again.

Rumble. Rumble. Rumble. Crunch.

The wrecking ball hits. A couple of floors above me I'd guess. I fall. I drag the suitcase towards me. Even if it's all for nothing. Even if I don't make it out of here I have to know. I want to see the flesh.

The zip is stuck. The case is full of something. I pull hard. The wrecking ball is about to hit again.

Crash. It does. Throwing me to the ground. It's getting closer.

I grab the case and pull the zip. Out she comes. A purpled body. Or what's left of it. Bloated. From rigor mortis and everything that happens after the heart stops beating. She only vaguely looks like herself because of what's called Casper's law. I read about it once. Lowell must have got her into that freezer quickly. So the air didn't get to her too much after death.

I push her back in the case and drag her towards the stairs.

Crash. Concrete falls just next to me. Narrowly missing us. Sonya and I.

I'm not going to make it downstairs, so I'm heading up. Dragging her slowly upwards as the wrecking ball hits again. Bang!

I want to call Dad and tell them to stop everything, but I've given him my phone. I want them to stop of their own accord, but I don't think they know I'm in here. I want to shout out of a window but they're all boarded up. I've got to tell them somehow.

On the sixth floor, I drag the case to the middle of the room and find a pole. I grab it and ram it against a metal slat. But it doesn't give. Somewhere outside the wrecking ball is winding up for another hit. And this is the one that might be the end of me. I take a run up and smash the pole into the metal slat. It gives just a touch. Just enough.

I wrench it away from the wall and push my head out of it.

'Stop! I'm in here! Stop!' I shout. But I'm so far up,

I don't think they'll hear. I see the machines below and then hear them shout too. In the distance.

'Stop! Stop!' they echo. I think they hear me. I peer out again. I can see people running onto the site. But the man in the wrecking ball, doesn't seem to see them, it's coming towards me. Right towards me. I grab the case and drag it to the back of the room as the wall gives way.

Bang! It's a brutal hit. My ears ring and sting with a high-pitched noise and the next thing I expect to feel is the fast fall to the ground where my bones will break. At least the case will be found. At least his fingerprints will be all over it. At least Dad can call it in and they'll know. I have the body. Lowell's marks all over it. Even though I am about to die, I've made sure that Jean and Sonya's killer is found. That they won't be simply lost. That justice will be done.

I open my eyes and see the thick cloud of brick dust part. The next thing I see is the blue sky and the whole estate before me. The floor before me is all but destroyed. But on a tiny ledge at the back of what was once a living room, I lie, holding a suitcase, with a body half sticking out of it. For the whole world to see.

I glimpse the skyline. The city far off on the horizon. But below that and far closer the workers are shouting at me. Saying they'll find a way up. Telling me to stay there.

The sky ahead is so, so blue. It's beautiful.

As I look to the dots below, I see police cars arrive. I seem to have drawn quite a crowd. I see the faces from the neighbourhood. The ones I know and love. They've finally all come out to play.

The world seems to spin in front of me as I lean against

the wall behind me. As my eyes close, I think how nice it is to feel a bit of community again.

I hold on tight, as the dust and wind blows past.

I see a flock of swifts in a distant crescent silhouetted against the sky.

It's been such a strange few weeks.

Hasn't it?

Part Eleven: The Life List

1 December.

Calidris alba, Chordata – **Sanderling (a small plump sandpiper) – Bright, fresh and cold, 6 deg – Singular – White with dark shoulder patch – 18 cm – Lonelyish, far from the coast, wandering.**

I rub my hands together. The winter chill breezes fiercely across the platform as I step off the train and head for home. I've felt quite alone since it all happened. I suppose that was to be expected. I lost my husband. My best neighbour too. Though 'best' is a debatable label, I realise.

I'm not *so* alone though. Terrence is here. I didn't know if they'd let a dog on a train, but they did. I realise I should've checked this before leaving. But here we are. I still don't know much about dog etiquette, but I'm learning. I'll get there in the end.

I took him for a groom for the first time the other day. He feels nice to the touch. You'd like him. He looks very lovely. Very neat. I've even got a walker for him for when I'm at work.

I got that new job. Same shit. Different office, of course. But there's more money. A far more dynamic atmosphere. Well, slightly more dynamic atmosphere. Well, they have a ping-pong table. But I like it there. I needed a new start.

I've taken up jogging. It's very impressive. I see them all out there. David Kentley, Mr Smith, Cary. We're on nodding terms. In fact I've had coffee with a couple of them at the park. I'm quite active in the building now, you see. I'm the building rep. That's right. I've taken Lowell's old job. It's a bit of a bloody coup, of course. But what did he expect? It's a tough job to do from prison. And I've started a Neighbourhood Watch. Seriously. We're a fantastic community now. Well, we're a much better community. Well, some of us know each other's names. But that's a start.

This journal serves another purpose too. It's a thanks, to you. For everything. For putting up with all my illusions. For so long. For coming back for me. For redeeming me. At last.

I'm not going to get teary. I promised me I wouldn't. That's not what this journal's for, in the main. It's to address things clearly. To keep a record of where I'm at. How I'm doing. It's a good thing. And I'm going to keep it up. But it's not for wallowing in sadness. But, I wish you were here. I really do. It was so good to see you. To get everything straight. I wish you were still here.

But you've gone to a better place. A much better place. Southern Brittany. Sorry, I realise now I made it sound a bit like you'd died. Which you didn't, of course. But then, you know that. Obviously.

I bet it's at least a bit warmer over there, it's brass monkeys here, freezing. I thought I might come over in February, it's always the crappiest month in London. The coldest and dreariest. But I thought there might be something to interest me where you are. A few spots of sunlight for a little bird to sit in. If the offer's still open, that is. Someone even wants to come with me. But we'll see.

That building is completely down. Alaska House. There's nothing left of it at all. Not even a brick. It's disappeared. Not even its ghosts remain. Then they broke ground on its replacement: 'Aqua View'. It's going to have a sauna and steam room. They had a sales party in my building. People came to look around. Eighty per cent of it was sold in twenty-four hours. Imagine that? They're going like hot cakes. This place is big business.

Meanwhile the others still wait on in their homes. I never see them. But I know they're there. On the rare occasion I do see them, the ones I met – Chris, Sandra, Thompson – we don't say much to each other. We just nod sagely. A silent understanding from those who knew. Who helped me in some way.

The others are more forthcoming. The ones I didn't know before. The middle-class types of the newbuilds. They've read about me in the paper. Like I did, with Jean, I suppose.

So I smile and nod to them. Answer questions if they chance to ask anything. Things to do with the 'evil look in his eye'. They ask if I 'could tell straight away'. Did I get a funny chill whenever he walked past me in the corridor? And I say no. He seemed very nice actually. Very ordinary. He was just like you or me.

It's strange, you'd think it might be bad publicity, but people are pretty hardy round here. And most of them wouldn't chance moving while the property prices are going up. I think they thought I'd move somewhere, but I'm not going to. I like it here. I'm more determined than ever to see how it all takes shape.

I got some compassionate leave after it all happened. Thought I'd go on holiday, but in the end I stayed here. I re-watched all the Hitchcock films. Every one. I know that doesn't sound like the healthiest thing to do, but I'm going to finish my book on Hitch. So I thought I'd brush up. At least it keeps my eyes from straying towards my binoculars. For now.

I'm introducing them to a friend. Poor guy. He hadn't seen any of them. Can you believe that? I'm really opening his eyes. He loves them. On the first night he came over, we watched a double bill of *Vertigo* and *I Now Pronounce You Chuck and Larry*. The latter one was his choice, obviously.

You remember Phil, right? We've been kind of seeing each other. He's a great guy. Well, he's an all right guy. No. He is. He's great. He's been so good to me. He's been there since it all happened. He likes me a lot, Dad. But we're taking it slow. I think I need to. I think that's definitely for the best.

He drives me to see Helen. I don't know why. I could get the Tube. But he says he wants to keep me safe. And it's to show he'll always be there, before I go in and when I come out. In a good way, not like a stalker or anything. Although I had thought about that possibility from time to time, before I got things clear in my mind. Before I saw him for real. The way he really is.

I've been going to see Helen every week. To make sure I see everything the way it is. I think I'm the best I've ever been. Physically and mentally. She agrees. No illusions. Nothing. And some closure. I'm putting a few things right. Which is partly why I've just been where I've just been. To see Mum. I'm not angry at her now. For letting go. The pills, the locked bathroom door, the hot bath. I forgive her it all. I put some flowers down for her and said my peace. It felt so nice to accept it all. Properly. For the first time.

The one thing I haven't got closure on is the possibility of an accomplice. The other set of footsteps in the dark. The one who must've moved the suitcase to the building before it was destroyed.

He still could be about. I don't know. Perhaps he made a run for it. I don't know.

If you ask me, though, I still think it was Brenner. Of course I do. But the police officer – Detective Andrews, the brown-suited bookkeeper, who was so apologetic about everything that happened, who apologised for a possible lack of professionalism at the station early on in the case – he couldn't find any other set of prints on the body or the case. Or anywhere. So, despite my protestations, that was that.

This thought does haunt me every so often. It creeps up on me when I feel most safe. I wonder whether he's watching me. Keeping a close eye. Waiting to strike. From one of those buildings over there. Watching my every move.

It could be any of them. Any face that passes me by. Everybody that walks past me in the hallway. It could be them. I don't know.

I think about it every so often. When I'm home late at night. When I put my key in my door and the lift opens behind me. When I see someone in the building I don't recognise. Or even someone I do. But I wouldn't say I'm solely afraid. That's not quite the feeling. I'd say I'm interested. Fascinated. Curious.

And if he does, if he exists, I want him to come for me. I'm ready.

I pick up my binoculars. I haven't touched them for a while. I stare at Brenner. He's in there right now. There he is. I don't need the binoculars to see. But it's symbolic. I want him to know I'm watching.

I flick my bedroom light off. Then on. Then off. Then on.

Signalling to him. That I'm here. As a lighthouse might. Beckoning him to turn. I stare.

He gets up and wanders around. He doesn't scare easily. But then he doesn't scare me either. I want the confrontation. I crave it. And so I wait.

A lone Sanderling passes above us. Perhaps he's lost. Poor bird. He's a coastal wading bird. He's a circumpolar Arctic breeder. Highly gregarious. So strange, but nice, to see him here.

I turn the light off. And on. Then off. Then on.

Off.

On.

Off.

On.

In spite of everything, things look so much better.

How well we all are here. What different people we have become.

I look at him. It's such a mystery. It fascinates me.

Then he turns. Looks right at me. We share an expressionless gaze. He lifts his hand slowly.

And, as I smile, my hand rises too. And waves.

Acknowledgements

Thanks to Catherine for her wonderful thoughts, general wisdom and a world of other things too.

To Al and Antonia, and particularly their children Evan and Darcy, for being the most consistent source of real life danger and violence I face on a regular basis.

To Jim for not going ahead with the long-mooted novel *Lennon and Presley Detective Agency*, leaving me as the sole author in the family to date.

To Juliet Mushens for being the best trinity of editor, agent and friend one could wish for.

To all at the Woodberry Wetlands for teaching me about the birds.

Everyone at HQ for their incredible support, dynamism and hard work from the very first moment we met.

My parents for everything, particularly for working for 50 years so their son could have the temerity of doing two Batchelor of Arts degrees when it was still economically possible to do so, which only qualified him to read books and act in detective-based TV shows. And for being my greatest champions and friends.

In ways big and small, there have been many people kind enough to read or listen to my words and not berate me for wasting their time. Every moment was immeasurably valuable to me. So, thanks to: Chris Farrar, John Hollingworth, Tom McHugh, Jules Stevens, David Hart, Fred Ridgeway, Jo Kloska, Richy Riddell, Natasha James, Jack McNamara, Jane Boston, Alex Odell, Dan Ings and Ben McLeish.

If there is anyone else who thinks themselves largely responsible for me getting to write this thing that has given me so much pleasure whom I have neglected to mention, I'm sure you're right and I apologise unreservedly.

HQ

One Place. Many Stories

The home of bold, innovative
and empowering publishing.

Follow us online

 @HQStories

 @HQStories

 HQStories

HQ Stories

 HQMusic2016

HQ_SM